THE ART OF THEATER

New Directions in Aesthetics

Series editors: Dominic McIver Lopes, University of British Columbia, and Berys Gaut, University of St Andrews

Blackwell's New Directions in Aesthetics series highlights ambitious single- and multiple-author books that confront the most intriguing and pressing problems in aesthetics and the philosophy of art today. Each book is written in a way that advances understanding of the subject at hand and is accessible to upper-undergraduate and graduate students.

THE ART OF THEATER

JAMES R. HAMILTON

Blackwell
Publishing

BLACKWELL PUBLISHING
350 Main Street, Malden, MA 02148-5020, USA
9600 Garsington Road, Oxford OX4 2DQ, UK
550 Swanston Street, Carlton, Victoria 3053, Australia

The right of James R. Hamilton to be identified as the Author of this Work has been asserted in accordance with the UK Copyright, Designs, and Patents Act 1988.

First published 2007 by Blackwell Publishing Ltd

1   2007

Library of Congress Cataloging-in-Publication Data

Hamilton, James R.
   The art of theater / James R. Hamilton.
      p. cm. — (New directions in aesthetics)
   Includes bibliographical references and index.
   ISBN-13: 978-1-4051-1353-3 (hardback)
1. Theater—Philosophy.   I. Title.

   PN2039.H357 2007
   792.01—dc22

                                   2006026271

A catalogue record for this title is available from the British Library.

Set in 10 on 12.5pt Galliard
by SNP Best-set Typesetter Ltd, Hong Kong
Printed and bound in Singapore
by Markono Print Media Pte Ltd

The publisher's policy is to use permanent paper from mills that operate a sustainable forestry policy, and which has been manufactured from pulp processed using acid-free and elementary chlorine-free practices. Furthermore, the publisher ensures that the text paper and cover board used have met acceptable environmental accreditation standards.

For further information on
Blackwell Publishing, visit our website:
www.blackwellpublishing.com

To Ben Tilghman

CONTENTS

Part II: The Independence of Theatrical Performance

5 Basic Theatrical Understanding

6 The Mechanics of Basic Theatrical Understanding

PROLOGUE

Synopsis

Even though we commonly speak of theatrical performances as being *of* particular literary works – works of dramatic literature – most of the time we do not in fact engage with theatrical performances in that way. When we talk about or discuss characters in plays we are usually thinking of them as we saw them in this or that performance or set of performances. We recount and discuss plots of plays we have seen but have never read. We do of course ask, "Who wrote that play?" But even when we say, "I'd go see anything written by Ibsen," we obviously do not mean we would go *see* the *written text*; it is the performance that interests us. There is some sort of disconnection between what we officially say are the 'works' of theater and what we actually do.

This book is an affirmation of what we actually do. The thesis of the book is that theatrical performance is, and in reality always has been, an art form in its own right whose works are identified and assessed without reference to the literary texts that, for several centuries in European culture, have been mistakenly taken to be the real works of which theatrical performances were *merely* performances.

The book has three parts.

In the first part I sketch out the main issues and methods in the book. I present a history of those changes in theatrical practice that brought the thesis of the book into view. I state the thesis precisely by contrasting its commitment to a specific view about the relation between texts and performances with standard views of the text–performance relationship. And I explain what it takes for a practice to be an art form. I present some idealized cases to work with and argue for three constraints on any adequate account of theatrical performance. And finally I set forth a guiding intuition regarding the central interaction between spectators and performers in theatrical performances, "enactment," and the factors of enactment that shape the means arranged by performers by which spectators are led to grasp performances.

The argument of the second part of the book concerns the independence of theatrical performance. If theatrical performance is an art form independent of literature, then we must identify works of the form without reference to the texts, if any, that are employed in them. I argue that a proper account of how spectators understand theatrical performances shows us how they do in fact identify them.

I argue there is a basic level of comprehension of theatrical performances that does not require more than what is provided in the moment-to-moment tracking of the performance as it is happening on the stage. Then I argue that the mechanism by which that tracking takes place involves convergence by even quite disparate spectators onto a common description of what has taken place in the performance. And finally I argue that, because of the way those convergences are secured, the resulting descriptions of what has taken place amount to basic-level identifications of performances as works.

The argument for the claim that we are able to identify works without reference to the texts they use is incomplete if we do not also have an account of how audiences identify elements of a performance (for example, characters, images, props) across performances in a production, across productions employing the same script material, and across performances utilizing different script materials (for example, the same characters in different stories). I offer a solution that relies on the recognition capacities of audiences in everyday circumstances and on the fact that theatrical performances are live events in space and time.

The argument of the third part of the book is for the view that the independent practice of theatrical performance is a form of art. If theatrical performance is an art form, then we must identify and explain, within the context of particular performances, both the achievements that are made or that fail to be made and the relevant details and groupings of details that demand aesthetic appreciation. I argue that a full appreciation of any theatrical performance is a complex matter consisting in part in the grasp of both the performance kind and of the means by which it is produced and in part in the assessment of the actual and the intended significance of the performance.

Something is seen to be an achievement only against a background of some kind. In the case of theater, there are two kinds of background – one having to do with content traditions in which a performance is presented and the other having to do with the skill sets and artistry required to produce a performance of a given kind. To attain a full appreciation of a particular performance as a work of art, audiences need to bring with them an understanding of both of these relevant backgrounds. But they also need to make plausible conjectures connecting the sense they make of the performed object with the sense they make of the performers' activities in presenting that object. To do that, I argue, audiences must be able to comprehend what it is that performers do. I present a story of what performers do, consistent with various ways performers comprehend it themselves, but described primarily in a way that makes sense of how audiences grasp what performers do and how they connect their sense of the performed object with their sense of the performers' activities. The linchpin, I argue, is to be found in the idea of a theatrical style, in reckoning how theatrical style is related to performer choices, theatrical conventions, and performer intentions, and in reckoning how conjectures about style guide spectators' appreciative judgments about performances.

At the end of all this, one might still wonder how we are to think about performances that are conceived – by some performers and some audiences – as performances *of* works that have had another life as works of literature and have had a life as reliable ingredients for long traditions of theatrical performance. The book concludes by showing how to resolve this issue within the conception of theatrical performance as an independent art form.

Sources

Elements of chapters 3 and 7 were first worked out in my entry on "Theater" for *The Routledge Companion to Aesthetics*, 2nd edition, ed. Berys Gaut and Dominic McIver Lopes (London: Routledge, 2001), pp. 585–96. Elements of chapter 4 were developed in "Theatrical Enactment," *Journal of Aesthetics and Art Criticism* 58/1 (Winter 2000), 23–35. Elements of chapter 5 were developed in "Understanding Plays," *Staging Performances*, ed. D. Krasner and D. Saltz (Ann Arbor: University of Michigan Press, forthcoming), pp. 221–43. I am grateful to the respective editors for permission to use this material here.

Acknowledgments

I work in a small undergraduate-only department that has hired extremely well. Some of the people we have hired have moved on, some have stayed; but the upshot is that I have been the beneficiary of talking out these ideas with a fair number of very talented philosophers. We have hired the best people we could and all we ask of them is that they be willing to read each other's work, even well outside their research specializations, and give solid philosophical and authorial critiques of that work. We benefit from each other. Many of the arguments in this in this book were improved as a result of cool and careful discussion with my colleagues.

Some bear special mention, however. The book is dedicated to Ben Tilghman, who always helped me to stay true to my core philosophical instincts. Robin Smith, now at Texas A&M, encouraged me to make contact with a broad range of work being done in the profession. Phil Clark, now at Toronto, read very early versions of several of these chapters. His comments helped me keep track of the fact that "the order of discovery is rarely the order of presentation." Laurie Pieper read the entire first manuscript and gave advice that strengthened the main line of argument. Doug Patterson read and gave detailed advice concerning two chapters I was struggling with during the re-writes. Amy Lara and Jon Mahoney read and critiqued several conference papers that later became parts of chapters. I also have had the strong encouragement of our current department head, Marcelo Sabatés. He, like Ben Tilghman before him, pressed me to stay focused on my initial philosophical instincts.

In 1989, at the behest of my wife and high school aged children, I founded the Manhattan Experimental Theater Workshop for high school students. Part classroom and part production company, MXTW, as it is locally known, teaches techniques of writing and performing in the theater to very bright and passionate young men and women. It is a kind of theater laboratory for participants as well as theater audiences in Manhattan, Kansas. For me, it has been a constant source of fun and new ideas for and about the theater. Most importantly, were it not for the experience of planning, directing and producing the MXTW, I do not think I would have fully comprehended the truth of the central thesis of this book.

In 1981, I had the privilege of studying in a National Endowment for the Humanities Summer Seminar on avant-garde theater taught by Herbert Blau, which formed the first stimulus for much of my work in the philosophy of theater. I studied topics in the history of theater, on a National Endowment for the Humanities sabbatical Fellowship, at SUNY-Stony Brook, where Bill Bruehl, the chair of the theater department afforded me an office and access to the library, rehearsals, and faculty discussions. There I learned much of the historical background relied on my work. In 2003, on a Big 12 Fellowship I spent two weeks at Texas Tech University working with Aaron Meskin and Danny Nathan on elements of several of the key chapters in the second part of the book. I am deeply grateful for their good critical assistance.

I wish also to thank the staff at Blackwell – Jeff Dean, Danielle Descoteaux, and Jamie Harlan – for their patience and kindness. Glynis Baguley has provided invaluable service as a copy-editor.

And finally I wish to thank Dominic McIver Lopes and Berys Gaut, the editors of the New Directions in Aesthetic series, for encouraging me to submit a book proposal to Blackwell for this project in the first place. This book would never have been completed without Dom's timely and always sage advice.

PART I
THE BASICS

1

THE EMERGENCE OF THE ART OF THEATER: BACKGROUND AND HISTORY

1.1 The Backstory: 1850s to 1950s

It is not difficult these days to find a book about actor training. Europe once had a long tradition of apprenticeship training, but no systematic actor training such as is found in Kathakali in India or in Noh training in Japan from as early as the 1500s.[1] A little over a century ago, the idea of systems of actor training was nearly unheard of in Europe. Then along came Stanislavski, and Nemirovitch-Dantchenko, Meyerhold, and others. But above all, Stanislavski. His work changed the way anyone in Europe thought about theater if they thought about theater at all.

The institution of theater was in tremendous flux in the late nineteenth century. Naturalists in both literature and theater had rejected the predecessor art because they perceived it as incapable of representing the changing social facts they were confronting. Instead they had begun to employ the language that ordinary people spoke and to treat themes of the everyday, especially concerning familial relations. They aimed to plumb the depths of human nature that they believed lay beneath the veneer of our civility if not of civilization itself.

Broader cultural trends led to the development of a new focus in literature and theater. Many among the educated classes believed that the now established scientific understanding of the natural world could with equal success be applied to the social order. The widespread acceptance of the theory of evolution in biology led to attempts to extrapolate its general ideas to social phenomena. Increasing democratization of European culture led many to think not only that the consent of ordinary individuals is the source of political authority but also that the nature of ordinary individuals was – had to be – worth thinking about. As Europe democratized, inevitably a feminist movement emerged as well, demanding for women what was becoming increasingly available to men of all classes. Each of these social trends had a powerful influence on the contents and styles of the new work of the theatrical Naturalists, such as Zola, Strindberg, and Ibsen.[2]

The economics of late nineteenth-century theater institutions also contributed to the pressure on theatrical practices. As had happened earlier to painting, sculpture, poetry, and music, theatrical performances increasingly drew their support from private companies' sales of subscriptions to seasons of performances. The subscription concert that, in music, began in the early eighteenth century (for example with Handel) is, in theater, a phenomenon of the late nineteenth century. It is usually traced to the first fully independent traveling company, the Meiningen Court Theater, under the direction of George II, Duke of Saxe-Meiningen. The company began to tour Europe in 1874, initiating the now familiar prominence of directors and producers.[3]

The late nineteenth century was also a period of stylistic upheaval in theater. Earlier in the century Romantic theater practices had been challenged by the successes of melodramatic theater that, like the Naturalism to come, would bring the lives of ordinary people to center stage, albeit sentimentally not scientifically. Scribe's "well made play" – a device for structuring theatrical performances – was enormously effective because of the way it set up and linked various elements in the presentation of theatrical narratives, and its adherents were getting their second wind in the latter part of the century.[4] "Realistic social drama" had already emerged before the specific devices of Naturalism came to the fore. And, finally, no sooner had Naturalism arisen than a new movement, Symbolism, arose to challenge it and its focus on ordinary individuals, the family, and everyday language.

What emerged in this fertile artistic climate, with all its disparate threads and pressures, was a clear need for more systematic actor training. A simple example demonstrates the need. Whereas eleven rehearsals were provided for a production of Ibsen's *A Doll's House* in 1879, four years later the same theater company allotted thirty-two rehearsals for a production of his *An Enemy of the People*.[5] More rehearsal time was needed to allow actors time to give attention to the ordinary characters who were becoming the center of attention. Into the space created by the need for actor training stepped, preeminently, Konstantin Stanislavski.

Stanislavksi's passionate attention both to the emerging science of psychology and to the needs of Naturalistic theater texts, notably those of Chekhov, is well documented. He is known to have been impressed by the scientific discoveries of Pavlov and Ribot;[6] and his reputation was made, in large part, by a single production of Chekhov's *The Three Sisters*,[7] and sealed by his production of *The Seagull*.[8] He reflected on the discoveries of the new psychological theories and on the needs of the plays that demanded his attention. These reflections led him to insist on a new approach to rehearsals – an approach that emphasized the attitude to the inner lives of characters for which he became known and insisted on the director's absolute control of the vision of each play.[9] Stanislavski sought this control not because of the pragmatic need to organize a company in new economic conditions, as the Duke of Saxe-Meiningen may be thought to have done. Stanislavski's aim was, in some sense, artistic.

For much of the twentieth century, theoretical practitioners who asserted that theater is an art were making a normative claim. That is, they set forth their visions of what theater could and should be doing; but they set those visions forth in the form of a descriptive claim about what theater *is*.[10] A case in point is E. Gordon Craig. Although best known for his contribution to scenography, Craig is also remembered for setting out a vision of theater that rejected Naturalism and sought a theater composed of symbolic gesture.[11] Among his contributions is an argument for directorial control, grounded in the thought that if there is an art there must be *an* artist. Most significantly, Craig argued for an alternative to the play text as the basic block on which the art of theater is built. He introduced the idea that there must be something that is what theater both is and could be about that is not the province of playwrights.[12] Notoriously, the alternative he imagined was ultimately to drive him to renounce acting; for on the one hand he observed that human beings, who are by nature free, cannot be a material, a medium for an art form; on the other hand, he believed acting is "impersonation" which is not a form of creating; and, hence, he reasoned, *acting* is not an art.[13]

Vsevolod Meyerhold and Jacques Copeau held less striking views in some respects, but they are still good examples of how the art of theater was understood by revolutionary theorists who developed acting systems. Meyerhold and Copeau were of a mind in rejecting Naturalism as an appropriate form for their respective national theaters.[14] Like Craig, Meyerhold and Copeau both sought to discover what Craig had called the "laws of the art of theater."[15] And like Craig, each thought those laws would be based on specifically theatrical elements – such as movement – to which words, texts, the work of playwrights would be subservient.[16] But whereas Meyerhold looked back to the mime, the *Commedia dell'Arte*, and the art of the *cabotin* for inspiration regarding the laws of the true theater,[17] Copeau thought the laws of the art had yet to emerge and that they would only do so in a future context of a sincere effort of renewal, "a return to principles," that enabled "preparation of the means suitable to the play of a broader, freer and more audacious dramatic imagination." And this, he thought, would not be possible at all without substantial changes in society – both society at large and the societies of actors in training.[18]

This brief historical sketch has focused upon theoretical practitioners who called for theater to be an "art." These calls amounted, in fact, to a series of prescriptions for what theater can be or can do that found expression as descriptions of the "art" of theater. From the writings and practices of these figures also emerged the idea that theater can exist independently of those literary texts that had been its proper object, so to speak, for many years. But the sense in which that independence is possible was neither fully nor coherently worked out.

1.2 The Decisive Influences: Brecht, Artaud, Grotowski

Visions of what theater can and should be continued to drive changes in theatrical practices throughout the twentieth century. As Copeau had predicted, these visions themselves were driven by perceived transformations in the social realm. No figure illustrates this better than Bertolt Brecht. Even in his earliest work, when Brecht writes of theater for a new audience he means what he calls a "scientific audience," an audience that seeks to understand what is going on rather than merely empathizing with characters, without conscious and critical understanding of their situations. This new attitude of audiences, he maintained, demanded new kinds of performance.[19] His middle work employed an arsenal of devices to achieve the kind of distance from identification with the emotional states of characters that Brecht thought suitable for this new audience.[20] Some of the techniques are quite simple, but were extraordinary at the time: for example, having actors deliver their lines in the third person or transposed into the past tense, or recite aloud the stage directions as they were being executed.

Even in his late work, when he was chastened about his earlier enthusiasm regarding the makeup of the "new audience,"[21] Brecht was still convinced there had to be ways to analyze plays and perform them so as both to entertain audiences and to instruct them in the scientific understanding of social practices to which he was committed. Brecht's late practices involved the development of what he called "model books" – descriptions of conversations that led to productions, and detailed pre-scriptions for how those productions were to be mounted – of both his own scripts and others'. One useful technique was to see how far his analytic framework and the performance techniques could go in achieving the desired kind of production, without changing any lines.[22] But, if that technique played out without the desired results, Brecht felt completely at liberty to change and rearrange quite a lot of the original lines. A strik-ing aspect of Brecht's career, despite his free and radical revision of other playwright's materials, is that he never explicitly called for a new theater in which words would – as Meyerhold, for example, thought – be sub-servient to distinctively theatrical elements.

Antonin Artaud, on the other hand, is for us most famous precisely for such calls. Known less for his own directing and performing than for the call for theater to "be given its own concrete language to speak,"[23] Artaud is the pivotal character in this sketch of the history of theatrical perfor-mance in the twentieth century. Again not for any theatrical production or even actor training that he actually undertook, Artaud came to be seen – came to be read[24] – as the singular proponent of theater independent of literature. He was not the first to ask why theater had been bound to "what can be expressed in speech, in words," rather than to "everything specifically theatrical."[25] Artaud had no clearer alternative worked out for this than had Craig or Meyerhold or Copeau. And it has been argued that, when he made his positive proposals, they were confused and shot through with unacknowledged cultural prejudices.[26] What makes him pivotal is that, for a variety of reasons, theater people heeded this call in a way they had not heeded its predecessors. Perhaps chief among those reasons was a sense that Western systems of thought had failed to deliver the good life and that a more 'spiritual' approach would have a greater chance of success. And the ground was fertile. Many theater people in Europe and the USA in the early 1960s, when Artaud became widely known, thought that a more spiritual approach could be found in 'Ori-ental' thinking; and it was to non-Western sources that Artaud himself had appealed. A correlative leading idea that caught fire among those reading Artaud was the demand that performers develop "an affective athleticism."[27]

Among the most influential of the figures heeding Artaud's call was Jerzy Grotowski. Grotowski put into practice – into a system of actor training and performance – Artaud's paired thoughts: first, that practi-tioners needed to discover what is "specifically theatrical" and to make theater that put theatrical material into the foreground and texts into the background;[28] and second, that performers should become a kind of focal point of energy, burning, to which audiences were to be witnesses. To achieve this, he called for a "poor" theater, a theater that relied only on the means brought to it by the performer.[29] To identify what was specifically theatrical, he asked what theater could do without: and he claimed it could do without costumes, sets, makeup, lighting effects, and "yes, without a text . . . [for] in the evolution of the theatrical art the text was one of the last elements to be added."[30]

It is fitting, then, that Grotowski is known for directing performances based in traditional theatrical texts, but radically adapting those texts in accord with his principles and methods. Among the texts so used were Marlowe's *Dr. Faustus*, Calderón de la Barca's *The Constant Prince*, and Wyspianski's *Akropolis*. Writing in the introduction to the program for *The Constant Prince*, Ludwik Flaszen wrote that "the producer does not mean to play *The Constant Prince* as it is . . . He aims at giving his own vision of the play, and the relation of his scenario to the original text is that of a musical variation to the original musical theme."[31] The producer, Grotowski, saw the texts he employed as giving him themes on which to 'play' variations. This idea governed the text–performance relation in the practice of the Polish Laboratory Theatre.

Grotowski himself was unable to sustain the practices he devised in actor training as practices of theater. After his work with the Polish Lab Theatre, he turned to creating "paratheatricals," rituals that were created by and for the performers. What exactly this expressed about his ideas is still difficult to assess, in part because others who followed took up many of the ideas developed in the Lab Theatre and continued a distinctively *theatrical* practice with them.

Brecht, Artaud, and Grotowski are the decisive influences on the events to follow. This is not because they inspired most theatrical performances thereafter. In fact, their ideas have not directly inspired many subsequent performances at all. But they inspired several specific and well-known performances and practices that clearly made possible the way of thinking about theatrical performance I defend in this book.

1.3 The Decisive Years: 1961 to 1985

Robert Corrigan's essay, "The Theater in Search of a Fix,"[32] published in 1961, was an exploration of the "Theater of the Absurd," a movement, largely European, that had sprung up in reaction to widespread cultural disillusion following World War II. His 1973 book of the same name[33] was an examination of the longer history of theater in search of an analysis of the changes in theater practices that took place in the 1960s and early 70s. He was to return to the phrase "theater in search of a fix" in a 1984[34] essay aimed at explaining both why theater was turning away from the experiments of these decades towards a more traditional text-based practice, and what the new poetics of theater could be. Corrigan's writings are intimately engaged with the changes I describe next. He presents us with several key ideas which have informed the debates of theoretical practitioners in these two decades about what to do and how to do it. And these turn out, once again, to be normative ideas about what theater could be – specifically concerning the relationship between art and life – but presented as reflections on "the nature of theatre."[35]

In 1979, just over a decade after the first performances of The Performance Group's *Dionysus in 69* at the Performing Garage in New York City,[36] Gerald Hinkle published a small book[37] whose title – *Art as Event: An Aesthetic for the Performing Arts* – contains in a nutshell both the changed situation of theatrical practices and the idea about theatrical performance that they had brought into view. The book itself would largely fall into obscurity.[38] And not until 1995 would the idea of art as an event and specifically as performance – an idea now applied to all the arts – come to have a serious and detailed defense.[39]

The changes that prepared the ground for this idea were, as we have seen, the result of over ninety years of ferment in the practices and theory of theater. Brief descriptions of just three emblematic performances from this period illustrate what happened to bring our thesis explicitly and clearly into view. Those three performances are: The Performance Group's *Dionysus in 69* (1968); Kraken's *Elsinore* (1976); and the American Repertory Theatre's *Endgame* (1984).

Dionysus in 69 was attributed to Euripides. But the performance did not so much 'interpret' *The Bacchae* as simply use it as the source for most of its language and many of its images. The result was that "the play [had] been so interwoven with something at least seeming [to be] private interaction between performers & pseudo-personal approaches to the audience that the tension between them [came] to seem a legitimate subject of primary attention."[40] Scenes were added that do not appear in Euripides' play. The company "[kept] most of the lines, [dropped] the plot, & [gave Euripides] an argument: the dialectic of the hip as illustrated by the story of the seduction & destruction of a prig. Variation of theme dominates the fable . . ."[41] During the course of the production's run, beginning in the spring of 1968 and lasting more than a year, a number of the techniques employed in the performance underwent substantial overhaul.[42] Euripides' words were mostly all there, "but the order and the emphases were different . . . The events and speeches of the play are incoherently jumbled up; often several speeches are spoken or chanted or sung at once."[43] *Dionysus in 69* was no ordinary production of Euripides' *The Bacchae.*

Nor was Kraken's *Elsinore* anything like an ordinary production of Shakespeare's *Hamlet*. As Herbert Blau, Kraken's director, tells it, the company began work during the fall of 1975, as a residence company at Oberlin College in Ohio. The work was largely improvisational and "the text was prepared . . . out of the improvisational studies done by the actors. The images were recorded during rehearsals, analyzed and sorted out, but none of the writing was done until after about six months of work."[44] *Elsinore* was presented at the New Theater Festival in Baltimore, Maryland, in June, 1976 and again in June, 1977. The first performance was received favorably. Richard Mennen described it as "an example of company-based textual experimentation . . . a tightly scored, physical piece with a text, derived from *Hamlet*, which was more response to than a reinterpretation of the play."[45] Ruby Cohn's review in the following year is more expansive and more detailed about the aims of Kraken's theater practices.

> Boldly, Kraken jettisons that mainstay of Western theatre – an actor playing a role. Kraken's actors play scenes, concerts, attitudes, emotions, but they do not play characters, and they do not present a story. Though their springboard is Shakespeare, Kraken belongs to the New Theatre, which is rooted in Artaud's theory and Grotowski's practice – a new theatre that is at once poor and elitist, physical and mythic, intelligent and passionate, but spatial rather than temporal. It is a theatre of risk, demanding utmost concentration from an audience, whom it challenges to feel, perceive, reflect.[46]

As even these brief descriptions of the first two performances suggest, by the 1960s and 70s something had given way in – or perhaps as a result of – the idea of performances as 'interpretations of plays' that had been a dominant mode of understanding theater practices and theatrical performances for well over a hundred years.

These performances could have been only an aberration. They were consistent with other experimentation in theater at the time, a good deal of which was built by companies of performers who, more or less democratically, built performances – sometimes employing multiple texts, even texts without identifiable authors – and began to challenge, if not change, some fundamental practices of theater.[47] But still one might think these were merely the excesses of a misguided form of thinking rampant in the turbulent 1960s.

And, in fact, between these performances and the American Repertory Theatre's production of *Endgame*, in 1984, many of the most pro-gressively experimental groups in theater had begun to move back to using texts by playwrights more or less as the playwrights had written them. ART's production was one of those that signaled this return. It was directed by JoAnne Akalaitis, a director and performer with one of America's most experimental arts collectives, Mabou Mines. And yet it signaled a return to playwrights because it employed almost all and only the words written by Samuel Beckett in the script for *Endgame*. As Gerald Rabkin puts it, "according to the traditional theatre model, the production was meant to interpret with fidelity the 'text and spirit of the play'."[48]

However, a controversy arose when Beckett's American publisher, Grove Press, threatened to go to court to stop the production. Despite its use of Beckett's text, not significantly more altered than he himself had done when directing his own work,[49] Beckett thought Akalaitis's setting of the play in an abandoned subway station and the adding of incidental music (by Philip Glass) was "a complete parody of the play as conceived by me."[50] But, given the faithfulness to the text, and the wide latitude taken by directors in interpreting texts written for the theater in the pre-ceding 50 years, it is hard to see what legal standing Beckett might have had. Beckett may have held that the text includes all that the author wrote – not just the words that come out of the mouths of the characters, but also the stage directions and indications of setting. In practice, however, most directors, including Beckett himself in some cases, hold that "the text" refers only to the words that could come out of the characters' mouths and some few essential stage directions.

There is irony here: for the controversy over *that* production, which had signaled a move back to scripts by playwrights, was to solidify the possibility of a new way of thinking about the limits of interpretation and the nature of theatrical performance more decisively than the more aggres-sively 'liberated' theater practices of the 1960s and 70s had ever been able to achieve.

Not every theater practitioner was happy about it. ART's production inspired one professional director to write a blistering polemic against "radical interpretations" in which "directing . . . seeks to control the text, instead of subordinating itself to the text."[51] Whether such a distinction can be made with sufficient clarity and precision is highly problematic. Any interpretation of a script must involve the interpreter in thinking through what she herself thinks, even if she thinks that she is subsuming her thoughts to that of the playwright. It is hard not to wonder just where, and how, to draw the line between when that thinking is and is not legitimate. To make matters worse for this distinction, at least as applied to ART's production, it is widely agreed even by detractors of the production that the "primitivism" employed by its director, JoAnne Akalaitis, had captured much of the "reflexivity of the play."[52] So, although Beckett thought the production a parody of his conception, it still had captured much of the play's "spirit."

Rabkin[53] notes that had Beckett pressed his claim that Akalaitis's production was a "parody," or had Akalaitis put her production forth as an "adaptation," the legal issues would have gone away. Courts have given far more latitude to productions under either of those descriptions. The fact that Akalaitis insisted hers was an "interpretation" has far more to do with how she viewed her practice and how she viewed her prior relationship with Beckett than with what this production was. And what this reveals is that parodies, adaptations, and interpretations cannot always be distinguished from one another.

In the end, what is important about ART's production is that, precisely because of the very public *and quasi-legal* nature of the controversy, the nature of theater practice shifted. Before ART's *Endgame* and Beckett's legal challenge, there was a fierce debate regarding the scope of legitimate interpretation. The Beckett–Akalaitis controversy changed the terms of the debate, so that it focused on the scope of what belongs to the playwright and what belongs to the performing company. The question became "Whose play is it? Who owns it?" To the legal form of this question there is a clear answer. But it was the artistic version of the question that was of greater interest. That was a new thought.

At this point, most of the elements that brought our thesis into view were in place. The text/performance link, once thought settled by determining when a performance was 'faithful' to the text, turned out to be anything but settled. Theater people saw how performers could "own" their performances. The detailed preparation of every moment in a performance, begun by Stanislavski, was intensified by more focused attention to the actor's body and movements. Yet it was to take a further development for the idea of theater *as art* to become something other than a normative hope.

1.4 The Final Threads: Absorption of New Practices into the Profession and the Academy

As Copeau predicted, the pressures for changes in theater's aims and practices have not always come from reflection on the relation of theater to the other arts. They have sometimes done so, but more often the pressure has come from developments in culture and politics and from the desire of theater people to find the means to address those developments. It is difficult, for example, to imagine *Dionysus in 69* or even *Elsinore* ever happening without being linked to the widespread societal unease in Europe and America regarding both the apparent ending of colonial dominance and the savagery of the wars between Euro-American forces and Asian powers that threatened to challenge their dominance. In the United States, the depredations of personal and institutional racism had become open to public view and revulsion. And both of these factors played a role in a new burst of feminist activism, now directed at matters much broader than the right to vote. These new developments in the wider society would continue to have an impact on the themes and concerns of theater people, most of whom would seek the means by which to respond. As already noted, one thing that happened was a return to the use of texts produced by playwrights and to the controlling hands of directors.

Acknowledging this return should not obscure other changes that extended the influence of what happened in the decisive years. For the return took place in an environment that was changed in many ways, not least by performances from those decisive years.

The first big change in the environment was in the way theater people conceived of actor training. The acting practices employed by Akalaitis in ART's production of *Endgame*, along with other elements of avant-garde theater, had become a staple of subsequent theater practice and performance practice more generally. Often overlooked in theoretical writing about ART's "scandalous" performance, Akalaitis's handling of space and movement belonged to an approach to preparation and performance[54] that was to become folded into the mainstream in actor training. Her view was that "the primal element of theatre" is "bodies moving in space onstage."[55] Even though this may seem a description of a primal element more apt to dance[56] than to theater, the starting and stopping game used in *Endgame* – to cite just one example – is effective as a piece of *theater* and is exemplary of the new focus on bodies and movement that has come to be essential to many forms of actor training.[57]

An important aspect of this change is that these practices are rarely, if ever, still considered *the* vocabulary of theatrical performance. More often they are taken to be supplemental to actor training *per se*. Part of the reason for this is that feminists have "rediscovered" Stanislavski. More precisely, although Stanislavski's methods had been "officially" rejected because of their historical links with masculinist works,[58] some feminists have discovered that their own practices had been making use of the core Stanislavkian approach to acting after all.[59] Others have noted that mainstream theater, especially professional and academic theater in the United States, had mostly not participated in any rejection of roughly Stanislavskian training. David Krasner has argued that Method Acting, the American inheritance of Stanislavski, was never constrained to "fixed characterization" that would be "useful only for realism."[60] The fact is that the new modes of performance developed in the decisive years have largely been subsumed under actor training as "movement and vocal training," or at least partnered with actor training as an enriching resource for the performance vocabulary.

The second big change in the environment was the introduction of "theory" into departments of theater in the academy. At the time ART produced *Endgame*, the arguments about the limits of interpretation, on every side, were pretty thin. Rabkin notes that in the 1980s the kind of critical theory – structuralism and post-structuralism in particular – that was ascendant in departments of literature was hardly known at all in departments of theater.[61] But it did not take long for academic writers on theater to catch up with what was happening in the theaters. One result was the quick adoption of a semiotic analysis of performance that had already been developed on the European continent by such figures as Erika Fischer-Lichte, Patrice Pavis, Anne Ubersfeld, and Kier Elam. Semiotic theorists championed a view – discussed in the next chapter – about the text–performance relation that is called the "two-text" theory. And they held that the performance text was every bit as much a work of art as the written text to which it corresponded. One lesson of *Dionysus in 69*, *Elsinore*, and especially of *Endgame* had clearly been learned.

Another result of the advent of "theory" was the push to transform theater departments into departments of performance studies.[62] Richard Schechner and Barbara Kirschenblatt-Gimblett were early champions of this movement.[63] Their descriptions of and prescriptions for some of these transformations show that, even though it is possible and perhaps natural to see theater as a species of performance,[64] more often performance and theater were seen to be at odds, the latter employing "acting" and the former employing "performing," or at least "not-acting."[65] Oddly enough, a driving thought here was a suspicion of theater, shared now by perfor-mance-minded and theater-minded writers.[66]

But the perceived opposition between performance and theater was not a function of anything about theater practices *per se*. Artists who had worked outside the mainstream had for many years turned to performance as a way of challenging whatever the prevailing gallery or museum struc-tures were prohibiting.[67] While this classical avant-garde used performance as such a vehicle and while "performance art" was sometimes regarded as "a new form of theatre,"[68] a genuinely *theatrical* avant-garde existed as well and had done since the early part of the twentieth century.

There are competing views about what links the various moments of that theatrical avant-garde together,[69] and disputes about where to place various movements and practitioners. But there is no disputing that the pressure since the 1960s towards performance as a new category for think-ing came both from traditional artists challenging prevailing gallery struc-tures and strictures and from theater practitioners challenging common expectations of what a theater should be. That there is no essential medium that defines performance,[70] nor any essential medium that defines theater,[71] means that the division between performance and theater is largely, as Marvin Carlson and Philip Auslander argue on other grounds, a function of theoretical commitments that are extraneous to the practices either of theater or of performance art.[72]

Nevertheless, one thing emerges, ironically, from all this: whatever theory of performance one adopts, there is general agreement that not every performance is artistic and that theatrical performances *do* belong among those species of performance that *are* artistic. Those who disdained theater, seeking to replace theater programs with performance studies, usually dismissed theatrical performance as belonging to a Western con-ception of the "aesthetic."[73] Those who defended theater programs did so, in part, because they thought, as Auslander and others do, that theater is the root form of performance and the means to discover whatever art there is in performance more generally.[74]

I do not take a stand on those debates, for what is of interest in this book is the fact that the history I have been tracing – including the history of these debates – has revealed theatrical performance to be a form of art in its own right, independent of literature. And it is the meaning and truth of that discovery that is the central, indeed the only, concern in this book.

This is not to say that these pressures, and the debates concerning what those pressures were and how they played out, are unimportant. Quite the contrary. They are the substantive engines that drove, and continue to drive, all interesting changes in theater practice and content. My interest, however, is in what those pressures and debates have revealed. In this book I am concerned to explain that revelation and to defend it as true.

The history of theatrical innovation from the late 1800s through the late 1900s has the following upshot: without always or often intending to, theater's theoretical practitioners have put us into a position to see that a claim which a hundred years ago would have seemed completely outrageous, or at best extraordinarily hyperbolic, is true.

Theatrical performance is an independent form of art.

Moreover, this claim is true not only of our contemporary theater. It has always been true; but for a long time we did not see it. The changes in theatrical practice we have been tracing have merely made it manifest. I shall argue that spectators have always demonstrated this by practices of reception.

Now it is up to us to state and explain precisely what that means.

Notes

1 Alison Hodge, ed., *Twentieth Century Actor Training* (London and New York: Routledge, 2000), pp. 1–2.

2 Christopher Innes, "Introduction," in *A Sourcebook on Naturalist Theatre* (London and New York: Routledge, 2000), pp. 1–27 (especially 3–19).

3 John Osborne, *The Meiningen Court Theatre 1866–1890* (Cambridge: Cambridge University Press, 1988).

4 Innes, *A Sourcebook*, pp. 33–8. Innes provides a useful timeline of major events in the period during which Naturalism had its official heyday in theater – from the 1850s through the early 1900s – with references to events before and after. The success of Sardou continued the influence of Scribe well into the late nineteenth century.

5 Christopher Innes, "Contextual Overview," in *A Literary Sourcebook on Henrik Ibsen's 'Hedda Gabler'*, ed. Christopher Innes (London and New York: Routledge, 2003), pp. 13–14. A similar fact is reported about two productions of Chekhov's *The Three Sisters*, one involving the practices of standard Romantic theater and the other, directed by Stanislavski, less than a decade later. Sharon Marie Carnicke, "Stanislavski's System: Pathways for the Actor," in *Twentieth Century Actor Training*, ed. Alison Hodge (London and New York: Routledge, 2000), pp. 11–36.

6   Not everyone notices this. Sue-Ellen Case, *Feminism and Theatre* (New York: Routledge, 1988), p. 122, mistakenly identifies the relevant psychological theory as Freud's.

7   Hodge, *Twentieth Century Actor Training*, p. 4, and Carnicke, "Stanislavki's System." Another view, one that links Stanislavski less with the emerging science of his day and more with the distinctively Russian feel of both Chekhov and Tolstoy, is presented in R. I. G. Hughes, "Tolstoy, Stanislavski, and the Art of Acting," *Journal of Aesthetics and Art Criticism* 51/1 (1993), 39–48.

8   In fact, the Moscow Art Theatre has a figure of a seagull over its entryway. I am grateful to an anonymous reviewer for pointing this out to me.

9   Nemirovitch-Dantchenko reported, in recounting the similarities in viewpoint he found he shared with Stanislavski, that each was astonished at the practices of rehearsal that had been in place before the advent of their new approaches. Nemirovitch-Dantchenko devotes several pages to describing the absence of any discussion of what the play is about in those practices, the way that the director's influence is increasingly absent after the initial blocking of the scenes, and how, in the end, those rehearsal practices ensure that "the actors will arrange the play by themselves." Vladimir Nemirovitch-Dantchenko, *My Life in the Russian Theatre*, trans. John Cournos (New York: Theatre Arts Books, 1968), pp. 94–6; first published in 1936).

10 Hodge, *Twentieth Century Actor Training*, p. 2.

11 Jane Milling and Graham Ley, *Modern Theories of Performance* (Basingstoke, Hants.: Palgrave, 2001), pp. 28–9.

12 He likens the theater to a garden that the men of theater have not tended well, thereby creating a situation in which "it has been annexed by anyone who wished to make use of it . . . playwrights . . . musicians, . . . painters." E. Gordon Craig, "Plays and Playwrights, Pictures and Painters in the Theatre," in *On the Art of the Theatre* (London: William Heinemann, 1911), p. 121.

13 E. Gordon Craig, "The Actor and the Über-Marionette," in *On the Art of the Theatre*, pp. 55–8. This argument depends on a failure to draw a distinction between an "artistic medium" and a "vehicular medium." But Craig may be forgiven this, since that distinction was not fully understood until very recently. See David Davies, *Art as Performance* (Oxford: Blackwell, 2004), pp. 56–60.

14 Milling and Ley, *Modern Theories*, p. 55.

15 Craig, "The Actor," pp. 71ff.

16 At least at one point in his career, Meyerhold takes a position that is almost a direct echo of Craig's – although they are at some distance and probably did not know of each other's view. Specifically, the thought each expresses is that the work of literature (for Craig it was Shakespeare, for Meyerhold it was mystery writers) would be better off were it not contaminated by the theater – and the theater would be the better for the lack of such works as well. Craig, "Plays and Playwrights," pp. 118–22, and Vsevolod Meyerhold,

"The Fairground Booth," in *Meyerhold on Theatre*, ed. and trans. Edward Braun (London: Methuen, 1969), p. 121.

17   Meyerhold, "Fairground Booth," pp. 124–7.

18   Jacques Copeau, "A Private Place," in *Copeau: Texts on Theatre*, ed. and trans. John Rudlin (London and New York: Routledge, 1990), p. 29.

19   Bertolt Brecht, "Shouldn't we abolish aesthetics?" in *Brecht on Theatre*, trans. and ed. John Willet (London: Eyre Methuen, 1964; paperback ed., 1978), p. 21; the essay dates from 1927.

20   Bertolt Brecht, "Short Description of a New Technique of Acting which Produces an Alienation Effect," in *Brecht on Theatre*, pp. 136–47; the essay was written in 1940 but not published at the time. For the specific techniques mentioned, see p. 138.

21   Bertolt Brecht, "Notes on Erwin Strittmatter's play *Katsbraben*," in *Brecht on Theatre*, pp. 247–51, most notably p. 250; the notes from which this essay was taken were written in 1953.

22   Bertolt Brecht, "Study of the First Scene of Shakespeare's *Coriolanus*," in *Brecht on Theatre*, pp. 252–65, notably p. 259; this essay was written in 1953.

23   Antonin Artaud, "Metaphysics and the Mise en Scene," in *The Theater and its Double*, trans. Mary Caroline Richards (New York: Grove Press, 1958), p. 37.

24   Milling and Ley, *Modern Theories*, p. 96, put it this way: Artaud "exists for us in writing."

25   Artaud, "Metaphysics," p. 37.

26   W. B. Worthen, "Disciplines of the Text/Sites of Performance," *TDR* 39/1 (1995), p. 14.

27   Antonin Artaud, "An Affective Athleticism," in *The Theater and its Double*, pp. 133–41.

28   Jerzy Grotowski, "The Theatre's New Testament," trans. Jorgen Andersen and Judy Barba, in *Towards a Poor Theatre*, ed. Eugenio Barba (New York: Routledge, 2002), p. 28.

29   Jerzy Grotowski, "Towards a Poor Theatre," trans. T. K. Wiewioroski, in *Towards a Poor Theatre*, ed. Eugenio Barba (New York: Routledge, 2002), pp. 15–25, especially 19–21.

30   Jerzy Grotowski, "The Theatre's New Testament," p. 32. One should take Grotowski's idea of finding theater's essence with a grain of salt. Theater is not a "natural kind" like gold or water. So it has no defining essence. It does have traditions, of course, and against some traditions one or two elements might well stick out as "definitive" of the practice; but that is far from providing necessary and sufficient conditions. See James R. Hamilton, " 'Illusion' and the Distrust of Theater," *Journal of Aesthetics and Art Criticism* 41/1 (1982), 39–50.

31   Ludwik Flaszen, "*The Constant Prince*," in *Towards a Poor Theatre*, ed. Eugenio Barba (New York: Routledge, 2002), p. 97.

32 Robert W. Corrigan, "The Theatre in Search of a Fix," *Tulane Drama Review* 5/4 (1961), 21–35.

33 Robert W. Corrigan, *The Theatre in Search of a Fix* (New York: Delacourte Press, 1973).

34 Robert W. Corrigan, "The Search for New Endings: The Theatre in Search of a Fix, Part III," *Theatre Journal* 36/2, The Margins of Performance (1984), 153–63.

35 Ibid., p. 156.

36 Despite the name, it was first performed in 1968. See the review by Stefan Brecht in *The Drama Review: TDR* 13/3 (1969), 156–8.

37 Gerald Hinkle, *Art as Event: An Aesthetic for the Performing Arts* (Washington, DC: University Press of America, 1979).

38 But its central claims are referred to as a point of departure for an extended analysis of a performance by the Metropolitan Opera, in Marvin Carlson, "The Ghosts of Versailles," *Theatre Research International* 25/1 (2000), 3–9.

39 Hinkle's book was not widely reviewed. But the review by Arnold Berleant, *Journal of Aesthetics and Art Criticism* 38/3 (1980), 345, was prescient. Berleant suggested that "it might even be instructive to take the performing arts as the reigning model" for all art. This idea has now been taken up and worked out in detail in what will become a highly influential book by David Davies, *Art as Performance.*

40 S. Brecht, review in *TDR*, p. 156.

41 Ibid., p. 158.

42 Dan Issac, review of the book *Dionysus in 69*, ed. Richard Schechner, *Educational Theatre Journal* 22/4 (1970), 435.

43 While the description quoted is accurate of *Dionysus in 69*, it was actually written about the other main performance by The Performance Group in 1969, *Makbeth*. Julius Novick, "*Makbeth*: 'Taken from Shakespeare'," theater review, *Educational Theatre Journal* 22/2 (1970), 208.

44 Herbert Blau, "*Elsinore: An Analytic Scenario*," *Cream City Review* 6/2 (1981), 57–99; quotation from p. 57.

45 Richard E. Mennen, review of the 1976 New Theatre Festival, *Educational Theatre Journal* 28/4 (1976), 555.

46 Ruby Cohn, review of two pieces by Kraken, *Educational Theatre Journal* 29/4 (1977), 556.

47 Here one might mention only *Serpent* and *Terminal* developed by the Open Theater group in 1967 and 1969, respectively. The former was built upon improvisations on texts from the Book of Genesis, the latter from a variety of texts, including medical descriptions of the embalming process.

48 Gerald Rabkin, "Is There a Text on This Stage? Theatre/Authorship/Interpretation," *Performing Arts Journal (PAJ)* 9/2–3 (1985), p. 146.

49 Ibid., p. 158.

50 Quoted in Rabkin, "Is There a Text?", 146. A slightly fuller excerpt is in Jonathan Kalb, *Beckett in Performance* (Cambridge: Cambridge University Press, 1989), p. 79.

51 Terry McCabe, *Mis-Directing the Play: An Argument against Contemporary Theatre* (Chicago: Ivan R. Dee, 2001), p. 16.

52 Kalb, *Beckett in Performance*, pp. 82–4.

53 Rabkin, "Is There a Text?"

54 Deborah Saivetz, "An Event in Space: The Integration of Acting and Design in the Theatre of JoAnne Akalaitis," *TDR* 42/2 (1998), 132–56. See also Nicole Potter, "Introduction," in *Movement for Actors*, ed. Nicole Potter (New York: Allworth Press, 2002), p. ix.

55 Saivetz, "An Event in Space," p. 135.

56 Noël Carroll, "Dance," in *Oxford Encyclopedia of Aesthetics*, ed. Jerrold Levinson (Oxford: Oxford University Press, 2003), p. 583. This is the "provisional" and "impressionistic" definition with which Carroll begins the entry. The rest of the essay discusses a variety of alternative ways to thicken the definition. See also Francis Sparshott, "The Philosophy of Dance: Bodies in Motion, Bodies at Rest," *The Blackwell Guide to Aesthetics*, ed. Peter Kivy (Oxford: Blackwell, 2004), pp. 276–90.

57 Saivetz, "An Event in Space," p. 143. See again, Potter, "Introduction," who writes, "In performance, the actor's body, and all that it entails – alignment, shape, senses, impulses, sounds, gestures – tells the story. If the body is the place of synthesis, it is as important for the student, teacher and director to be aware of an array of approaches [to movement] as it is for them to have knowledge of diverse styles of theater and acting techniques" (p. ix).

58 Sue-Ellen Case, *Feminism and Theatre*.

59 J. Ellen Gainor, "Rethinking Feminism, Stanislavsky, and Performance," *Theater Topics* 12/2 (2002), 163–75, and Deb Margolin, "Mining My Own Business: Paths between Text and Self," in *Method Acting Reconsidered: Theory, Practice, Future*, ed. David Krasner (New York: St. Martin's Press, 2000), pp. 127–34.

60 David Krasner, "I Hate Strasberg: Method Bashing in the Academy," *Method Acting Reconsidered: Theory, Practice, Future*, ed. David Krasner (New York: St. Martin's Press, 2000), pp. 3–39.

61 Rabkin, "Is There a Text?," pp. 149–50. The thought is echoed by Herbert Blau, "The Impossible Takes a Little Time," *Performing Arts Journal (PAJ)* 7/3 (1984), 29–42, especially 30.

62 Shannon Jackson, *Professing Performance: Theatre in the Academy from Philology to Performativity* (Cambridge: Cambridge University Press, 2004) presents an analysis of what happens in academic – that is, bureaucratic – discussions when "performativity" is the name of a movement in literary studies and "performance studies" is the name of a potential academic department. The first chapter, "Discipline and Performance: Genealogy and Discontinu-

ity" (pp. 1–39), is especially illuminating regarding the history of depart-
ment-making in the academy.

63 Richard Schechner, "A New Paradigm for Theatre in the Academy," *TDR*
36/4 (1992), 7–10. This brief manifesto has been a lightning rod for the
debates on this issue. See also Richard Schechner, "Performance Studies: The
Broad Spectrum Approach," and Barbara Kirshenblatt-Gimblett, "Performance Studies," in *The Performance Studies Reader*, ed. Henry Bial (London
and New York: Routledge, 2004) pp. 7–9 and 43–55. See also Sue-Ellen
Case, "Theory/History/Revolution," in *Critical Theory and Performance*,
ed. Janelle G. Reinelt and Joseph R. Roach (Ann Arbor: University of
Michigan Press, 1992), pp. 418–29.

64 James Hamilton, "Theater," in *Routledge Companion to Aesthetics*, 2nd
edition, ed. Berys Gaut and Dominic McIver Lopes (London and New York:
Routledge, 2001), pp. 585–96.

65 Michael Kirby, "On Acting and Not-Acting," in *Art of Performance: A Critical Anthology*, ed. Gregory Battcock (New York: E. P. Dutton, 1984), pp.
97–117.

66 Marvin Carlson, "The Resistance to Theatricality," *SubStance 98/99* 31/2–3
(2002) (special issue: *The Rise and Fall of Theatricality*, ed. Josette Féral),
238–42.

67 Roselee Goldberg, "Performance: A Hidden History," and "Performance:
The Golden Years," in *Art of Performance: A Critical Anthology*, ed. Gregory
Battcock (New York: E. P. Dutton, 1984), pp. 24–36 and 71–94. The first
essay argues that performance had been used in the classical avant-garde in
the early twentieth century to work out problems of "the viewer's perception
in art" (p. 25). The "golden years" are the years we are discussing here, the
1960s and 70s.

68 Cee S. Brown, "Performance Art: A New Form of Theatre, Not a New
Concept in Art," in *Art of Performance: A Critical Anthology*, ed. Gregory
Battcock (New York: E. P. Dutton, 1984), pp. 119–24.

69 Arnold Aronson, *American Avant-Garde Theatre* (London and New York:
Routledge, 2000); Bert Cardullo and Robert Knopf, eds., *Theater of the
Avant Garde 1890–1950* (New Haven: Yale University Press, 2001); David
Graver, *The Aesthetics of Disturbance* (Ann Arbor: University of Michigan
Press, 1995); James Harding, *Contours of the Theatrical Avant-Garde* (Ann
Arbor: University of Michigan Press, 2000); Christopher Innes, *Avant Garde
Theatre 1892–1992* (London and New York: Routledge, 1993). Innes, for
example, argues that what unites the trends in the historical theatrical avant-
garde is a tendency to "primitivism," understood as "the exploration of
dream states or the instinctive and subconscious levels of the psyche; and the
quasi-religious focus on myth and magic, which in the theatre leads to experiments with ritual and the ritualistic pattern of performance" (p. 3).

70 Noël Carroll, "Performance," *formations* 3/1 (1986), 63–79, especially
64–5.

71 Hamilton, "Theater," pp. 592–5.
72 Carlson, "Resistance," 242. Philip Auslander, *From Acting to Performance: Essays in Modernism and Postmodernism* (London and New York: Routledge, 1997), pp. 2–3.
73 Schechner, "A New Paradigm," pp. 7–8.
74 Auslander, *From Acting to Performance*, pp. 3–4.

2

THEATRICAL PERFORMANCE IS AN INDEPENDENT FORM OF ART

2.1 Theatrical Performance as Radically Independent of Literature

The claim that theatrical performances are works of art independent of literature must be connected to a view about the relation between texts used in theatrical performances and the performances themselves. Although there are a number of more specific and detailed models of the text–performance relation, they fall into four general and ideal kinds: the literary model, the two-text model, the type/token model, and the ingredients model. Few theorists now defend the literary model despite its considerable strengths. Many theater and performance theorists accept the two-text model. Most philosophers engaged in analytic aesthetics accept something like the type/token model as roughly on the right track. I argue for the ingredients model and the radical independence of theatrical performance that is associated with that model.

The literary model

Adherents of this model hold the following claims to be true.

(1) Theatrical performances are presentations of works of literature, typically but not exclusively works of dramatic literature.
(2) Audiences establish the identity of a performance by reference to the literary work it presents.
(3) A performance is a performance of some work just in case it is faithful to that work.

(4) Theatrical performances are not works of art; instead, the works of art presented in theatrical performances are the works of literature that are performed.

(5) Works of dramatic literature are distinctive in that they typically have two modes of presentation – as works to be read and as works to be performed.

The literary model need not be construed as denying that theatrical performances involve considerable artistry or that theater practitioners are genuine artists. What *is* denied is that the artistry of performers issues in works of art which are distinct from the literary works that are presented.

This model expresses three important and related ideas about the ways audiences engage with theatrical performances. First, it provides a straightforward way to characterize what audiences do when they assert what performance they saw. Audiences always see works of literature illustrated or interpreted by means of the theatrical arts, whether or not they are aware of that fact. So, when they identify a performance they have seen, they always do so by reference to the literary text whose illustration or interpretation they saw. Second, this model explains how it is that, in seeing a performance of a play, audiences see the play itself. And, third, the model explains how audiences identify different performances as being of the same play.[1]

But the literary model faces two serious obstacles. First, there are the difficulties in sorting out what counts as faithfulness to a text. While there may be no coherent non-historical standard for faithfulness, I know of no principled reason that rules out a historicized account of fidelity. On a historicized account, a standard of fidelity will be any internally coherent agreement demonstrably consistent with the aims of theater practitioners and the expectations of audiences at a particular historical moment. Thus, for example, *we* might think that Naturalistic performances and even Brechtian performances could be faithful performances of *A Doll's House*, but that a performance such as Mabou Mines's *Dollhouse* – with its unusual casting and chanted passages – pushes the line, and that anything beyond that kind of performance (such as we might imagine Grotowski to have done, making use of Ibsen's text as mere material or pretext for an image theater production) can never be construed as faithful to, and hence a performance of, Ibsen's work at all. But in a possible culture with a different standard of fidelity, rooted in quite different "cultural norms [of] theatrical production . . . and reception,"[2] audiences might view the matter differently. They might, for example, acknowledge the fact that

Mabou Mines's production relied on roughly correct perceptions of Ibsen's intentions with respect to the images in his own script and, so, decide the performance meets *their* standard. Had Mabou Mines's production instead stressed *our* preoccupations with those images – as would be the case had Grotowski actually directed it – audiences in *that* possible culture could find the performance failed to meet their standard of fidelity and that it was not a performance *of* Ibsen's work.

The idea of historicized standards of fidelity is not inconsistent with anything in the first three claims the literary model holds true; but it probably violates the spirit of that model because it puts considerable pressure on the fourth claim. That is, the idea that "the 'of' of theatrical activity is subject to a fair degree of oscillation" – the idea that fidelity is always "a question both of the possible and the allowable"[3] – may give greater privilege to performer artistry than would fit comfortably with an absolute denial of artwork status to performances.

More importantly, even a historicized standard of fidelity is subject to a direct and devastating challenge. For such a standard relies on works of dramatic literature being far more stable than they are or ever have been. Most of the classical works of Western dramatic literature exist in multiple *original* versions. This is because they were originally written as scripts for performance and only later edited, almost never by the author, as works for reading.[4] As originally written, most scripts are provisional, subject to change by performers and directors, and frequently improved upon as vehicles for the stage by this process. Many plays exist in multiple "authoritative versions."[5] So it is not clear to *which* work a performance is to be judged faithful.

A still more serious challenge to the literary model has to do with theatrical performances that are not faithful to the works of which they are performances and with performances that are of no previously existing work. Consider: any performance faithful to the text of Ibsen's *Hedda Gabler* – by some historically grounded standard of fidelity – would be a performance of *Hedda Gabler*. It might be a bad performance of that work, but it would still be a performance of that work. But, were the second and third claims true and were a performance *not* faithful to the text, then that performance would fail to be a performance of *Hedda Gabler*. It might be a good theatrical performance, but it simply would not be a performance *of* Ibsen's drama at all. But, if the first claim of the literary model is true, it must still be a performance *of some work of literature*. And the trouble is, it is not at all clear what work that could be.

A proponent of the literary model might suggest we can secure literary works for such performances because, on principle, a script is always retrievable from a performance. The thought is that some spectator, skilled at stenography, could always retrieve the spoken text that is essential to the identity of the work being performed.[6] There are several problems with this suggestion. First, it is a plausible strategy only if scripts can be reliably reconstructed from performances; and there are good reasons to doubt this can be done. The retrieval idea depends on the stenographer's ability to separate clearly two sets of elements in a performance: those that are the result of instructions for performance that may come from the text or from the director and those that are the verbal component of the work of literature. But this is put into question by possible Brechtian performances of the piece; and even with Naturalistic performances it is not always possible.[7] Second, even if this sort of retrieval were possible, that fact provides no reason to think of the retrieved script as a work of dramatic literature. Third, even were we persuaded to accept a retrieved script as a work of dramatic literature, that script need not have the right kind of intentional connection to the performance. For comparison: even if we could reconstruct a script from a particular improvisational theatrical performance, we need not think – and we characteristically do not think – that the performance was a performance *of that script*. And, finally, the problem is exacerbated by the fact that there are performances that simply cannot be construed, under any analysis, as performances *of* any work at all: this class of performances includes works of *Commedia dell'Arte* and mime, well-understood historical instances of theatrical performances which do not involve performances *of* any work, and it also includes many instances of experimental theater work in the 1960s and 70s.[8]

The two-text model

Like the type/token model to be discussed below, this model takes its cue from the widely shared idea that most texts used in theatrical performances are *written to be performed*[9] and tries to spell out that idea in greater precision and detail.[10] The two-text model conceives of the relation between a play and its performances as consisting in the relation between two different kinds of languages: a play consists of linguistic signs and a performance of theatrical signs.[11] Concerning the performance this means, more precisely, something like the following:

> by 'performance text' is meant a theatrical performance, considered as
> an unordered (though complete and coherent) ensemble of textual

units (expressions), of various lengths, which invoke different codes, dissimilar to each other and often unspecific (or at least not always specific), through which communicative strategies are played out, also depending on the context of their production and reception.[12]

This idea of a performance-as-a-text rests, ultimately, on the further idea of reading human actions as texts. This founding thought has been given rigorous explanation by some;[13] others have relied on it as simply an analogy.[14]

Adherents of this model hold the following claims to be true.

(1)   Typically, *but not always*, theatrical performances are translations, "transformations," or "reconstitutions" of the contents of corresponding written texts.
(2)   When a theatrical performance corresponds to a written text, audiences establish performance identity by reference to the text of which the performance is a translation, completion, instantiation, or execution.
(3)   Because there can be no univocal translation, transformation, or reconstitution of a corresponding written text, the fidelity standard required by the literary model is "useless."[15]
(4)   Theatrical performances or productions are works of art in their own right.
(5)   The written texts translated into performance texts are usually works of art, specifically works of dramatic literature.[16]

Two features of the two-text model are immediately evident. First, it promises fuller resources for dealing both with those performances that do not meet a fidelity standard (and, so, on the literary model are not *of* a given text) and with those performances that are simply not of a text at all. This model acknowledges right off that there will be such cases and attempts to make room for them. Second, this model holds that theatrical performances are artworks in their own right, where that claim is taken to mean performances can be identified and assessed in terms that are appropriate to the aesthetic, artistic, and social experiences that audiences get from other kinds of art.

Any special advantages of the view are those that accrue to the idea of human action as texts. Most notable among the latter is the possibility of a serious methodological alliance between performance studies and those social sciences for which the idea of human action as readable, like a text, was originally developed. A further advantage is that the two-text theory appears to sever the "fidelity" tie between written texts used in a performance and the performance texts that can arise out of them.

The two-text theory faces insurmountable difficulties. First, it is unclear that the two-text theory actually achieves an escape from the fidelity standard. If a performance is a translation or even a reconstitution of a written text, it is still the written text that is responsible – at some level – for the performance. If the claim that the fidelity standard no longer has any utility was intended to mark an escape from the authority of authorial intentions, the two-text theory will for this reason have failed.[17] Second, some have argued that there are non-semiotic performances. These performances formally realize a written text. But they resist being *read* as meaningful performance *texts* because the selections of features in those performances are either a matter of chance or the result of other techniques having no semantic content.[18] Thirdly, the two-text model appears to fail at one of those things the literary model does well, namely, showing how seeing a performance of a play is seeing the play itself. On this model one never sees the play, only a translation, transformation, or reconstitution of the play.[19] And finally, by putting the performance in the relation of translation, transformation, or reconstitution of the written text, the two-text model not only fails to escape "the hegemony of the [written] text," but for that reason also fails to make good on the idea of theatrical performances as works of art in their own right, at least if that was to mean their artistic status is equal to that of the written text.[20]

Despite these weaknesses of the two-text model of the text–performance relation, some model grounded in the idea that texts are written for performance is likely to be attractive. For, all versions grounded in that thought attempt to put the right weight on the artistry involved in producing theater.

The type/token model

Some have thought about the text–performance relation in more explicitly ontological terms and have sought to explain it by employing the distinction between an instance of a kind and the kind itself.[21] This distinction is frequently captured by reference to "types" and their "tokens." Adherents of this model hold the following claims to be true.[22]

(1) Theatrical performances are instances ("tokens" or "tokenings") of plays, understood as "types"; and plays may be initiated in a number

of ways, for example by writing a text or by staging an individual performance.

(2) Audiences establish the identity of a performance by reference to the play-types that are tokened in the performance.[23]

(3) When a play is initiated by an author writing a text for performance, the author's text sets forth what will count as a performance that tokens the type; so the writing of that text counts as having written a play.

(4) Theatrical performances are works of art in their own right.

(5) Two competing views of the art-status of the texts that initiate theatrical performances are associated with this model. One of these holds that, when a play is initiated by a text, there is only one work of art, namely, the fully instantiated or completed work in performance that also contains, as a crucial part, significant elements of the text itself. For this reason, we should think of this as a "one-artwork" view.[24] On this view, a text written for performance is not a work of art in its own right; it must be completed or instantiated in performance in order to be a work at all. In contrast, a "two-artwork" view holds that, when a play is initiated by a work of dramatic literature, the theatrical performance is a token of the play-type but so also is the written text; so the written texts of dramatic literature still have two modes of presentation, as texts to be read and as texts to be executed in and as performances.[25]

The strength of this model is that it succeeds where each of the foregoing models succeeds and also where they fail. The type/token model gives a straightforward story about what audiences do when they assert what performance they saw; and that story explains both how it is that, in seeing a performance of a play, audiences see the play itself and how it is that audiences can identify different performances as being of the same play. In seeing any performance of a play one is seeing a token of the play, an instance of it; so one is seeing the play. Moreover, this model provides resources for dealing with those performances that are simply not of a text at all. In these cases what counts as a play-type is something initiated *by a performance*; and what count as further performances of that play is determined by the play-type that is initiated by the first performance. And, finally, the model can be used to push the thought that theatrical performances are artworks in their own right. For one can easily see that this model allows separate criticism of the play-type, of the means by which the type is tokened, and of its performance-tokens – as well as of the integration of these elements.[26]

One thing the type/token model does not do that the two-text model seeks to do is to sever the 'fidelity' tie between written texts used in a performance and the performance texts that can arise out of them. There must still be some standard by which to determine when a given performance actually tokens forth the play-type.[27] And so it will face some of the same challenges the literary model faces. First, there is no reason to think the standard of faithfulness is any clearer when we think of texts as initiating a play than when we think of them as literary works. Nor should we be any more sanguine about the stability of such texts written to initiate play-types than about that of texts considered as works of dramatic literature. So it will be unclear exactly which version of the text initiates the play-type in any case.

Second, a separate account will have to be devised to handle those performances that do not meet any kind of fidelity standard, and are so divergent from the elements constitutive of the play-type that they cannot plausibly be regarded as even defective tokenings of that type. Clearly, these cannot be regarded as performances *of* a given play. Proponents of the type/token model handle these cases as follows: these performances may be analogous to musical inventions or "fantasias"; they may be performances of totally different plays; and in some cases they may be instances of performance art (about the play, for example) rather than instances of theatrical performances of the play.[28]

The *ad hoc* character of these solutions is not problematic from the point of view of ontology. But it does pose epistemological problems. For it is unclear in such cases how audiences are to identify the performances they are seeing. Apparently they must first identify the performance and then, presumably by comparing to the play-type, conclude the performance is aberrant in one of these ways. A similar epistemological problem confronts this model's solution to the case of those performances that are simply not initiated by a text at all. In those cases what counts as a play-type is something initiated *by a performance*; and what counts as further performances of that play is determined by the play-type that is initiated by the first performance. The question is how audiences are to identify the first performance. Viewed ontologically, the performance is of a play-type that is being initiated by the performance; but viewed epistemologically, as the audience first encounters the performance, it is unclear how they are to think of it and so identify it.

But, of course, audiences have no problem identifying performances of this kind. Whatever the correct ontology of performance is, the epistemology is pretty clear. In fact, even when a play has been, as this model has it, initiated by a written text, most of us are in this situation: if I have seen only one performance of *Hedda Gabler* that is what *Hedda Gabler* is for me; if I go to another play billed as "Hedda Gabler" I will conclude I saw the same play as on the first occasion if I think the same story was presented and if I and other people come out talking about the story and characters pretty much in the way I did on the first occasion.

It is by explicit reference to our experiences of performances that most of us do, in fact, identify the performances we have seen by what we say to each other when we come out of theaters.

The ingredients model

Adherents of this model think of the texts used in theatrical performances as just so many *ingredients*, sources of words and other ideas for theatrical performances, alongside other ingredients that are available from a variety of other sources. Works of dramatic literature, in particular, are not regarded as especially or intrinsically fitting ingredients for performances. As ingredients they are but one kind among many possible sources of words for a theatrical performance. Textual dialog provides, in other terms, "another piece of information."[29]

There may be extrinsic reasons for regarding works of dramatic literature as especially useful kinds of ingredients for theatrical performances.[30] But imagine this situation: a number of cooks are put in a room with a bunch of potential ingredients of various kinds in order to figure out and prepare a meal. They have no recipes, no performance directives, no elements amounting to constitutive rules defining what the meal they produce should look, sound, smell, or taste like. They have nothing but their own abilities as cooks, their knowledge of the ingredients themselves, formed by knowing what other cooks have done with those and similar ingredients, and their ideas of the kinds of dishes or meals they want to prepare. This is exactly analogous to the situation that faces individual painters before a canvas. And it is the situation facing theatrical performance companies when setting out to create a performance on the ingredients model of the text–performance relation.

More specifically, then, adherents of the ingredients model hold these claims to be true.

(1) Theatrical performances are not presentations *of* works of literature, nor are they 'performance texts' arrived at by the transformation *of* a written text, nor are they the completion or execution *of* works that are initiated – in any substantive sense – in written texts of any kind.

(2)   Performance identity is established by reference to aspects of, or facts about, the performance itself and sometimes to aspects of and facts about other performances too.

(3)   A performance is, accordingly, never a performance *of* some other work nor is it ever a performance *of* a text or *of* anything initiated in a text; so no faithfulness standard – of any kind – is required for determining what work a performance is of.

(4)   Theatrical performances are artworks in their own right.

(5)   A text used as a source of verbal and other ingredients in a theatrical performance may have another life as a work of literary art. But it need not. Moreover, whether the text has a literary life of its own is a question logically unrelated to the use of any materials from that text in a theatrical performance. That is, there simply is no theatrical mode of presentation of works of dramatic literature: as works of dramatic literature they are *only* texts to be read.

This last observation need not be construed as determining *how* such literary works should be read. They may be literary works, but the question remains: does the fact that they were written for performance contribute features that should be considered in thinking about how to *read* them?[31]

The first important difference between the ingredients model and the others is that it drops the idea that theatrical performances are *of* something *extraneous to the performance*. The leading problems facing each of the previous models we discussed arise from the idea that performances are intentional, that they are almost always *of* something other than the performance itself. This model avoids those problems straight off. And it is fairly intuitive.

Clearly not everything we regard as a performance is intentional. Consider what you have in mind when you compliment your friend after watching her deftly wriggle out of a very public and socially awkward moment. "Good performance," you say, after the dust has settled. You feel no need to think there must be a something *of which* hers was a performance. There is no such need in such a case. The ingredients model generalizes this idea to all theatrical performances.

The intentional idiom can reappear without reference to texts. Suppose you see your friend extracting herself in the same way on another occasion. In that case you might be inclined to compliment her, saying, "You did it again!" By the pronoun "it" you intend to refer to a social routine of some sort she seems to have for getting out of tough social situations. The social routine your friend has performed is analogous to the performed routines of gymnasts; and many of those have names. And once a routine has a name, the intentional idiom "of" may easily reappear in reference to routines.

The second main difference between the ingredients model and the others is that this model accepts the common practice of audiences, that they establish performance identity by means of reference to the performance itself, as the only relevant account of performance identity. This claim needs a good deal more support than is gained by pointing out that this appears to be the way audiences actually do go about identifying performances. For not just anything we say to each other when we come out of the theater is taken as identifying a performance. That is one reason the appeal to an extraneous something or other *of which* a performance was a performance has been very strong. Further support for that appeal is supplied by the fact that some performances are hard to identify with any precision at all *as individual events occurring at specific places and times* because of their interactive nature[32] or because they involve a relationship between audience and performance that is intermittent, fragmented, and of no set duration.

I defend the ingredients model in chapters 5 through 7 of this book. I argue that a proper account of how we understand theatrical performances shows us how we do in fact identify them. More specifically, I argue for three claims. First, in chapter 5, I argue that there is a basic level of comprehension of theatrical performances that does not require attention to more than what is provided in the moment-to-moment flow of performance as it is happening on the stage. In chapter 6, I argue that the mechanism by which that tracking takes place involves convergence by even quite disparate spectators onto a common description of what has taken place in the performance; and I further argue that, because of the way those convergences are secured, the resulting descriptions of what has taken place amount to basic-level identifications of performances as works.

The argument for the claim that we are able to identify works without reference to the texts they use is incomplete, however, if we do not also have an account of how audiences identify elements of a performance (for example, characters, images, props) across performances in a production, across productions employing the same script material, and across performances utilizing different script materials (when, for example, the same characters appear in different stories). In chapter 7, I offer an analysis of how spectators identify elements across performances that relies on the recognition capacities of audiences in everyday circumstances and on the fact that theatrical performances are live events in space and time.

2.2 Theatrical Performance as a Form of Art

If a practice is a form of art, it can be expected to produce works of art. One common conception of a work of art is that it is "an enduring thing, created in some medium (such as oil on canvas) by an author (such as a painter) in order to be beheld in a particular kind of way (namely, to be viewed aesthetically)."[33] Clearly, seeing theatrical performance as a form of art having performances or productions as its "works" challenges some aspects of this conception. The idea that works of art are all "enduring things" has already come under pressure, of course, if not by music then certainly by dance.

One might want to insist that for a practice to be productive of works of art, we need to specify the essential medium/media of all the products belonging to the form and perhaps to do so in a way that sets or at least explains the limits to what can be expressed in the specified medium/media.[34] Alternatively, one might want to insist that we have to specify the sensory mode(s) to which the aesthetic features of the products of the practice primarily appeal. But this idea of a fixed medium, perhaps appealing to a specific range of the senses, for each work of art or each art form is simply untenable. So the fact that there is no obvious single medium of theatrical performance – despite the fact that very nearly all theatrical performances employ human beings as performers – is not a new challenge to the common conception.[35]

As to viewing something aesthetically, the key idea I will employ for thinking about this is that for a practice to be regarded as a practice of making art, the products of the practice – its works – must be observable, appreciable and evaluable *as achievements*.[36] We appreciate works of art, in no small part, because we appreciate the achievements they embody. And, although we rank works of art far less frequently than may be supposed, we do sometimes evaluate works of art; and a measure we use appears to be that there is more achieved, in some sense, in better works than in lesser.

To be sure, many other human practices, none of which are artistic in any direct sense, are valued because of the achievements they allow human beings to make. Gymnastics is an obvious example. Nevertheless, it seems correct to connect being an achievement to works of art and to most of what we say and do with them. But this fairly minimal conception of what it takes for a practice to be considered a practice of art-making needs to be enriched in two ways.

First, to correctly appreciate anything for the achievement it embodies, we must understand what that achievement is. This requires a grasp of the background against which any work is, or is not, an achievement and against which one is able to determine the kind of achievement for which one should be looking. With respect to the latter, this involves knowing not only what to appreciate but also how to appreciate it – both what is to be looked for and how to go about looking.[37]

Second, an interest in achievement in works of art involves an interest in details, an interest in answering the question why certain details are present and others are not, and in answering the question what a given detail can tell us about the whole work.[38] This may be thought to mean restricting attention to what is under the intentional control of the artist within each individual work and assuming a fairly narrow sense of being under intentional control. But the position for which I will argue does not commit us to these restrictions.[39]

In the case of theater, being able to answer these questions means being familiar with traditions of content and of performance practice, and of their interconnections. In chapter 8, I articulate and defend success conditions for having a deeper understanding of a theatrical performance than that which is sufficient for identification of the work. I show that deeper understanding of a performance comes in the forms of understanding traditions of contents and understanding traditions of performance practices. By reference to the mechanism by which we acquire deeper understanding, I show, further, that these must be different kinds of understanding and require knowledge of different kinds of information. Finally, I argue that, although deeper understanding is necessary for a full appreciation of a theatrical performance, it is not sufficient for it. What a spectator needs, I argue, is an interpretive grasp of the interconnections between what a performance presents and how and why the performers have gone about presenting it the way they have.

In chapter 9, I set forth a view about the general kinds of choices performers make in developing theatrical performances and I use that view to justify provisional definitions of theatrical conventions and theatrical styles. In chapter 10, I defend the view that while a number of different things may properly be called "interpretations" of a theatrical performance, only one of those is genuinely relevant to the question whether theatrical performance is a form of art. And I connect that idea of interpretation with a grasp of styles.

In chapter 11, I entertain and respond to a deep skeptical worry about the view I have put forward regarding the grasp of styles and even the understanding of conventions. I examine the provisional definitions of theatrical styles and theatrical conventions by contrasting them with leading theories of social conventions and artistic styles in the philosophical literature. And I defend a characterization of the full appreciation of theatrical performances against the skeptical worry. I show that that characterization is consistent with the ideas, set forth here, that appreciation of works of art is a matter of assessing achievement, against a background of relevant information, and that appreciation proceeds by answering the kinds of questions about details that explain what is going on in any given work and why that is what is going on.

In the Epilogue I return to "the myth of 'of'." What leads many to think the literary or the two-text model of the text–performance relation must be correct is nothing more than an adherence to a set of performance practices that have dominated the theatrical tradition for the past several hundred years. Those practices have been so dominant, and so fruitful, that it is hard to think otherwise than in these terms. I use material developed in chapters 9 and 11 to define "theatrical traditions" and show that it is essential to a tradition that most people working in them become blind to other ways of doing things. I then present and defend a definition of "the text-based tradition." I show that only a very few facts about the text-based initiation of a performance constrain that performance. What actually does the constraining in that tradition, I will argue, has to do with the ways that changes in conventions alter what can be learned from a performance.

Once the text-based tradition and false views about what constrains performances within that tradition no longer have us in their thrall, we have a way of describing its characteristic theatrical performances within the general scope of the view defended in the book. By focusing on the very same material we used to determine what a full appreciation of a performance consists in, we are able to notice that some performances in the text-tradition are performances in which companies have chosen to constrain their other choices *as though* the false views were true.

A major advantage of this approach is that, while we can continue to judge performers' success in terms of the text-based tradition, just as we could before, we can also judge something else about the performers' success. Namely, we can explain and evaluate the choice to be so constrained in the aesthetic and cultural environment in which a company find themselves. Where the text-tradition had obscured the fact, the most basic decisions about how to employ a text are finally seen as choices concerning which spectators can make appropriate aesthetic and artistic judgments.

Notes

1 David Saltz, "When is the Play the Thing? – Analytic Aesthetics and Dramatic Theory," *Theatre Research International* 20/3 (1995), 266–76. Saltz shows that this is also a central concern of at least one variety of two-text model (268).

2 John Rouse, "Textuality and Authority in Theater and Drama: Some Contemporary Possibilities," in *Critical Theory and Performance*, ed. J. G. Reinelt and J. R. Roach (Ann Arbor: University of Michigan Press, 1992), p. 146.

3 Ibid.

4 See Marjorie Garber, *Shakespeare After All* (New York: Pantheon Books, 2004), pp. 8–19, and Leah Marcus, "Localization," in *Puzzling Shakespeare: Localization and its Discontents* (Berkeley: University of California Press, 1988), pp. 1–50, especially 26–32.

5 Philip Gaskell, "Example 12: Stoppard, Travesties, 1974," in *From Writer to Reader: Studies in Editorial Method* (Oxford: Oxford University Press, 1978), pp. 245–62.

6 Although he has other issues in mind than establishing faithful texts *retroactively*, Nelson Goodman suggests this in *Languages of Art* (Indianapolis: Hackett Publishing Company, 1976), pp. 210–11.

7 This is not the claim that we do not have a notation for capturing the performative aspects of the performance, defended by Patrice Pavis in "The Discourse of Dramatic Criticism," trans. Susan Melrose, in *Languages of the Stage* (New York: Performing Arts Journal Publications, 2nd printing, 1993), pp. 111–30. Goodman acknowledges as much. It is instead an entailment of a claim defended by Patricia A. Suchy that there are cases when it is impossible to separate the instructional material from the verbal component *in the scripts* of some important contemporary plays: "When Words Collide: The Stage Direction as Utterance," *Journal of Dramatic Theory and Criticism* 6/1 (1991), 69–82. I will argue later that, once we grasp the mechanism by which even basic comprehension of a theatrical performance is secured, we will see immediately why Goodmanian retrieval is impossible.

8 Marcus, "Localization," p. 39.

9 This is true both far and near. See Garber, *Shakespeare After All*, p. 12, for Renaissance practices, and W. B. Worthen, "Disciplines of the Text/Sites of Performance," *TDR* 39/1 (1988), 13–28, especially 16–17, for contemporary practices.

10 I do not place much emphasis here on the question whether a literary or a theatrical mode of understanding the idea of a text as written for performance is most appropriate. For the purposes of this book, that is beside the point. Harry Berger argues that the more theatrical mode of understanding what this means leads to an impoverished understanding of plays because it relies upon the limitations imposed by the conditions of performance, including especially the limitations imposed by what an audience can take in during

the time of a single performance: *Imaginary Audition: Shakespeare on Stage and Page* (Berkeley: University of California Press, 1989). See David Saltz, "Texts in Action/Action in Texts: A Case Study in Critical Method," *Journal of Dramatic Theory and Criticism* 6/1 (1991), 29–44, for a solid examination of the tension between these two modes.

11   David Saltz, "When is the Play the Thing?", p.266.

12   Marco De Marinis, "The Performance Text," from *The Semiotics of Performance*, trans. Aine O'Healy (Bloomington: Indiana University Press, 1993), pp. 47–59: reprinted in *The Performance Studies Reader*, ed. Henry Bial (London and New York: Routledge, 2004), pp. 232–51; the quoted text is on pp. 232–3. Others holding a two-text theory are Erika Fischer-Lichte, *The Semiotics of Theater*, trans. Jeremy Gaines and Doris L. Jones (Bloomington: Indiana University Press, 1992), pp. 173–217, and Patrice Pavis, *Languages of the Stage*, pp. 25–35, 135–43.

13   Paul Ricoeur, "The Model of the Text: Meaningful Action Considered as a Text," *Social Research* 30 (1971), 529–62.

14   Catherine Bell, "'Performance' and Other Analogies," from *Ritual Theory/Ritual Practice* (Oxford: Oxford University Press, 1992), pp. 37–46: reprinted in *The Performance Studies Reader*, ed. Henry Bial (London and New York: Routledge, 2004), pp. 88–96; the reference is to 92–3.

15   Fischer-Lichte, *The Semiotics of Theater*, p. 206. See also Andrew Parker and Eve Kosofsky Sedgwick, "Introduction," in *Performativity and Performance*, ed. Parker and Sedgwick (New York: Routledge, 1995), pp. 1–18.

16   Fischer-Lichte, *The Semiotics of Theater*, pp. 185, 191, 191–206, Pavis, *Languages of the Stage*, p. 140, and Kier Elam, *The Semiotics of Theatre and Drama*, 2nd edition (London and New York: Routledge, 2002), pp. 190–1. However, I see no reason the view must be tied to this position.

17   Worthen, "Disciplines of the Text," pp. 14, 20–2.

18   Michael Kirby, "Non-Semiotic Performance, *Modern Drama* 25/1 (1982), 105–11.

19   David Saltz, "When is the Play the Thing?", p. 273.

20   Ibid., pp. 273–4.

21   This does not require a commitment to Platonic realism about kinds. One can be a nominalist about kind *terms* and still draw the relevant distinction. It is useful to remember that Nelson Goodman (*Languages of Art*), who is responsible for first applying this kind of analysis to works of art, is a dyed-in-the-wool nominalist.

22   A number of analytic philosophers have proposed some sort of type/token analysis of the text–performance relation, beginning with Nelson Goodman, *Languages of Art*. The view I present here is something of a composite of the three best views: those of Paul Thom, David Saltz, and Noël Carroll. In the end, I think Saltz's view is the stronger – in part because he brings practical experience in the theater directly to bear on the details of the analysis he

gives and in part because his nominalist convictions about types are success-fully sustained – but nothing I say either for or against this model depends on that judgment.

23 Saltz argues correctly – at "What Theatrical Performance Is (Not): The Interpretation Fallacy," *Journal of Aesthetics and Art Criticism* 59/3 (2001), p. 303 – that what play-types take as tokens are really productions, not per-formances. Productions, in turn, act both as tokens (to plays as types) and as types (to their individual performances). This refinement is not germane to the discussion at hand, so I do not focus upon it.

24 Paul Thom, *For an Audience: A Philosophy of the Performing Arts* (Philadel-phia: Temple University Press, 1993), pp. 76–80. I thank John Fisher for suggesting I think of these as "one-artwork" and "two-artwork" views.

25 Noël Carroll, *A Philosophy of Mass Art* (Oxford: Oxford University Press, 1998), p. 212.

26 Ibid., p. 213.

27 Saltz, "When is the Play the Thing?", pp. 271–3, and Thom, *For an Audi-ence*, pp. 111–12.

28 Stephen Davies, "John Cage's *4′ 33″*: Is it Music?", in *Themes in the Philoso-phy of Music* (Oxford: Oxford University Press, 2003), pp. 11–29, and David Saltz, "When is the Play the Thing?", p. 272.

29 Michael Kirby, "The New Theatre," in *The Art of Time: Essays on the Avant-Garde* (New York: E. P. Dutton, 1969), pp. 75–98, especially 90ff.

30 See Thom, *For an Audience*, pp. 60–73 and 139–53, for a defense of the view that, even though performances can occur without works, a practice of performances including works, especially "works for performance," is a more valuable practice than practices that exclude them. For an argument that a tradition of performances without works would restrict performance possi-bilities, see Robert Hapgood, "Script and Performance," *PMLA* 114/2 (1999), 224–5, a reply to W. B. Worthen's "Drama, Performativity, and Performance," *PMLA* 113/5 (1998), 1093–1107.

31 See n. 10 above.

32 Philip Auslander, *Liveness: Performance in a Mediatized Culture* (London and New York: Routledge, 1999), pp. 47–8. See also Marco de Marinis, "The Performance Text," in Bial, *The Performance Studies Reader*, p. 235.

33 Thom, *For an Audience*, p. 28.

34 Richard Wollheim, "On the Question 'Why Painting is an Art?'," in *Aesthet-ics: Proceedings of the 8th International Wittgenstein Symposium, Part I*, ed. Rudolph Haller (Vienna: Hölder-Pichler-Tempsky, 1984), pp. 101–6.

35 James Hamilton, "Theater," *Routledge Companion to Aesthetics*, 2nd edition, ed. Berys Gaut and Dominic McIver Lopes (London and New York: Rout-ledge, 2001), pp. 585–96, entailed by the argument at 592–5.

36 This idea is suggested by, among others, Denis Dutton. See his "Artistic Crimes: The Problem of Forgery in the Arts," *British Journal of Aesthetics* 19 (1979), 302–14.

37 For further discussion of these points, see Allen Carlson, "Appreciation and the Natural Environment," *Journal of Aesthetics and Art Criticism* 37/3 (1979), 267–8, and Paul Ziff, "Reasons in Art Criticism," in *Philosophy and Education*, ed. I. Scheffler (Boston, 1958), pp. 219–36, especially §1, 220–33.

38 Roger Scruton, "Photography and Representation," in *The Aesthetic Understanding* (London and New York: Methuen, 1983), pp. 102–26, especially §8, 116–19.

39 For a discussion of these points with respect to Scruton's views about photography *per se*, see Nigel Warburton, "Individual Style in Photographic Art," *British Journal of Aesthetics* 36/4 (1996), 391–2.

3

METHODS AND CONSTRAINTS

3.1 Idealized Cases that Help Focus on Features Needing Analysis

We imagine idealized theatrical performances in two ways and for two quite different purposes. One way is related to the practice of "production analysis." Production analysis aims to imagine fairly full-blown performances when it is not possible to attend an actual performance. The aim is "to clarify *possible meanings and effects*, primarily for readers, critics, and theatergoers" and the result "should be improved understanding of *the performance potentialities* of the play at issue."[1]

Philosophers, in contrast, use idealized cases in order to abstract those features of actual cases that they think need explanation. Which aspects of a case need explanation will depend on the question being asked. That is, given a well-formed question about a group of actual cases, not every feature of each case will need to be explained, but only those relevant to the question.[2] This is the mode in which I now ask you to imagine groups of cases of which each is a set of variants on Ibsen's *Hedda Gabler*.

These groups of cases are idealized, or artificial, in three ways. First, each reflects one kind of use of Ibsen's text. Although some developments in theater practice since the beginning of the twentieth century have involved the recycling of earlier texts from the tradition of dramatic literature, other new performances have been based on texts well outside the tradition of dramatic literature and even outside of any literary tradition whatever.

Second, these idealized cases reflect practices involving the use of scripts. But much of the performance art tradition and some of the

theatrical performance tradition has eschewed anything like scripts altogether. Nor is that anything new in the history of theater. It almost goes
without saying that mime employs no scripts. The *Commedia dell'Arte*
and vaudeville traditions are based on stock routines and consist largely
of sequences of improvisational variations of the stock routines. Sometimes the sequences themselves are improvised or, as in some fully improvisational theater, given over to the audience to determine.

Finally, the developments in theater that these idealized cases reflect
were motivated by specific challenges – aesthetic, social, and political –
facing theater and culture at very specific times. But these idealized cases
altogether ignore the motivating aspects of any actual cases.

I ask you to imagine these idealized cases primarily because I hope it
will highlight important aspects of theatrical performances that are relevant to the questions I address: in what ways are theatrical performances
independent of literature and film, and in what ways are theatrical performances appreciable as works of art? All other features of any actual performances involving Ibsen's scripts for *Hedda Gabler* are either ignored
entirely or invoked only to contribute to a focus upon the relevant
features.

I choose to employ Ibsen's work – even if only in translation – because
I think it safe to assume that performances using that script are familiar
even to most theatrical novices. As Christopher Innes writes,

> *Hedda Gabler* was published [in German] in December 1890 and first per-
> formed at the Residenztheater, Munich, January 1891. Since then it has
> become the most frequently performed of all plays (with the possible excep-
> tion of one or two by Shakespeare). With over sixty productions, many of
> which have enjoyed long runs or toured extensively, *Hedda Gabler* has
> appeared almost continuously somewhere on the American or European
> stage over the whole of the last century.[3]

I have developed these cases in part to make the otherwise bewildering
array of new performance practices more available to theater novices by
providing gradually more distant contrasts with an example of theatrical
performance with which they should be familiar. The performance studies
and theater studies literatures are replete with descriptions of actual cases
that are relevant; and anyone familiar with that literature should be able
to locate them and see how the idealizations presented here are related
to the questions addressed in this book.

For those unfamiliar with Ibsen's story, here is a sketch of the main
outlines of the plot. As the action opens, Tesman and Hedda have returned

from what she regards as an unsatisfying honeymoon trip to a house he has purchased for her in the mistaken belief that she wanted a house in which to make a home, with him. Tesman is a mediocre university professor who has dedicated most of that honeymoon to his abstruse researches. Hedda is strong-willed, aristocratic, and passionate, with a reputation for irresponsibility. She has indeed had wilder days and now sees nothing but a boring, emotionless desert before her. Adding to the intensity of her feelings is the fact – only obliquely referenced in the script – that she is pregnant and that she wishes she were not. She is entangled with the lives of others in this story, including Tesman, his aunts (one of whom is dying), Brack (a judge and seducer), Lovborg (Tesman's professional rival and a former suitor of Hedda's), and Mrs. Elvsted (a recent widow who is now hopeful for Lovborg's attentions). Hedda acts in ways guaranteed to create even more tangles in their lives. When Lovborg thinks he has lost the manuscript of the scholarly work that will finally secure him the position he craves, Hedda's action is crucial and emblematic. Her response is to give him one of her target pistols with the encouragement to shoot himself. Irresponsible that may seem, but in Ibsen's telling, Hedda seems also to be aiming at finding something that could be done, once for all, by any of them, that would be "a free and fearless action."[4] At the end of the play, Hedda is profoundly disappointed to discover that Lovborg has shot himself only accidentally and not deliberately as she had initially supposed. Hedda burns the manuscript of Lovborg's book that has come to her hands. And she kills herself with the other pistol.

   Here is the first idealized case.

Hedda-to-Hedda

The company arrives at the theater ready to rehearse the play in which they have been cast. The stage manager distributes the scripts. Each performer is to play a character and finds her or his lines in the script by reading the speech prefixes in the text. The director describes the scene. As prescribed by the author, the play will take place entirely in the living rooms in the house Tesman has purchased. The director has been thinking about the play for several months. She has done a serious study of the performance history of the play and has determined that the company will follow at least all those stage directions that can be attributed to Ibsen himself. All other stage directions in their scripts are the products of previous performances; they will ignore these and will determine their own stage movements in the course of rehearsal. The director may at this point suggest any line changes she has been considering and give a general sense of the interpretive ideas that are to govern the performance. The company will do a read-through and the rehearsal process is under way.

The actors may approach their roles using a "twin-track" idea of acting. Michael Frayn and David Burke describes this as follows:

> Acting is mostly a twin-track mental activity. In one track runs the role, requiring thoughts ranging from, say, gentle amusement to towering rage. Then there is the second track, which monitors the performance: executing the right moves, body language, and voice level; taking note of audience reaction and keeping an eye on fellow actors; coping with emergencies such as a missing prop or a faulty lighting cue.[5]

Another approach might be to acknowledge that acting *can be* a twin-track mental activity, but insist on attempting as nearly as possible a performance on only the first of the two tracks: setting it up so that, as far as possible, the execution of the role is unconscious, once set in motion; ignoring the audience; playing through in such a way that the response to what happens in the environment is always entirely from the responses of the character. Crudely put, we can call this the "single-track" approach to the role. Theater practitioners sometimes refer to these approaches as "external" and "internal" approaches to roles. Many people will have heard of so-called "method acting" and will correctly associate the various techniques that go by this name with at least some variety of what I am calling the "single-track" approach.

These approaches are variations of a single case. But, to retain recollection of the distance between twin- and single-track approaches within the case let us call it "Hedda-to-Hedda."

Gabler at a Distance

The company arrives at the theater for the beginning of rehearsal. The stage manager distributes the scripts and the performers find their roles in the script by referring to the speech prefixes. As in *Hedda-to-Hedda* cases, each performer will portray one or more characters (if double-cast, for example). But as the director begins to lay out the interpretation she has in mind, they discover that at times an actor may say another character's lines, prefacing them with either "And he said . . ." or "And she said . . ." As the company rehearses, additional line reading techniques are introduced. Occasionally, a performer will be called on to preface her or his own character's line with "And I said . . ." The performers may be asked to state the stage directions Ibsen wrote in the script and others of the director's invention, so that each character sometimes describes what she or he does as she or he is doing it. During the rehearsal process, the company comes to employ other techniques that are consistent with whatever effects are achieved by the techniques already mentioned. In all the rest, the performance practices are the same as the familiar stage practices found in performances of the *Hedda-to-Hedda* type.

Some people have thought that the span from the single-track to the twin-track approaches to acting described in *Hedda-to-Hedda* encompasses the full range of possible theatrical performances. That this is not the case, if it ever has been, can easily be seen by imagining *Gabler at a Distance*. Performances of the *Gabler at a Distance* type may seem to owe more to story-telling practices than to the practices of theater. But many theater people – only perhaps most notably Brecht[6] – have tried out something like this kind of performance practice for purposes that prevent them from performing a narrative more straightforwardly.[7]

Spontaneous Beauty

The company arrives at the theater to begin rehearsals. As the stage manager distributes the scripts, one actor discovers he has a script that amounts to a narration of much of the story in Ibsen's text. Moreover, he has quite a few lines that are signaled by the speech prefixes of other characters in Ibsen's original script. A second actor has a script with many, but not all, of the lines designated in Ibsen's text by the speech prefix "Hedda Gabler." The company realizes there is only one other actor, who has been assigned exactly the same lines as the second actor but whose script begins with the words, "You will be Hedda's 'ghost': as such you will express Hedda's emotions through gesture, occasional verbal doubling of the actor portraying Hedda, and appropriate non-verbal sounds; these will be developed in the course of rehearsals." Others who make up the company are told they will form a group of visible puppet-handlers. As the director explains her concept of the play, the performers discover that Hedda will sometimes be portrayed by a puppet – or even by several puppets of varying sizes. The actor playing Hedda is to speak Hedda's lines only in the least emotional tones so that Hedda's *alter ego* – or "ghost" –, who is always present when Hedda is on stage, expresses all of Hedda's felt reactions to events in the story. A final group of performers have been cast because of their musical skills. They will accompany the performance by producing sounds that sometimes give insight into the inner lives of the characters and that at other times are simply sound effects. So, for example, the percussionist would make the sound of

gunshot at the end of the play when Hedda shoots herself. Perhaps this
sound would be followed by a cry from the actor portraying Hedda's
"ghost."

Let us call cases of this kind "Spontaneous Beauty." This particular
version of *Spontaneous Beauty* uses techniques from Japanese *bunraku*
traditions. But a number of twentieth-century directors and groups used
techniques from Chinese, Indian, and Balinese traditions for staging
scripts from the Western narrative tradition. These include Antonin
Artaud, Gordon Craig, Mabou Mines, and Alfred Jarry. We will have them
in mind when referring to this class of cases.

The first three idealized cases involve practices from the mainstream of
the European tradition, broadly speaking, including practices from the
early stages of the twentieth-century theatrical avant-garde. They are all
cases of narrative theatrical performances. The remaining cases push
beyond those practices, both because they are non-narrative performances
and because of the techniques they employ. So they provide us with a
fuller sense of the task facing any philosophical discussion of theater as an
independent art form.

Burning Child

A company of performers have been working with dance theater techniques in a workshop setting for many months before they begin to reflect
on Ibsen's script. In the course of their encounter with the script, they
decide they will use only lines from that script (including Ibsen's stage
directions). But they also decide they will assemble a new text by asking
each member of the company to think about those lines he or she believes
express, or could be an appropriate reaction, to deep social problems of
contemporary life. Meanwhile, during their physical work they develop
images from the action in the script, using their own bodies and those of
their fellow performers – images that they take to be essential to the new
text they are crafting out of Ibsen's script. At one stage in the process,
they provisionally settle on two sets of images. One set centers on the
burning of Lovborg's manuscript and the other on the table in Ibsen's
script's living-room. After intense debate, they choose to make images of
the burning of the manuscript central to their performance because it is
often regarded as the "moral climax" of Ibsen's play[8] and because it
reflects the destruction of Hedda's unborn child that she literally accom-
plishes with her suicide later in the play. They choose to retain some
images of the table because it is around that table that so many of the

telling reflections of social depravity revolve. They see Lovborg, Judge Brack, and Tesman as violating Hedda, each in his own way, each without either recognition or apology. The images they develop centering on the table reflect this sense of violation and betrayal. Finally, having assembled a text, having decided who will say what and how it will sound, they work out a sequence of their images, into and out of which they can move over the course of delivering the text. They choose to structure the sequence using a musical or visual analog of the classic structure of problem–development–climax–denouement for organizing the sequence of images. Once narrative is abandoned, it is likely that such a structure will be abandoned as well; but it need not be. This company aims to create the tension and release patterns characteristic of narrative theater, but without the narrative.

Let's call this class of cases "Burning Child." We will have in mind any performance that is developed by means of a process like the one described and that makes use of the techniques of "the theater of images."[9] So this would include some of the work of Richard Foreman, Mabou Mines, and Robert Wilson, as well as Jerzy Grotowski.

Something to Tell You

A company takes every line in Ibsen's script and rewrites it as a sentence that some member of the company could say truthfully in front of and to an audience. The company makes most of those sentences simple declarative sentences. They write as conditionals sentences forming a certain number of key passages. The company thinks of places in which the same sentence could be repeated for interesting acoustic effect. The company decides who says what sentences, bearing in mind that each sentence could be said by more than one of them. The company now works on rhythmic and dynamic patterns, listening together to a lot of rock and roll and jazz, paying attention to rhythmic patterns and opportunities for musical irony in their script. The company organizes the resulting text for the performance using an explicitly musical form – for example, the result could be a set of themes and variations. The company rehearses and performs with the aim of creating the kind of sonic experience one gets from music.

This class of cases, that I propose we call "Something to Tell You," is even further removed from *Hedda-to-Hedda* than is *Burning Child*. One mark of the difference between this kind of performance and the preceding cases is the fact that the conditions of theatrical performance are referred to explicitly within the performance itself. I have patterned this group of cases on the self-referential theatrical performance described in the prologue to *Offending the Audience*, by Peter Handke. It is helpful to know that this passage from the prologue is both a description of what the performers do and do not do in the piece and also itself part of the piece performed. Here is some of that prologue:

> We are speaking directly to you. Our dialogue no longer moves at a right angle to your glance . . . You are no longer disregarded. You are not treated as mere hecklers . . . There are no asides here . . . We don't step out of the play to address you. We have no need of illusions to disillusion you. We show you nothing. We are playing no destinies. We are playing no dreams. This is not a factual report. This is no documentary play. This is no slice of life. We don't tell you a story. We don't perform any actions. We don't simulate any actions. We don't represent anything. We don't put anything on for you. We only speak. We play by addressing you.[10]

Something to Tell You is a way of imagining using the script of *Hedda Gabler* to reflect the style of Handke's *Offending the Audience*. And, of course, its themes would be very distant from Ibsen's.

Pistols and Other Doors

A company lists all the sentences and sentence fragments in *Hedda Gabler*, numbers them, and then selects the order of their appearance in the text using some randomizing technique.[11] The company is not prepared to rely entirely on chance ordering; and so they edit the resulting text, looking for ways to enhance rhythmic effects, plays on words, jumbles of interesting-sounding nonsense, language that is just on the edge of sense and then flies off in unexpected directions. Before the rehearsal process begins, the company debates and decides to stress some underlying theme, namely, the risk of absurdity in any apparently sensible venture. This company's performance, like that in *Something to Tell You* cases, aims at creating sonic effects. But the company also aims at generating visual effects that sometimes underscore and sometimes undermine those moments of actual sense-making that occur in the script. The company chooses to create a routine that mixes dance and traditional stage move-ment techniques; and they have done this for reasons relating to the overall structure and themes they wish the piece to express. In the end, the performance style seems to owe more to dance technique than to practices of traditional stage action.

As Michael Kirby notes,[12] styles of theater that owe more to Grotowski and Open Theatre – here exemplified by *Spontaneous Beauty, Burning*

Child, and to a lesser extent *Something to Tell You* – have dominated the theatrical avant-garde. It is important that we have an example of a form of theatrical performance that has largely been marginalized, even in the avant-garde. This is why we imagine the idealized class of cases I propose we call "Pistols and Other Doors." This final idealized case is brought in to reflect the facts that, in the early twentieth century, Gertrude Stein, Tristan Tzara, and other surrealist and dada performance artists explored the techniques of *Pistols and Other Doors* for crafting scripts for theatrical performance and that, in the period following World War II, Eugène Ionesco used some of these same techniques, albeit to very different ends.

Other varieties of theatrical performance

Each of these examples has called attention to *performers* engaged in some style of theatrical performance. *Hedda-to-Hedda* cases call for a number of different acting styles and strategies most of which are variations on single-track or twin-track approaches to roles. Cases like *Gabler at a Distance*, which include Brechtian analyses and performances, require acting strategies of a very different sort. *Something to Tell You* and the others call for radical changes in the performers' approaches to the performance as well.

But the interaction between audiences *and performers* is not all that goes on in a theatrical performance, however central that interaction may be to the phenomena we wish to survey. So I will conclude this tour of the terrain with three examples that widen our fund to include other aspects of what goes into a theatrical performance.

In the first two examples, what count theatrically are lights, sounds, and spaces. Each of these two pieces was created in the Italian Futurist movement near the beginning of the twentieth century. Of greater interest is that neither of them involves performers enacting anything.

In *Detonation: Synthesis of All Modern Theater*, by Francesco Cangiullo, the curtain opens to reveal a suggestion of a crossroads on an otherwise bare stage. After a long pause, there is a gunshot. The curtain closes.[13]

In *Colors*, by Fortunato Depero, the curtain opens to reveal four regular geometrical solids, in four different colors. As sounds are made – presumably piped in from performers speaking into microphones off stage – each object shimmers and shivers. When the sounds cease, the curtains close.[14]

For the third example, consider the remark attributed to Jerzy Grotowski: "in our theater, the actors' sweat is their makeup."[15] Standard textbooks on makeup present this aspect of the craft as aiming either at making expressions more readily visible in large theater houses or at creating something like moveable character masks – for example, using makeup to change the apparent age of the actor or prostheses to change the shape of the actor's face. In light of the standard story, Grotowski's remark may be taken as a hyperbolic expression of his refusal to disguise his actors, to mask their features. But whatever he means, he seems to have something in mind that could count as an exploration *in theater* of one of the means of theater.[16]

Self-consciously theatrical reflections on the means of theater could be extended to costumes, sets, and props. And one need not look as far as the Futurist provocations to find examples. Indeed it has become something of a staple of contemporary theater to play with the way the costumes, sets, and properties enhance features of the performance so as to contribute to the company's aims. Consider the difference between a performance from any Agatha Christie script produced with a standard box set and realistic properties (guns, scarves, letters, safes, and chessboards) and a performance from the same script, taking place on a number of levels and ramps backed by a lit scrim, in which the performers mime all the business that involves props. Someone might well ask why this might be done and wonder what kind of interpretive goal could underwrite such choices. But the point is that it could be done. And so familiar have we become with theatrical exploration of theatrical means that we would not wonder that it was done, but only why it was done.

3.2 Three General Facts about Theatrical Performances and the Constraints they Impose on any Successful Account of Theatrical Performances

The analyses I present in the rest of this book are shaped to conform to three general and obvious facts about theatrical performances. Those three facts are: (1) theatrical performance is a social form of art, (2) performers and audiences are disposed to interact in the standard conditions under which theatrical performances are seen, and (3) theatrical performance is a temporal form of art.

Theatrical performance is a social form of art

Theater involves public gatherings. It takes place in public spaces, spaces that are socially and often legally set aside for its performances. The word "audience," as it is used in the familiar locution "audience for art," does not necessarily mean actual gatherings of people. But as used with respect to theater, it does. Theater is an inherently social activity.[17]

The thesis that theater must involve gatherings of people seems to be compatible with the claim that a theatrical performance may take place with only a few audience members, only one, or even none at all. For the thesis asserts something like a dispositional property having to do with a contrast between the practice of theater and the practices of the other performing arts.[18]

The precise nature of the property can be brought out by observing a distinction between "audience practices" and "non-audience practices." An "audience practice" is the conduct of an activity requiring some level of skill for its execution with a view to presenting the activity, some of its features, or its products to an audience. A "non-audience practice" is the conduct of an activity that also requires some level of skill for its execution with a view to *realizing* the activity, some of its features, or its products, but with no view to being presented to others.

A non-audience practice of playing music might be observed by an audience. Passers-by might overhear a group of musicians playing by themselves. And that music may be listened to by those passers-by with just the same kind of attention and pleasure as they would have had if they had gone to a concert hall to hear it performed.[19] This does not, by itself, transform our musicians' non-audience practice into an audience practice of playing music. Similarly, a group of musicians, on-stage in front of an audience which has paid to hear them, may feel they are playing only for themselves, but this does not transform their activity into a non-audience practice.

The point is this: whereas playing music and dancing commonly can have both audience and non-audience forms of practice, theatrical playing has no common non-audience form of practice. The thesis that theater inherently involves gatherings of people just comes to the claim there are no common non-audience practices that are recognizable as the making of theater.

Some might object that games of make-believe should count as a common non-audience practice of theater. For make-believe, or the propensity to engage in make-believe, is among the raw ingredients in human nature that are often utilized in theatrical craft. But, whereas we do not hesitate to think of people at a party, for example, as dancing or singing, when children engage in games of make-believe we do not think they are making theater, but carrying out an activity only for themselves.

Any account of theatrical performance, especially one that treats it as an art form, must be constrained by the fact there is no non-audience practice of theater. It must, that is, make plain and explain the social nature of theater.

Audiences and performers are disposed to interact in the conditions under which theatrical performances are observed

Theater is a social institution in another sense. It is well known that performers and audiences interact in the context of a performance. Audiences watch, listen, and react to theatrical performers. Performers shape what they do with a view to the fact that audiences will observe them. Performers are also disposed to modify what they do in response to the reactions of an observing audience.

One might be tempted to acknowledge this and still think of analyzing performers' and audiences' impulses in more individual terms and then think of them as harnessed and put to use in the social institution of theater.[20] For example, we might think that the mechanism by which audiences receive what is presented to them consists in nothing more than watching, listening, and making sense, and that the disposition to react to performers is extraneous to the mechanism by which content is grasped. We might think that the mechanism by which performers present what audiences are to receive is nothing more than shaping what they do, and that their knowledge that they will be watched and listened to and will respond to audience reactions is extraneous to the mechanism by which they deliver their performances.

Problems arise immediately if these are the stories we are inclined to give. First, watching and listening to performers *is* reacting to them. So, clearly, we already have to adjust the story. We might seek to distinguish between reacting to performers when that is the means by which content is grasped and reacting to performers when it is not the means by which content is grasped. This seems right enough. Suppose a performer turns to sneeze ostentatiously, looking and smiling directly at some members of the audience. If some spectators were expecting a performance of the *Hedda-to-Hedda* type, then they are likely to react to this as a distraction from the content of the play. But, if the performance is of a kind with *Gabler at a Distance* and they still think the ostentatious sneeze is a distraction, then they are likely to miss the content that was there to be grasped by reacting to the performer in that moment. Were we to ask them what they saw and heard in the two cases, our spectators would give the same answer: "the performer turned to sneeze ostentatiously, while looking and smiling directly at some members of the audience." So the difference, we want to say, is a matter of how our spectators reacted to the performer. The problem is that, when we try to make that distinction precise, it threatens to become the circular claim: "reacting to performers is the means by which audiences grasp content just in case it is the kind of reacting to performers that allows audiences to grasp content."

Second, performers tend not to think of their own disposition to respond to audience reactions as extraneous to their craft. Indeed, some of them think of it as one of the chief issues the craft is to deal with. This may seem consistent with thinking of the disposition as a (potential) distraction. If, for example, we think of what performers do as fundamentally a matter of imitation or pretense, the fact that they will respond to audience reactions will be nothing more than a distraction. But we will then have difficulty explaining exactly what the performer is doing in the scene just described; for turning to an audience and ostentatiously sneezing seems to require recognizing that audiences will react. So the fact that performers respond to that kind of reaction seems to be a central aspect of whatever story we tell about what is going on in that performance.

In the next chapter, I articulate an intuition about what it is to "attend to" another human being. I analyze the phenomenon of "attending to" and suggest it is the underlying story about what happens between performers and audiences in theatrical performance.

Some traditional theories of theater seem to have derived authority from the idea that what they take to be the underlying human mechanism of performing, which they identify as imitation or pretense, is entirely natural. And, of course, imitation and pretense are natural impulses. But attending to people and responding to being attended to by others are impulses just as natural as the impulses to imitate or to pretend. The latter impulses, however, are inherently social in a way that the former need not be. One can imitate a wolf without expecting to be watched by another human being; one cannot intend to be attended to without expecting to be watched by another. On the account I develop in this book, the social institution of theater is not laid on top of more basic material drawn from individual impulses; instead, it is a social enterprise arising out of equally natural but social impulses.

Theatrical performance is a temporal art form

Theatrical performances require time for their presentation. Theatrical performances require time for their reception. The time in which an audience receives the theatrical performance is the same time as that of its presentation.

Theatrical performances consist of events arranged in a sequence. The sequence of events in which a given production of a play is performed need not always be the same from performance to performance. We can imagine a production in which the scenes are numbered and, upon arrival for each evening's performance, the company settles on the ordering of the scenes by drawing from a hat numbers corresponding to the scenes. Clearly, in this production one night's performance could be different from every other night's performance. Just as clearly, however, each night's performance will have been arranged and experienced by the audience in just that one particular order, albeit an order that was randomly chosen at the outset of the performance.[21]

Unless the performers make a mistake, audience experience the sequence of events in theatrical performances in the order in which the performers have arranged the events to be experienced. Moreover, the events are experienced at roughly and typically the pace the performers have arranged for them to be experienced.[22]

In all of these respects theatrical performance may be said to be a *temporal* art form.[23] Here is another. An individual moment in a theatrical performance, a "zero-duration-time-slice," is not usually considered something in the performance that is to be experienced for itself. A theatrical performance could be filmed and, as a result, single moments of individual scenes could be observed and even appreciated as pictures in their own right. But these would be freeze-frames of the *film* of the performance, and not "non-temporally extended parts" of the performance to be observed for their own sakes; for of a theatrical performance there is nothing that corresponds to that description.[24] This is not to deny that performers can stop the action in a play and allow for something to register with the audience. Such "freeze-frames," if that is what we want to call them, not only are possible, they may be very effective bits of theater. But they are not presented or experienced as moments to be understood on their own in isolation from the rest of the sequence of events comprising the performance. Indeed their value as bits of theater will be experienced precisely because of their connections to and contrasts with the remainder of the events.

A further pair of features of theatrical performances follows from the foregoing. First, there is no stepping back from a theatrical performance and taking it in as a whole in a single observation. Second, nor is there any flipping backwards and forwards through the performance to check if one got it right the first time, to remind ourselves who the character now present to us really is or to discover what will later become of her.[25]

Reference to these practices or capacities, characteristic of what one can do with movies and novels but not with theatrical performances, may be thought useful for distinguishing theatrical performance from those other forms of art. I offer no opinion about that. I focus on these practices to articulate a constraint on any account of the mechanisms by which audiences grasp theatrical performances. Whatever mechanisms we propose for that must be operationally possible under the constraint that theatrical performance is a temporal art form in the ways in which I have described.

Notes

1 Judith Milhous and Robert D. Hume, *Producible Interpretation: Eight English Plays, 1675–1707* (Carbondale: Southern Illinois University Press, 1989), p. 10. See also Andrew Sofer's discussion of this practice in *The Stage Life of Props* (Ann Arbor: University of Michigan Press, 2003), pp. 3–6.

2 One way to disagree with a philosopher's idealized case, accordingly, is to argue that some features standing in need of explanation do not appear in it.

3 Christopher Innes, ed., *A Routledge Literary Sourcebook on Henrik Ibsen's* Hedda Gabler (London and New York: Routledge, 2003), p. 1.

4 Henrik Ibsen, *Hedda Gabler and Other Plays*, trans. Una Ellis-Fermor (London: Penguin Books, 1961), p. 357.

5 M. Frayn and D. Burke, *The Copenhagen Papers: An Intrigue* (New York: Picador, 2003), p. 29 (originally published as *Celia's Secret*, London: Faber and Faber, 2000).

6 Bertolt Brecht, "The Street Scene," in *Brecht on Theatre*, ed. and trans. John Willett (New York: Hill and Wang, 1964), pp. 121–9.

7 Theater people sometimes refer to the difference between, on the one hand, the single-track approach to *Hedda* and, on the other, both the double-track approach and the distancing techniques associated with Brecht as the difference between "representational" and "presentational" acting. Since philosophers use these terms in very different ways, I avoid addressing or employing this terminology altogether.

8 Innes, *Routledge Literary Sourcebook*, p. 155.

9 B. Marranca and G. Dasgupta, eds., *The Theatre of Images* (New York: PAJ press, 1969).

10 P. Handke, *Kaspar and Other Plays*, trans. Michael Roloff (New York: Farrar, Straus and Giroux, 1969), pp. 8–9.

11 Samuel Beckett is said to have organized one of his late pieces in this way. The story is that he wrote a story of some 60 sentences, numbered the sentences, put the numbers from 1 to 60 in a hat and pulled them out. The

result was the ordering of the first half of the script. The order was reversed for the second half. This may be apocryphal.

12 This discussion is found in Michael Kirby, *Futurist Performance* (New York: E. P. Dutton, 1971), p. 7.

13 Ibid., p. 247.

14 Ibid., pp. 278–9.

15 This may be a kind of theatrical urban legend. I have not found the remark in anything I have read by Grotowski.

16 Since Grotowski has his actors work on creating masks using their own facial musculature, it is unlikely that what I have written here is what he meant even if he did say it. It is, of course, possible that he said it and that his thought about makeup is not coherent; and that may be worth exploring. But the general point still stands that one can imagine self-consciously theatrical explorations of any of the standard means of theater. See Jerzy Grotowski, *Towards a Poor Theatre*, ed. Eugenio Barba (New York: Routledge, 2002), pp. 20–1.

17 Elements of this section were initially worked out in my entry on "Theater" for *The Routledge Companion to Aesthetics*, 2nd edition, ed. Berys Gaut and Dominic McIver Lopes (London: Routledge, 2001), pp. 585–96.

18 A "dispositional property" is a property a person or thing may have even though, under many conditions, the property is not expressed. For example, "soluble in water" is thought to be a dispositional property of sugar – even though sugar does not dissolve in water under all circumstances. The thought is that, under suitable conditions, it *would* dissolve. For present purposes, I believe we can ignore the question of what ontological view to adopt regarding dispositions. See J. L. Mackie, *Truth, Probability, and Paradox* (Oxford: Oxford University Press, 1973), ch. 4.

19 Kendall Walton, "Style and the Products and Processes of Art," in *The Concept of Style*, ed. B. Lang (Philadelphia: University of Pennsylvania Press, 1979), pp. 72–103.

20 Bernard Beckerman does this in his *Theatrical Presentation: Performer, Audience, and Act*, ed. G. B. Beckerman and W. Coco (New York and London: Routledge, 1990). In the "Prologue," he notes how Leon Battista Alberti, in Book VIII of the *Ten Books on Architecture*, correctly characterizes the nature of theater as that of a kind of "social exchange," notably as one of a variety of public shows or performances (p. x). But in a later chapter, when he attempts to discriminate among this variety of performances in order to determine what defines the sub-class to which theater belongs, he writes, "Still other shows present people *pretending* to do something . . . whatever they do is a representation of some other action . . . such shows are *shows of illusion*" (p. 15, emphases in original). Despite substantial differences in approach, Bert States, in *The Pleasure of the Play* (Ithaca, NY, and London: Cornell University Press, 1994), takes much the same line when he asserts that, on the one hand, audiences are presented with performers "pretending"

in such a way that audiences are invited to believe that the actors are what they pretend to be (p. 25) while, on the other, audiences are presented with performers who are clearly engaged in a craft in such a way that audiences are invited to believe that the actors are not what they are pretending to be. These two "semic registers" constitute the puzzle, according to States, that the audience is always trying to grapple with in the theater.

21   The example is not, in fact, imaginary. Robert Corrigan, in discussion, has described such a production of *Woyzeck*. And this is the standard technique – indeed allowing the audience to pick the order of scenes – in the long-running show of Chicago's Neo-Futurists, *Too Much Light Makes the Baby Go Blind*.

22   The qualifiers "roughly" and "typically" are required because the performers may, for a variety of reasons, perform the sequence of events, in whole or in parts, more slowly or more quickly than they had planned.

23   This list is not intended to be exhaustive. There are other respects in which time plays a role in various art forms, including theatrical performance. The most recent systematic discussion of these, on which I have drawn heavily in this section, is that of Jerrold Levinson and Philip Alperson, "What is a Temporal Art?", *Midwest Studies in Philosophy*, XVI (1991), 439–50. The first five claims about theatrical performances in this chapter reflect four of the time-related characteristics of arts that Levinson and Alperson discuss. See also comments on temporally inflected features of some art forms in Stephen Davies, "Is Architecture Art?", in *Philosophy and Architecture*, ed. M. Mitias (Atlanta, GA: Rodopi Press, 1994), pp. 41–3. Others who have remarked specifically about theatrical performance as a temporal form include: Sofer, in *Props*; Marco De Marinis, "The Performance Text," in *The Semiotics of Performance*, trans. Aine O'Healy (Bloomington: Indiana University Press, 1993), pp. 47–59, reprinted in *The Performance Studies Reader*, ed. Henry Bial (London and New York: Routledge, 2004), pp. 232–51; and Alice Raynor, "The Audience: Subjectivity, Community and the Ethics of Listening," *Journal of Dramatic Theory and Criticism* 7/2 (1993), 3–24.

24   The phrase is from Levinson and Alperson, "What is a Temporal Art?", p. 443.

25   To be sure, performers may choose to play some scenes out of sequence, repeating scenes from earlier in the sequence or playing scenes that will be played again. And this may allow an audience to be reminded of someone or to discover something in advance. But this is under the control of the performers and not the audience, and so is not the same phenomenon.

4

THEATRICAL ENACTMENT: THE GUIDING INTUITIONS

Not all theatrical performances involve performers. It follows that enactment – whatever it is that is goes on between audiences and performers – is not essential to theatrical performance. Nevertheless, performers are typically and centrally involved in theatrical performances. Indeed, most of audiences' understanding of the content of typical theatrical performances is gained by watching and listening to performers. For that reason I put it forward as encapsulating the central features of what happens in most theatrical performances. The goal is to provide a model of the central interaction in theatrical performances that fits within the constraints laid out in chapter 3 and that guides the analyses in later chapters.

I have chosen to use the word "enactment" to designate what goes on between audiences and theatrical performers for several reasons. The words "acting" and "representation," words commonly used in this connection, carry so much cultural or philosophical baggage that their use could interfere with an attempt to give a clear account of what it is that theater performers do. "Acting" has associations with a form of theater dominant primarily in late European culture. These associations are not helpful when thinking about either much earlier or very recent manifestations of theater in the European tradition and are even less so when examining non-European theatrical traditions. A philosophical account of theatrical performance should put us into position to consider the precise meaning with respect to theatrical performance of the term "representation."

The main problem with these words is that they are used to refer almost exclusively to what performers do, and not to the interaction between audiences and performers. So they tend to lead away from strict adherence to one of our principal constraints, that is, the need to explain the mechanism of theatrical performance in terms that keep clearly in view the dispositions of audiences and performers to interact.

Finally, the term "enactment" has the virtues of being less familiarly used and of having fewer associations or implications of these kinds. It is, therefore, a term that approaches greater descriptive neutrality with regard to the phenomenon we want to discuss.

4.1 Enactment: Something Spectators and Performers Do

The general account of enactment I propose is this:

> Theatrical enactment is the social practice in which audiences attend to the physical and verbal expressions and behavior as well as the 'non-expressive' movements and sounds of performers (human or mechanical) who, by those means, occasion audience responses to whatever the performers arrange for the audience to observe about human life (for example, stories and characters, or sequences of images and/or symbolic acts).

This statement is unrestricted in its scope. It may not seem immediately applicable to more familiar forms of theatrical performance, such as *Hedda-to-Hedda* and *Gabler at a Distance*. Accordingly, after explaining the sense of the key terms in the account, I will present a version of the account limited to narrative performances. That version will be derivable as an instance of the more general version, and will be suitable for analyzing examples ranging from *Hedda-to-Hedda* to *Spontaneous Beauty*.[1]

4.2 The Crucial Concept: "Attending to Another"

The crucial concept in this new account of theatrical enactment is the notion of audiences' "*attending to*" performers and what they do. This is the character of the fundamental interaction that takes place in theater.

There is nothing esoteric about attending to someone. We all do it. Think of the kinds of things going on when you attend to your sick friend, when you attend to your lover, when you attend to your nemesis at poker, and when you attend to someone on the street whom you have never seen before but whose behavior suddenly strikes you as odd, interesting, or entertaining in some unusual way. Consideration of three elements in the phenomenon will lead us directly to a compelling set of ideas about theatrical enactment.

> First, attending to someone involves watching for particular events and features, falling within a proper range of events and features, where the proper range in any particular case is defined by the kind of situation in which the watching takes place.

Attending to someone is connected to "watching and listening closely." It is a kind of focusing. If I have merely glanced in someone's direction, you are unlikely to describe me as attending to him. But I may focus my attention on someone without attending to him. If I am focused on my sick friend's odd habit of whistling through his teeth when he breathes, something that I have found mildly diverting in the past, I am not attending to my sick friend *qua* sick friend. Focusing attention on another is not enough to constitute the phenomenon in which we are interested. What is missing can be brought out as follows.

In attending to someone, one is watching or listening *for* particular events or features. Attending to someone is anticipatory. If it is your nemesis at poker to whom you are attending you will watch hopefully for some things she may do and watch with trepidation for others. And you should not be surprised if something for which you are looking appears.

In attending to someone, one watches and listens for things which fall into a *proper range*. If you attend to someone who is sick, you are likely to be looking for changes in mood or in vital signs, things that reflect his health; if you are attending to someone you love, for another example, you will be looking and listening for moods, for expressions of need or desire, and for evidences of dissatisfaction, things that affect and reflect the health of your relationship. More generally, as these examples suggest, we may say that attending to someone consists of being alert both to what is expressed and to what is only indicated.[2]

What makes a particular sort of expression or sign the proper kind of object to be watched or listened for in attending to someone depends on the kind of *situation conceptually connected* to the attending. This should not be confused with the empirical matter that one might have further ends to which the attending is related as means. For example, you may attend to a sick enemy with a view to withholding consolation and comfort upon the appearance of his need for these. But if you have not looked or listened for the kinds of changes in your enemy's condition that are related to his health, you have not been attending to him in the mode of attending to a *sick* enemy. This is a conceptual connection and defines the range of features for which one watches in attending to another.

Second, attending to someone requires being prepared to respond to that for which one is watching and listening. That preparedness and the responses themselves usually take physical form.

In addition to watching for a certain range of things related to the situation that defines the attending, attending to someone also involves being prepared to respond, to react, in ways related to what one has been looking for when it appears. Failure to respond to appropriately related changes in the condition or behavior of an attendee is *prima facie*, although defeasible, evidence that one has not been attending to her. Suppose your nemesis at poker tips her hand. Were you now either to fold when you see her hand is beatable or up the ante when it clearly is not, we could plausibly say you were not paying the right kind of attention to her.

Moreover, because many of our responses when attending to another are physical, attending to someone is itself usually physical. Attending to someone usually requires being physically alert, physically prepared. We would be puzzled were you to fail to respond physically to a watched-for change in the behavior of a lover, for example. If you don't get excited when she shows her affection or if you don't show disappointment when she gets absorbed in her video games and seems to have forgotten you, something is off. Failure to behave as though ready to respond to changes in the behavior of a lover might well lead an onlooker to conclude you had become emotionally detached from this person.

Third, people react physically and sometimes emotionally to being attended to.

Because attending to someone is usually physical in the foregoing ways, it also characteristically has a physical effect on the one attended to.[3] The physical effect on attendees is related to the effects on some people when they know they are being observed. Many people prefer not to be watched doing ordinary things and are made uncomfortable when they are.

Our reactions upon discovering we are being watched belong to a second kind of case. Such discoveries are sometimes unsettling and at other times pleasurable. Many times such discoveries induce in us some degree of self-consciousness in the tasks that, moments before, we had been undertaking quite *un*self-consciously.[4]

That people who are attended to respond physically is not surprising. It would be surprising, indeed, if attendees did not so respond, especially in cases where both attender and attendee are fully cognizant that one is attending to the other, as when one attends to a (conscious) sick friend.

The range of your sick friend's reactions may extend from the minimal to the more overt and self-conscious. She may, for example, press back against the cool hand on her fevered brow or actively reach for your hand to caress it even as it comforts.

We should also note that we can imagine cases in which one can accustom oneself, train oneself as it were, not to respond in the usual way when attended to.

Summary

When one person attends to another, then (1) these people are in a situation kind that defines a specific aspect of their relationship, (2) the specific kind of situation determines what one of them watches for among the expressions or signs produced by the other, (3) the specific kind of situation further determines what the one attending is expected to do upon the appearance of those relevant expressions or signs, and (4) if conscious, the person attended to usually exhibits changes in behavior that evidence awareness of being attended to.

4.3 What it is to "Occasion" Responses

The word "occasion" should be construed broadly. In some performances responses are induced and the audience is aware of the specific means by which the responses are induced. In other performances responses are induced without such awareness.

Consider, for example, whether spectators are always aware of how the focus shifts in a performance. Audiences are usually aware of shifts of focus when, for example, a performer strides directly to center stage while the others fall silent and still. But there are subtler methods of repositioning performers to occasion a shift of focus of which spectators may not be so aware. Some cases of enactments, perhaps most, involve both inducements of which the audience is aware and inducements of which the audience is not aware.

4.4 Audience Responses: Willing Suspension of Disbelief, Acquired Beliefs, or Acquired Abilities?

The expression "responses to what is presented" should also be construed broadly. It should be understood generally to include both propositional attitudes towards images, events, situations, characters, and actions, and sub-doxastic physical reactions to these same things, that is, reactions that do not involve beliefs or belief-like mental states.[5] It is, therefore, best thought of as acquiring an ability to describe what one saw and to react in ways appropriate to what is seen.

Clearly, audiences come to believe things about situations, characters and events in the stories they watch in narrative theatrical performances. They recognize the characters, they discriminate among the options open to the characters, they hope for better outcomes than they believe are possible, and so on. If they did not, we should think they had not understood the story they had witnessed.[6]

For this reason, we should reject outright the notion, made popular by Coleridge in the nineteenth century, that audiences engage in the "willing suspension of disbelief" when confronted with fictional characters and events on-stage. That idea was hit upon as a solution to the "asymmetry" problem, namely, that we seem to have genuine emotional reactions to figures on stage and what is happening to them, but do not do what we would do when confronted with people in similar situations in everyday life. The asymmetry problem is real enough but, in view of the fact that we cannot have understood what was happening to these figures unless *we thought* they were in danger, deserved our pity, were laughable, and so on, this solution will not do. So, audiences cannot be said to suspend disbelief, willingly or otherwise, about the figures and situations they encounter in theatrical performances.[7]

It is tempting to move in the other direction and emphasize only what beliefs audiences hold about characters and their situations and actions. However, it may be more accurate to characterize the cognitive states of audiences in terms of the acquisition of an ability – namely that, in watching and listening to a theatrical enactment, audiences come to be able to react in appropriate ways and describe what it was they saw with reasonable accuracy.

One reason to prefer the ability-characterization of the cognitive states of audiences over the belief-only characterization is that it seems likely that one could articulate the set of beliefs in question without displaying the relevant reactions, but much less likely that one could display the ability in question, tell a story for example, without also displaying those reactions.[8]

Another reason is that the ability-characterization seems to put the right kind of stress on the fact that audiences react physically to what is presented to them. Audience members squirm and grimace and guffaw, wince when, for example, they believe a character is about to do something stupid, lean forward in anticipation of bad people getting their just deserts, and occasionally cry for the losses characters suffer. But audiences also react physically to images, events, characters, their traits and conduct, without the kind of awareness that is typical of belief. And this is connected to the fact that they react to performers physically. A character may be felt to be in a stronger position in the story because the performer is positioned on stage in such a way as to occasion that feeling about the character. And, unless the audience member is sufficiently cognizant of the relevant bits of stagecraft, she will be completely unaware of both the feeling towards the performer and how the response to the character was occasioned. Even when audiences are unaware of their own felt reactions, their reactions demonstrate they are following the events, the sequences of images, or whatever is happening – and yet, because they are unaware, they cannot be said to hold beliefs about those matters.

If the beliefs in question are just about such things as whether Hamlet is truly mad or merely affecting an "antic disposition" and so on, it may be hard to see how having beliefs about what is going on in the play differs from acquiring the ability to tell what they take to be the story.[9] For present purposes it is enough that we are reminded that, whatever characterization we end up giving of the cognitive states of audiences, we must not overlook these reactions, forgetting the fact that audiences react physically to characters and their situations in stories. And, accordingly, we must show how those reactions can be said to be truly informative, that is, cognitive, reactions that enable audiences to understand what it is they are seeing.[10]

A final reason for preferring the ability-characterization is its greater generality. It can accept the belief-characterization as a species. As such it forecloses on fewer substantive questions about how particular theatrical conventions work. And, at this stage of the inquiry, it is a virtue to allow as much latitude as possible as regards the nature of audience involvement in theatrical enactment.

4.5 Relativizing the Account by Narrowing its Scope to Narrative Performances

"Plays"

Throughout the book, I frequently discuss plays first and then expand the discussion to include other kinds of theatrical performances. By "play" I mean only narrative theatrical performances. As is obvious by now, not all theatrical performances are narratively structured. That is to say, not all theatrical performances aim to tell stories, are expected to tell them, or are taken as telling stories. We might wish to call such non-narrative theatrical performances "plays." But in this book I will not have in mind that wider use of the term. Nor will I be using the word "plays" to refer to *scripts* for narrative theatrical performances.

Plays and stories

We need a characterization of stories, or narratives, to make precise what is meant by a "play." That characterization must be weak enough that it does not preclude clear examples of narrative performances that happen to possess more robust structures. For example, we need not insist that a story must have a beginning, a middle, and an end, at least if coming to an end entails full-stop closure. Nor should we insist – as Aristotle did – that it set forth a causal chain leading from the first events to the last. Nor should we demand that a story set forth a sequence of events of which a description seems to organize and explain the solution to some sort of problem.[11] There are three reasons for allowing greater latitude about what counts as a story.

One reason is that there is so little theoretical agreement on what a proper account of narrative looks like. As Paisley Livingston remarks, "Theorists arguing for a favored usage of 'narrative' typically appeal to our 'intuitions' concerning which examples should and should not count as a story. It is far from clear, however, that any detailed and coherent bed of intuitions awaits any of the theories."[12]

Another reason is that performers may choose to present a narrative in a way that goes against the grain of an audience's more robust expectations regarding stories. The performers could have a view about what particular narrative structure they wish the performance to achieve and it may be a view they take in recognition of and despite the more robust expectations of their audiences. This is the sort of thing performers of pieces like *Gabler at a Distance* might seek to achieve if they know their audience is expecting a performance of the *Hedda-to-Hedda* kind. We should not foreclose on those performance strategies or render them irrelevant to a performance by adopting a more robust conception of narrative structure. We want an account of narratives that allows unanticipated kinds of things to count as narratives.

The most important reason for adopting a weak characterization of what counts as narrative is that it leaves room for audiences to discuss and debate which robust narrative structure a performance has actually displayed. The ability to have that kind of discussion would seem to be crucial to whatever account we arrive at of audience appreciation; and insisting on a robust conception of narrative would preclude these kinds of discussion.

On the other hand, the characterization of narrative must be robust enough to allow us to distinguish between narrative performances and non-narrative performances.

For example, although many stories have structures that might induce a feeling of directionality, cases of non-narrative theatrical performances may easily give us the same feeling. Consider the structures of *Burning Child* and *Something to Tell You*. We imagined a company might structure *Burning Child* by using a musical or visual analog of the classic structure of problem–development–climax–denouement for organizing the sequence of images. We thought of that company as aiming at creating the tension and release patterns characteristic of narrative theater but without the narrative. We imagined a company might structure *Something to Tell You* by adopting musical forms such as theme and variations or classical ABA sonata form and then rehearsing with the aim of creating the kind of sonic experience one gets from music. Neither of these has a narrative structure, but each has a structure that is likely to give auditors a feeling of directionality and momentum.

Nor do we want to adopt a characterization of narratives in which causal connections within sequences of events constitute a sufficient condition for a narrative. Were we to do so, any presented sequence of events having any sort of explicit and effective causal structure would be a narrative and we would be committed to holding that many performances we take to be paradigmatically non-narrative would be narrative theatrical performances after all. And we would lose the very distinction we are trying to sort out.

But we are on the right track. For this much seems right: most stories have agents whose actions and changing traits together constitute whatever movement the story possesses. This is enough to get us a generous, but precise, idea of "a story" that we can use in discussing plays. Accordingly, I propose we adopt the following:

> A story is a series of events which are either the actions or inactions of agents, usually called "characters," or the results of the actions or inactions of agents.

Relativizing the general account

We might think the restricted version of the general account of enactment will be sufficient if it focuses, like the account of narrative, only on agency. If so, we would adopt the following:

Narrative theatrical enactment is the social practice in which audiences attend to the physical and verbal expressions and behavior of performers who, by those means, occasion audience responses to characters, situations, and events in stories.

This formulation does brings agents, the situations they encounter, and the events of stories into view as what narrative theatrical enactment aims to present. And its characterization of the primary objects of audience responses ties this version of the new account directly to the mainstream European theater of the past two hundred years.

However, although this formulation is adequate to performances in the tradition of *Hedda-to-Hedda* and *Gabler At a Distance*, it fails to capture something important about our third idealized case of narrative theatrical performance, *Spontaneous Beauty*. In *Spontaneous Beauty* the performer playing Hedda speaks her mind in the least emotional tones possible and the performance sometimes relies on musical accompaniment to give us insight into the inner lives of the characters, to what they are feeling. These are not captured by the foregoing characterization. We have proceeded in the right direction, but we have restricted the scope of the characterization too much.

Fortunately, there is an obvious way we can widen the scope of those features *of the performers* to which audiences could attend. We can add to the expressions and behavioral signs of the performers the non-expressive movements and sounds of performers in certain kinds of performance.

The characterization is still too restrictive to capture exactly the narrative/non-narrative distinction. There is still one very obvious respect in which the account fails to capture something important about *Spontaneous Beauty*. We will need to broaden the range *of objects* that may be the bearers of the features to which audiences attend. That is, we need to include animals, puppets, and other mechanical devices that may be made to act like human beings within the scope of the term "performers." We achieve what we need by adopting the following version.

Narrative theatrical enactment is the social practice of having audiences attend to the physical and verbal expressions and behavior, as well as non-expressive movements and sounds, of performers (human or mechanical) that, by those means, occasion audience responses to characters, situations, and events in stories.

Although the difference between narrative and non-narrative theatrical performances has something to do with theatrical means, it is mostly concerned with the kind of object – a story – to which audience responses are to be occasioned. We have obtained the right restriction of scope by restricting the range of objects of responses to agents and events propelled by agents of whatever kind. We have not precluded the possibility that narrative performances might present sequences of images or symbolic gestures. But we have allowed that, when those are all that a performance presents, we are in the fold of non-narrative performances such as *Burning Child*, *Something to Tell You*, and *Pistols and Other Doors*, to which our general account of enactment applies.

The ease with which the general version of the account can be relativized to narrative performances counts in its favor. The key terms that drive what is distinctive about either version of the account – namely, "occasioning," "audience reactions," and "attending to" – are analyzed in exactly the same way in both the restricted and unrestricted versions. All that was required to capture the narrower range of theatrical performances that have dominated European theater for the past several hundred years was to restrict the scope of what is occasioned and what kinds of things are thought to trigger the occasioning.

Someone might complain that the general account presents an analysis of theatrical enactment that makes theatrical performances seem more like dance and music performances, or even athletic events, and less like what goes on in the movies or in literature. I welcome this observation. For it is my conviction that theatrical performance as an art form *is* more like dance and musical performance than like the art of the movies or the literary arts. And it is to the defense of those claims, modeled on the account of enactment developed here, that we now turn.

Notes

1   The basic material for this chapter first appeared in *Journal of Aesthetics and Art Criticism*, 58/1 (Winter 2000), 23–35.

2   Attending to someone includes being alert to what may be *hidden* within the expressions and signs presented to us by another. Stanley Cavell suggests, in Part IV of *The Claim of Reason* (Oxford: Oxford University Press, 1979), pp. 361–70, that the way a body can hide expression of a soul is illuminated by the way seeing the duck aspect of Wittgenstein's figure prevents one from seeing the rabbit aspect.

3   This phenomenon is especially noted in two otherwise very dissimilar accounts of the concept of a person, those of David Wiggins, *Sameness and Substance* (London: Blackwell, 1980), and Peter Winch, "Eine Einstellung zur Seele," in *Trying to Make Sense* (London: Blackwell, 1987). See also Simone Weil's "The *Iliad*, Poem of Might," in *A Simone Weil Anthology*

(London: Virago Press, 1986) and Winch's discussion of her remarks in this regard.

4   A third kind of case includes our reactions when we recognize we are being looked at in certain stereotypical ways. For example, those subjected to "the male gaze" cannot help but react and will have had to learn to cope with their own visceral reactions to these experiences.

5   A "propositional attitude" is an attitude that takes a proposition as its object. Where p is any proposition whatever, one might fear that p, hope that p, doubt that p, wish that p, believe that p, and so on. Thus, fears, hopes, doubts, wishes, beliefs are propositional attitudes. Many philosophers think that belief and desire are the fundamental propositional attitudes, because it is held we can explain all the others in terms of those two.

6   Alex Neill, "Fiction and the Emotions," *American Philosophical Quarterly* 30/1 (1993), 1–13.

7   Paul Woodruff, "Understanding Theater," in *Philosophy and Art*, ed. Daniel Dahlstrom, Studies in Philosophy and the History of Philosophy, 23 (Washington, DC: Catholic University of America Press, 1991), pp. 13ff.

8   Ibid., pp. 16–17.

9   B. R. Tilghman pointed out this line of thought to me in discussion.

10 I take up this challenge in chapter 6.

11 Paisley Livingston, "Narrative," in *The Routledge Companion to Aesthetics*, ed. B. Gaut and D. Lopes (London: Routledge, 2001), pp. 275–84, and Peter Brooks, "Reading for the Plot," and "Narrative Transaction and Transference," in *Reading for the Plot: Design and Intention in Narrative* (New York: A. A. Knopf, 1984), pp. 3–36 and 216–37.

12 Livingston, "Narrative," p. 277.

PART II
THE INDEPENDENCE
OF THEATRICAL
PERFORMANCE

5
BASIC THEATRICAL
UNDERSTANDING

 To show that theatrical performance is independent of literature, and always has been, and to justify the ingredients model of the text–performance relation, we need to explain how it is that audiences can identify performances without reference to texts.

In one sense, nothing could be easier. We often just do identify performances without such reference, using instead the names of the performing company, the names of the actors, the dates and locations of the performances for our reference points. But descriptions of our common practices can cut the other way. For we may know that it is Shakespeare's play, or Ibsen's, or Wasserstein's that we have seen. And we often refer to authors as our reference points and so appear to refer to authors' texts in fixing performance identities after all.

What we need is a more principled explanation that shows us how we go about identifying performances independently of reference to texts. I believe we can find this explanation by examining closely what it is to understand a theatrical performance.

By "understanding" I do not mean getting a full measure of the significance of the performance for oneself or for others. Nor do I mean grasping what the performers or the director was aiming at, nor even what styles they employed and to what effect. Nor, finally, do I mean having a full appreciation of the performance's artistry.[1] Instead, I mean only what it is and what it takes for a single spectator[2] to get the gist of what is presented to her in the performance as it is happening.[3] I take this to be a fairly common sense of "understanding," not laden with a bunch of theoretical or ideological baggage.

In the first part of this chapter I articulate and defend a set of success conditions for what I refer to as "basic theatrical understanding." These are conditions under which only the least generous of us would say the spectator who met them did not "really" understand the performance.[4]

In the remainder of the chapter I argue that all that is required for the success conditions for basic theatrical understanding to be met is provided by what is presented to spectators during the course of a performance, moment to moment. Even when there are more complex structures embedded in a performance that a particular spectator does not understand, that need not be a reason for denying that she has basic comprehension of the performance.

In the last section of the chapter, I raise a problem for the proposed success conditions for basic comprehension. I will have shown what it takes for individual spectators to demonstrate basic theatrical understanding. But I will not have shown that every spectator, or even most of them, will demonstrate the same things in response to the same performances. And it is plausible to hold that, if one person genuinely understands something, then others can do as well. So we require an account of the mechanism by which theatrical understanding is achieved.

5.1 Minimal General Success Conditions for Basic Theatrical Understanding

The general success conditions for *basic understanding* of a theatrical performance are:

> A spectator has basic understanding of a theatrical performance if she (1) can describe the object that was presented over the course of the performance, (2) reacts physically in the right ways to what is happening in the performance as those things happen, *or* (3) adopts the moods responsive to what is happening in the performance as those things happen.

This formulation sets forth minimal success conditions for having understood a theatrical performance. That is, anyone who can do (1), or does either (2) or (3) would be said to have understood what she has seen or to understand what she is seeing by all but the least charitable of observers.

These success conditions may seem to overlook the obvious contribution to present understanding provided by prior preparation with specifically theatrical information, including such things as having read the script prior to attending the performance. I will argue, however, that whatever advantages a spectator has because of prior preparation, these do not enhance that spectator's ability to gain basic understanding of the performance. Nor does the lack of theater-specific preparation disable other spectators from gaining basic theatrical understanding of any performance. They may fail to understand the performance, but it will not be for lack of prior knowledge of substantial theater-specific information.

5.2 Physical and Affective Responses of Audiences as Non-Discursive Evidence of Understanding

Although minimal, these success conditions may still seem overly generous. Suppose a spectator, let us call him Glenn, comes out of a *Commedia* performance laughing so hard he cannot speak. When asked what he just saw, Glenn is unable to say. Suppose he is never able to reconstruct a story line or to describe anything we would take as showing he had understood the performance. Suppose Glenn not only found the performance funny, but still laughs every time he thinks of it.[5]

Now suppose we also discover in talking to Glenn that, just the week before, he had seen a theatrical performance and, although he could tell the story presented in the performance, and can do so now, he was then and has ever since remained utterly unmoved by it.

The first case is consistent with success conditions (2) and (3) for basic theatrical comprehension. But just as clearly it is a case in which we might hesitate to claim Glenn has understood the performance. In contrast, our second case presents a challenge from another direction because Glenn fails to react in ways that meet conditions (2) or (3). Nevertheless we should agree that Glenn had basic comprehension of the second performance.[6]

The problem highlighted by these cases lies with our acceptance of non-discursive elements among the success conditions for basic understanding. What is missing in the first case but is clearly present in the second is *discursive* evidence of comprehension.

The ability to describe what one has observed is a cognitive capacity. The reactions and moods a spectator experiences need not be cognitive. If they are not, one wonders why we should think of them as evidence of *understanding* at all.

Moreover, there is a natural causal story to tell about the first case, namely, that Glenn's reactions and moods in that case were merely caused.

No recognition of the triggers or even of the fact that there are triggers for these reactions and moods was needed in order for them to be induced. Insofar as there is no recognition, there is no cognition, and no understanding either. This suggests it is simply a mistake to take Glenn's reactions and moods as evidence of comprehension; and so we should jettison conditions (2) and (3) altogether.

I wish to resist this suggestion and to insist that physical reactions and adoption of the moods responsive to what has happened during the performance may be evidence of basic understanding of a performance. One reason for insisting on this is that performers count on observing precisely these kinds of reactions in order to gauge how the performance is going and what changes might be needed to steer the performance in the right direction.[7] If audiences' reactions and moods are never signs of comprehension then performers are surely mistaken to try to gauge those reactions for the reasons they do.

Further reasons for regarding physical reactions and mood shifts as evidence of cognitive grasp of a performance are seen in the following imagined cases.

Esmerelda leans back in anticipation during a *Hedda-to-Hedda* performance at the time Hedda crosses the room and pulls the pistol out of its case. Later, Esmerelda is unable truthfully to say that, at the time, she thought or feared Hedda was about to commit suicide. She may not even have been aware of leaning back and, being unaware of her own behavior, she may not be able to say why she did it. Don't we still want to treat Esmerelda's reaction as evidence that she comprehended what was about to happen?

Amanda is unable to describe what she saw in the performance of *Burning Child* in any exhaustive and coherent fashion. Yet Amanda may have exhibited behavioral reactions to what was happening in each moment during the performance of the kind we are interested in here. In contrast Beatrice, who also saw *Burning Child*, is able to give a description of what she has observed over the course of the performance. Moreover, Beatrice is able to cite specific reactions she had during the performance that prompted her, in part, to that description. When Amanda and Beatrice meet and talk after the performance, Amanda discovers that she had experienced the same reactions that prompted Beatrice to the description she gave of what had happened. Would we then not want to say that Amanda's reactions were evidence she had understood the performance as it was happening, every bit as much as Beatrice had?

These plausible cases illustrate what is at stake for a view that includes physical reactions and adoption of moods, as these occur *during a per-*

formance, among the success conditions for basic understanding of theatrical performances. We therefore have to go against some very powerful intuitions if we do not regard reactions and mood shifts as cognitive.

We may capture the intuitions I am relying on here by employing some of the machinery of counterfactual conditionals. If a spectator has a certain physical reaction or mood shift at a given moment during a performance, she could have had others at the same time, but did not. Some of those alternative but unrealized physical reactions or mood shifts are consistent with what she would describe were she, or any other basically comprehending spectator, to provide discursive evidence of comprehension. But other reactions and mood shifts are not consistent with such a description. Let us make this idea more precise in the following ways.

- Let "a reaction is consistent with a description" mean that the reaction is one among those reactions that would be appropriate responses to a recognition recorded in a description. For example, laughter is a response, and seeing the funniness in a joke or situation is recognition. On principle, what is recognized can be described.
- Let "a reaction is consistent with another reaction" mean that both are within the range of appropriate responses to recognitions given the same description.
- A spectator's reaction is evidence of comprehension if, had she not reacted as she did, she would have reacted in some other way consistent with her actual reaction *and* if the set of reactions she could have had is consistent with a correct description of what was presented, whether the relevant description is offered by that spectator or not.

By this means we can state precisely when a reaction or mood shift is *not* evidence of basic theatrical understanding: either the reaction is not consistent with other ways of reacting that are consistent with a correct description or it belongs to an entire repertoire of reactions that is inconsistent with a correct description.[8]

This strategy ties reactions and mood shifts to descriptions in a way that makes it clear why the discussion between Amanda and Beatrice was a case of one spectator learning what to say from another on the sole basis that their reactions were the same. It also allows us to demonstrate why Esmerelda's reaction to Hedda's behavior is a sign of comprehending what is about to happen: it is so precisely because her reactions to what is going on at that moment are consistent with all other reactions and mood shifts consistent with a description of Hedda as about to commit suicide, whether or not Esmerelda can provide that description. This strategy also allows us to rekindle our confidence that when Glenn laughed at the *Commedia* performance, but could not tell the story he had seen, he really had understood the comedy. He laughed because any other reaction he might have had would have been consistent with recognizing what there was to laugh at even though he could not describe what that was.

5.3 The Success Conditions for Basic Theatrical Understanding Met by Moment-to-Moment Apprehension of Performances

Having a basic theatrical understanding of a *play* requires only the following.

> *First*, understanding a play as it happens is centrally a matter of apprehending individual bits of dialog and stage action and the immediate progression from bit to bit.
> *Second*, the objects of basic theatrical understanding are *at the outset* nothing more than (1) the moment-to-moment bits of dialog and stage action and the transitions between them and (2) those bits of dialog and stage action prepared for and then delivered in a manner available for recognition later in the play.
> *Third*, the object of basic theatrical understanding of a play, as it comes to have a *developed* object over the course of the spectator's experience of the performance, is a story.
> *Fourth*, making sense of what is happening in the performance, for a suitably backgrounded spectator, requires nothing more than observing individual bits of dialog and stage action, as they occur, and the connections they have with immediately preceding and succeeding bits.
> *Fifth*, spectators assess whether what is happening makes sense by sensing whether the bits and the transitions between bits are cogent, moment to moment.[9]

These five claims conjointly state what is required for a spectator to meet the success conditions for basic theatrical understanding. They do not provide a mechanism for basic comprehension of a performance, but they state what that mechanism has to ensure – and what it may ignore.

These requirements for meeting the success conditions may seem too weak. On this account, grasping what is happening in a play is not a matter of apprehending such phenomena as flow of action, overall plot structure, the relation between flow of action and act structure, or any other such large-scale formal features that can be correctly attributed to a play either upon reflection and further study of the script or because of prior theater-specific training. Instead, all that is grasped is the bits in the moment and how the sequence of bits becomes apprehended as a story over the course of the experienced performance.

None of this should be taken to deny that plays and the stories they tell have large-scale structures. Stories do have, for example, episodic plots or plots exhibiting the structure of the "well made play"; and some stories do have a problem–development–climax–denouement structure. Nor do I deny that understanding those large-scale features and structures can be important background for successfully crafting a script or producing a play. Nor do I deny that understanding those large-scale features can occur during a performance.

But I do deny that having a grasp of those structures is a required for "getting" the basic elements of a play. I also deny that having a grasp of those structures is normally a part of what goes on when one has a basic understanding of what is going on in a play.

5.4 "Immediate Objects," "Developed Objects," and "Cogency"

Unlike my use of the term "understand," my use of the phrase "object of understanding" is slightly more technical. However, I mean by it to refer only to whatever it is someone might say was understood. When asked what Jones understood, *whatever* we correctly give in answer is what I am calling an "object of understanding."

"Immediate" and "developed" objects

It is typical for spectators of a play to grasp the story as it is being developed over the course of their experience of the performance. As each spectator tracks the performance, she is trying to make some sort of larger sense of the more immediate objects of her experience, the individual bits of language, gesture, and movement and the transitions between them. She is assessing the cogency of the transitions and she may be making guesses about a number of different things she has observed.

When it is unclear whether the performance is actually a play, special circumstances are created and spectators must guess whether there is in fact a story unfolding. For the present, however, we are confining our attention to plays and to spectators who already know that the performances they are watching are plays. In these cases spectators are doing little more than trying to figure out, to follow – from the bits and the transitions – what the story is, where it is going, what is likely to happen next, who is doing what, what will happen to whom, how some character will feel, and so on.

The idea is that the immediate objects of basic theatrical understanding include not only the bits of dialog and action and the transitions between them but also those bits of dialog and stage action that are setups for dialog or action that can be recognized later. This should be understood much as we grasp how the punch line of a joke is prepared for and perhaps only much later delivered. Understood in this way, we get a good approximation of the link between the immediate objects of basic theatrical understanding and the developed object of basic theatrical understanding of a play, namely, a story. But what counts as linking things up in the relevant ways requires a bit more explanation.

"Cogency"

Spectators make sense of what is happening in a performance by assessing the cogency of the individual moments and the transitions from moment to moment in the performance. They are guided by general norms in assessing cogency, although the basically comprehending spectator need not always be capable of expressing what those norms are.

What are the norms of cogency that guide spectators? Because cogency determinations are crucial for understanding, it is particularly tempting to think that assessments of cogency presuppose conscious apprehension of formal relationships in which the bits and the transitions figure.[10] But I have denied that spectators need any awareness of large-scale formal relationships and structures in order to have basic theatrical understanding.

It might be useful to say this: following a performance is like following a conversation. Clearly we do not need to already have a grasp of the full import of the conversation in order to follow it. To be sure, the import of the conversation can be evident *to someone else* when we recount the conversation to that person. But *we* need not be aware of the deeper import in order to have understood the conversation or to have recounted it. So that deeper import can have played no role in the assessment we made of the cogency of the bits of language and gesture that produced our ability to recount the conversation (and thereby to demonstrate that we understood it).

Some candidates we might consider as the norms against which we assess cogency within and between bits of language, gesture, action, and movement in a theatrical performance are whether the immediate objects and transitions give spectators a sense of (1) "necessity," (2) "continuity," (3) "progression," (4) "development," (5) "evolution," or (6) "directionality." Each of these candidates, including Aristotle's – option (1) – commits spectators to knowing more than they need to know. Each of these putative norms expresses an aspect of our orderly and coherent everyday sense of what follows what in human action. But our sense of what follows what is frequently exploited and even subverted in plays. This is another way in which theatrical performance can be a temporal art form. Theatrical performance allows for playing with time: the time of events in the temporally and causally well-ordered version of the story may be altered and shifted around, the time of the performance may itself be referred to and played against, and the time it takes to do a single action can be stretched or made unnaturally quick.[11] But for all that, such subversions still allow spectators to get the drift of things pretty well sorted out. Indeed the effectiveness of such exploitation and subversion usually depends on the ability of spectators to do so.

Exposure of assumptions by distancing techniques is characteristic of practices involved in performances in the stylistic mold of *Gabler at a Distance*. Playing against spectators' causal expectations might easily be regarded as just another distancing technique, suitable for use in a performance of this kind. A company might choose to stage certain key scenes in ways that play against their spectators' causal expectations regarding what follows what for a variety of reasons. They may think it creates more opportunities for insight into unacknowledged social assumptions than would a performance more nearly illustrating the views Ibsen had. Such subversions of expectations still typically allow spectators to track the story in the performance. And, once again, the effectiveness of these subversions depends on spectators' abilities to do so.

So it appears that the standard for assessing cogency in theatrical performances allows for some degree of incoherence in and among bits and transitions, especially incoherence as regards temporal and causal order.

Jerrold Levinson[12] presents a formulation of the basic test for cogency in the auditing of musical works that is suggestive. "[C]ogency of sequence," he claims, "is each part . . . leading convincingly to the next, each consequent appearing, upon familiarity, to be the natural, even inevitable continuation of each antecedent." This is on the right track. But it still commits us to a standard of cogency that insists we know more than we need to know for basic theatrical understanding.

There are two elements in Levinson's analysis of cogency: the part about each immediate object leading *convincingly* to the next and the part about each subsequent bit appearing to be *the natural or inevitable continuation* of the preceding object. And it would be useful to my proposal if these two elements in Levinson's formulation of "cogency" could come apart. For there is far more room for apparent incoherence in a genuinely cogent transition in theatrical performance than would be allowed if the transitions had to seem "natural or inevitable." Moreover, if we think a spectator who assesses a transition as cogent must see the sequence as the "natural or inevitable" consequence of its predecessor, then we require her to be able to trace, upon inquiry, not just some connections, but particular kinds of connections between the sequences. She must be able to trace, or at least think she can trace, causal, reasoned, or rule-governed connections, the kind of connections that entail naturalness or inevitability. And this seems to require too much.

The good news is that seeing a transition as convincing can come apart from seeing a transition as natural or inevitable. This is because are able to offer a plausible characterization of what we should take as evidence that a spectator had found some transition "convincing" without reference to the contents of her thinking and so, in particular, without reference to what kind of connections she may be tracing. Accordingly, I propose we adopt a norm definitive of "cogency" in terms of convincingness together with a statement of what it takes for a spectator to find a transition convincing.

> (1) A transition from sequence to sequence is judged "cogent" if it is found convincing to a spectator *and* (2) a transition will be convincing to a spectator if (a) the spectator does not object in some way to the transition, (b) the spectator can tell the story or describe the sequence of that region of the play without being blocked at that transition, or (c) the spectator, upon being questioned, is able to trace at least some connections, even if only thematic or imagistic, between the preceding and the succeeding sequences.

Now it is true that a spectator may also feel something, *feel* convinced by a cogent transition. And perhaps that is even typical. But such a feeling need not be present in order for a spectator to *be* convinced.[13] A spectator may demonstrate her sense of the cogency of bits and transitions without ever articulating that she has found the bits and transitions in question cogent. She will show this, perhaps, by what she does physically and involuntarily in response to the moment. Esmerelda, in the earlier example, leans back in anticipation during a *Hedda-to-Hedda* performance at the time Hedda crosses the room and pulls the pistol out of its case. This shows us she has found cogent both the moment and the transition leading to the next moment.

5.5 Objects of Understanding Having Complex Structures

Someone might object to the account I have given by pointing out a comprehending spectator may display her comprehension of a play by telling a story that is as complexly structured as the story that was presented. If the story recounted is as complexly structured as the story presented then the spectator must have such a structure in mind. So, this argument goes, the view I have proposed must be wrong.

A moment's reflection will show, however, that the second premise contains an ambiguity: it could mean being able to tell a story possessing a particular structure or being able to tell *that* the story possesses a particular structure. If the second premise is taken to mean the former, the argument is not valid. If the second premise is taken to mean the latter, the argument is unsound because the second premise would then be false. Only the former kind of knowledge need be involved in basic theatrical understanding. The latter kind of knowledge is characteristic of what we might expect a spectator to possess if she has some sort of richer or deeper understanding of a theatrical performance.

Another objector may still think audiences have to grasp large-scale features of stories in order to understand the story if only because some narratives employ shifts backwards and forwards in time. Temporal shifts seem to pose special problems for the view I have proposed because the view holds that all a spectator needs in order to comprehend a theatrical performance at the basic level is provided in the moment-to-moment presentation as it happens. How, one may ask, can what is provided in any given moment be enough for the spectator to recognize shifts in temporal location?

But so long as we recognize that spectators typically will *remember* immediate objects that have gone before, bits that include, for example, time markers, temporal shifts within theatrical narratives do not pose a problem for the view. We still need not attribute a grasp of the whole to a spectator, or even a grasp of very large-scale theatrical structures – including the fact that the narrative contains temporal shifts – in order to account for her understanding of these devices and of their significance in the moment for what is happening in the story.

This second objection might be pressed by insisting that the view I have proposed cannot explain how we understand sometimes very long stretches of a performance, including such things as the connections between a bit of action in the first scene and a bit of dialog in the last. One might think the fact that we do understand these kinds of things suggests that understanding the play requires us to have its large-scale form present to mind in the act of comprehending after all.

This is one of the places where the fact that theatrical performance is a temporal art form gets its bite. There is no such thing as "standing back" from theatrical performances in order to get the whole thing in focus in the way there can be with paintings and buildings. The sort of "going forward" and "going backward" in the way that is possible with novels, poems, movies, and even recorded music is not typically available in theatrical performances.

The point is not that it is difficult to *stage* the kinds of flashbacks or premonitions that can easily be achieved in novels and movies. That is not particularly difficult.[14] The point is that there are characteristic patterns to our *reception* of the objects presented to us in music, movies, novels, poems, and theatrical performances. Among these patterns is the fact that going backwards and forwards is typically under the reader's control with respect to novels and poems, for example, and that this is characteristic of how good readers read novels and poems. Going backwards and forwards is typically not under the spectator's control with respect to theatrical performances as they happen. Many spectators of theater clearly do achieve basic comprehension of long stretches and connections over time; and they seem to do so only by exercising their memory of what went before. Of course it is not uncommon for a spectator to remark that she did not get something that happened at the end of the performance, and to see it only when someone reminds her of what happened earlier. But that is not an argument for the view we must have apprehension of large-scale features to grasp such moments.

To be sure, in both music and theater there is the possibility of reflection both prior to and after auditing the performance and there are practices of using scores and scripts to aid the study of large-scale forms. I make no judgment about the correctness of Levinson's claim[15] that such reflection can only "facilitate basic *musical* understanding" and is "not an absolute prerequisite or *sine qua non* of aural synthesis." But I do claim this holds with respect to basic *theatrical* understanding.

5.6 Generalizing Beyond Plays

The account I have given of what is required to meet the success conditions for basic theatrical understanding of plays is a conjunction of five claims, one concerning what basic understanding consists in, two concerning the nature of the objects of basic understanding, a fourth claim concerning what is required for an spectator to make sense of a play, and finally a claim concerning how spectators go about making sense of a play. We can generalize this account beyond that required for understanding plays by giving wider scope to what might be the objects of basic understanding. I now propose a more general set of requirements for basic comprehension of any theatrical performance.

First, understanding a theatrical performance as it happens is centrally a matter of apprehending individual bits of language and movement and the immediate progression from bit to bit.

Second, the immediate objects of basic theatrical understanding are nothing more than (1) the moment-to-moment bits of language and movement and the transitions between them and (2) those bits as prepared for and then delivered in a manner available for recognition later in the play.

Third, the developed object of basic theatrical understanding of a theatrical performance is a complex object that is appropriate to the style of the performance.

Fourth, making sense of what is happening in the performance, for a suitably backgrounded spectator, requires nothing more than attending to the bits of language and movement, as they occur, and attending to the connections of such features with immediately preceding and succeeding bits.

Fifth, spectators assess whether what is happening makes sense by sensing whether the bits and the transitions between bits are cogent, moment to moment.

To accommodate several of our idealized non-narrative performance kinds I have made two adjustments to the requirements for basic comprehension. The first is to refer to "language" and "movement" rather than to "dialog" and "action" in the first, second, and fourth claims. The terms "language" and "movement" refer to general characterizations of the immediate objects of understanding, of which dialog and stage action are species.

The second adjustment is of a different order. I have made a more striking change in the third claim, namely, by making reference to the style of the performance.

One reason is that the developed objects of non-narrative performances may come in many different varieties. *Burning Child* and *Pistols and Other Doors*, for example, are performance kinds consisting of sequences of images that accompany non-narrative, possibly poetic, texts. Typically, they eschew the presentation of characters or events. The elements that any non-narrative performance may manipulate so as to be distinguished from these two different styles include the use of images (some theatrical performances abstain even from these), sources of texts,[16] the linearity or non-linearity of texts, the use of texts at all, the intelligibility or nonsensicality of texts, and the principles for ordering the sequences of what is to be heard and what is to be seen. Clearly, and just formally, there is room for variety here.

A second reason is that non-narrative performances in different styles can employ some of the same immediate objects but to very different ends. Here is an extended example. Suppose the sentence, "Ah, thoughts . . . they are not so easily mastered," is uttered both in *Burning Child* and in *Something to Tell You*. In Ibsen's script, this line comes up near the beginning of Act Four in the following sequence.

> HEDDA: Can't I help you with anything?
> MISS TESMAN: Oh, don't think of that! Hedda Tesman mustn't do that kind of thing. Nor dwell on the thought, either. Not at such a time, certainly not.
> HEDDA: Ah, thoughts . . . they are not so easily mastered.[17]

Neither *Burning Child* nor *Something to Tell You* employs characters or actions of characters. But the spoken material in each is developed in different ways. In *Burning Child* the company chooses lines that reflect reactions to deep contemporary social issues. In *Something to Tell You*, the company chooses lines that they think they can literally and honestly say in the present tense in front of any audience.

Nevertheless, we can imagine the performers in either of these performances presenting this same line in a similar-sounding six-part, six-repeats round so that each possible logical accent receives stress during one of the repeats.

> THEY are not so easily mastered.
> They ARE not so easily mastered.
> They are NOT so easily mastered.
> They are not SO easily mastered.
> They are not so EASILY mastered.
> They are not so easily MASTERED.

In terms of how the sentence is to sound, our two different performances would handle this sentence in the same way.

But, because the company of *Burning Child* sets out to develop images around a common theme that is at the same time a commentary on contemporary life, we can imagine the full sequence from Ibsen's script quoted above being part of the spoken elements and appearing as preparation for the single line that is presented as a round. In contrast a company planning in a way that is consistent with *Something to Tell You* – setting out to find rhythmic patterns in the text and developing sequences of sonic qualities – is far less likely to use anything more from that original sequence than the line itself. Moreover, to get a fuller sense of what goes on in *Burning Child*, we have to imagine what image, images, or transitions the company would plan to appear to its audience during the round. These other elements do not matter in *Something to Tell You*. The rhythmic telling is all.

For these two reasons, then, what particular developed object a spectator is to understand will be a function of the style of non-narrative performance presented. Since we cannot say in advance what those styles might turn out to be, we have to leave room for variation and experimentation in stating what is required for basic understanding of the developed object in a performance.

5.7 The Problem of "Cognitive Uniformity"[18]

What we have shown so far is that there is a coherent idea of basic theatrical understanding and that meeting the success conditions for such basic-level comprehension does not require more than the individual spectator's experience of the performance, moment to moment.

But we have not addressed a fundamental question, namely, why we should count meeting these success conditions for basic comprehension as evidence of understanding at all. The issue here is occasioned in large part by the "cognitive uniformity" constraint: "Whatever can be understood can be understood uniformly; any process that cannot be uniform in the required way is not understanding."[19] But the disparate nature of audiences may compromise the very possibility of understanding. Audiences can be made up of people with quite different social and personal backgrounds, and even a single spectator can respond differently to what is happening at different moments if she considers those moments from the points of view of different social roles she plays.[20]

One move we could make at this point is to abandon the idea that spectators do have basic comprehension of theatrical performances. Another is to abandon the cognitive uniformity constraint. I think we should do neither of these things.

The move I think we should make is to develop a model of how it is that spectators grasp what they do that shows why it is reasonable to expect they will converge on the same objects and the same characteristics of the objects of understanding. As a matter of fact, of course, spectators appear to agree, generally, on what they have seen and heard. But that fact by itself does not guarantee it is reasonable to expect that they should.

Accordingly, in the next chapter I demonstrate that, even granting wide disparities among spectators, there is a mechanism of basic theatrical comprehension and that this mechanism enables us to show why it is reasonable to expect what actually happens. That is, the mechanism allows us to show that every spectator has good reason to think that most other spectators are getting the same things she is. And for that reason, individual spectators may achieve genuine understanding.

Moreover, because that mechanism operates by securing convergence among individual spectators onto mostly the same things, individual spectators are able to identify the performance as the same performance identified by other spectators and to identify it without reference to anything other than what has been presented in the performance. And this, I will argue, is exactly what we need to identify performances without reference to the texts they may employ, if any.

Notes

1 The idea that identification is separate from appreciation – that our sense of "what was done" is separate from our sense of "what was achieved" – is argued for by David Davies, *Art as Performance*, New Directions in Aesthetics (London and New York: Blackwell, 2004), pp. 151–8, especially 154–5. Because I think our sense of "what was done" is determined by means of a basic-level understanding that is far more minimal than what Davies has in mind, the separation is even more stark in the case of understanding and appreciating theatrical performances.

2 Because there are substantive questions about the nature of audiences, for present purposes I will focus almost entirely on what it is and what it takes for a single spectator to understand a performance as it is happening. This chapter concludes with questions about the nature of audiences, and in the next chapter I answer most of those questions.

3 This way of putting the matter is very similar to that of Paul Woodruff, "Understanding Theater," in *Philosophy and Art*, ed. Daniel Dahlstrom, Studies in Philosophy and the History of Philosophy, 23 (Washington, DC: Catholic University of America Press, 1991), p. 15. On many matters I agree

with Woodruff. However, although our formulations of the target for our discussions is similar, he has what I think of as a "thicker" idea of understanding than that which I defend in this chapter. See n. 8 below.

4   Many of the elements of this chapter were developed first as an address to the ASA Pacific Division in April, 2001 and then as an address to the ASA in October, 2001. A more developed treatment is given in "Understanding Plays," in *Staging Philosophy: Intersections of Theater, Performance, and Philosophy*, ed. David Krasner and David Saltz (Ann Arbor: University of Michigan Press, 2006), pp. 221–43.

5   I owe these cases to a conversation with Bruce Glymour who encouraged me to consider a wider range of cases and to answer this particular objection to the proposed success conditions.

6   Woodruff would not agree. But that is because he has a "thicker" conception of what it is to understand than I am employing here. Again, see n. 8 below.

7   See M. Frayn and D. Burke, *The Copenhagen Papers: An Intrigue* (New York: Picador, 2003) [originally published as *Celia's Secret* (London: Faber and Faber, 2000)], pp. 28–30.

8   Woodruff claims that "understanding consists largely in having certain emotions," "Understanding Theater," p. 13. In part because he is committed to a cognitive theory of the emotions – and I wish to remain neutral about that – and in larger part because this is why his idea of understanding is "thicker" than what I am pushing here, I use the less controversial and weaker ideas of "reactions" and "mood shifts." Another reason is that, as should be clear from the account of enactment in chapter 2, I am concerned to ensure we keep the physical interactions between performers and audiences clearly in view. Emotional reactions surely are physical reactions to some extent. But it is easy to lose sight of this fact on many cognitivist theories of the emotions, and I believe we should not do so.

9   The view of understanding plays I will set forth is partially modeled on a "concatenationist" account of how we understand musical performances, developed and defended by Jerrold Levinson in *Music in the Moment* (Ithaca, NY, and London: Cornell University Press, 1997). I do not claim that Levinson is right about music. I borrow the rough structure of the view he presents and show that it has detailed application to the basic comprehension of a theatrical performance.

10   I borrow this formulation from Levinson, *Music*, p. 9.

11   Some of these possibilities for playing with time can be achieved more convincingly in film than in theater, but the theatrical performance is open to some of them at least. See Jerrold Levinson and Philip Alperson, "What is a Temporal Art?", *Midwest Studies in Philosophy*, XVI (1991), pp. 443–4.

12   Levinson, *Music*, p. 7.

13   Conditions (a) and (b), by reference to time frames that may follow the experience of the performance, invoke the fact that what feels convincing at

a given moment may later be re-evaluated. A transition that does not imme-diately feel convincing may, upon the later discovery of one's ability to tell the story without stumbling over the transition, be revealed as convincing after all. And, correlatively, a transition that feels convincing at the time may, upon later reflection, be revealed as not convincing.

14 The suggestion was made John Dillworth in commenting on an early version of the essay presented at the Annual Meeting of the American Society for Aesthetics in Minneapolis, October, 2001.

15 Levinson, *Music*, p. 228.

16 See, for example, several scenes in Susan Yankowitz, "Terminal," in *Three Works by the Open Theater*, ed. K. Malpede (New York: Drama Book Special-ists, 1974), pp. 38–65.

17 Henrik Ibsen, *Hedda Gabler and Other Plays*, trans. Una Ellis-Fermor (Baltimore: Penguin Books, 1961), p. 347.

18 I borrow this term from Woodruff, "Understanding Theater."

19 Ibid., pp. 19–20.

20 Alice Rayner, "The Audience: Subjectivity, Community, and the Ethics of Listening," *Journal of Dramatic Theory and Criticism* 7/1 (1993), 3–6.

6
THE MECHANICS OF BASIC THEATRICAL UNDERSTANDING

To defend the claim that theatrical performances are works of art in their own right, we must be able to show how they can be identified. By abandoning the idea that theatrical performances are "of" any written texts, we also abandoned the idea that theatrical performances are identifiable by appeal to the texts "of which" they are performances. The strategy I have proposed is to show how audiences identify theatrical performances by demonstrating how they understand them.

The first step was to present fairly minimal success conditions for attaining basic comprehension of a theatrical performance. The second was to show that spectators need make no reference to anything beyond what is happening in the performance in order to meet those success conditions. The next step is to show how spectators converge upon the same characteristics of the intermediate objects in a developing object in a performance and come to offer the same descriptions of the characteristics of that developing object.

6.1 The "Feature-Salience" Model of Spectator Convergence on the Same Characteristics

How is it that spectators at a play, for example, converge upon the same characteristics of agents as other spectators, and so come to tell the same story? To answer this question we need to resolve two problems, one concerning performers and one concerning spectators.

With regard to performers, we must know what informs a spectator that certain features of the performers are characteristics of or facts about one of the objects of the performance – traits of a character, for example – and that others are not. This is no mean feat. In an entertaining and widely used book on script analysis, David Ball notes that there is usually a good deal more information about characters in novels and people in real life than there is about characters in scripts. "In fact," he writes, "you probably know more about most acquaintances than *anyone* knows about Hamlet."[1] Characters, he tells us, are "minimally extant in scripts, skeletal accumulations of carefully selected traits . . . because the nature of any stage character is heavily determined by the actor in the part."[2] This means that many more of the features of a performer will also be characteristics of or facts about a character in the performed story than those referred to in the script on which the performance is based. Ball's observation puts pressure on us to be generous in considering which performer features are character features.

But consider the question, "Does Hamlet have blue eyes?" Surely, many performers who have played Hamlet have had blue eyes and many others have not. For each of those performers, there is a determinate answer to the question, "Does she or he have blue eyes?" But, unless and until a performance makes something of the question with respect to Hamlet, the question of Hamlet's eye color does not have a determinate answer. And, when it does, it has an answer only relative to a particular performance or production. The point is that the number of features of any given performer who plays Hamlet is far greater than the number of features that enable a performer to fit the description, "playing Hamlet." Many of a performer's features go unnoticed, and they are supposed to. These considerations put pressure on us to be cautious in considering which performers' features are characteristics of characters.

Given these opposing pressures, we might think audiences would have a lot of difficulty figuring out what features of the performers to attend to in order to grasp the characteristics of the characters. But they do not. So what is needed is some principled account of what individual spectators do that explains how these matters are managed.

The problem about spectators is that each spectator brings a different context and history to any given performance. A spectator may share some aspects of her background with all other spectators. They may all recognize that they are at a theatrical performance. If any one of them knows they are attending an off-Broadway production, probably they all know this. But they may not share other aspects of their backgrounds even with respect to theater: the kinds of theater one has seen could be quite different from and independent of the kinds another has seen; one may have seen a lot of performances by this company and they may be familiar to her, while another may be seeing one of their performances for the first time. Moreover, there are likely to be some aspects of one spectator's background that no other spectator will bring to the performance: one may have just taken a very difficult test and be mentally exhausted; another may be preoccupied with her husband's suicide. So, we may think, their experiences are so different they cannot have understood the play in the same way.[3] Yet, if there is to be genuine understanding by any one of them, then according to the principle of cognitive uniformity what is understood by one must be understandable by most others.

We have already prepared in chapter 4 for an approach to resolving these problems by appeal to the intuitions that theatrical performance is a social practice in which spectators attend to performers in order to gain what they can from the performance, and that attending to depends upon the existence of some sort of social circumstance that allows this to happen.

Building on the foundation provided by these intuitions, I propose a "feature-salience model" for analyzing spectator convergence on the same characteristics of what is going on in any theatrical performance. Consider a character in a play who has an eager thirst.

"Spectator S understands, when presented with feature f of performer J, that character C has an eager thirst" is true just in case, for some spectator S, some performer J, and some character C,

(1) S responds to feature f as salient, under conditions of common knowledge that spectators are attending a theatrical performance, for a fact or set of facts that would lead one to conclude that C has an eager thirst or that will be recognized as inconsistent with alternatives to C's having an eager thirst,[4]

(2) S concludes that C has an eager thirst,

(3) feature f is salient for C's having an eager thirst.

6.2 What it is to Respond to a Feature as Salient for Some Characteristics or a Set of Facts

The account of feature salience developed here is dependent upon the notion of salience employed in game-theoretical analyses of rational choice in coordination problems. In those analyses, a feature is said to stand out from others when there is a trigger that is not specific to the feature itself or to the problem itself that makes the feature stand out. Instead, the trigger is determined by contextual elements.

Consider the following example, a variant of David Lewis's "telephone game."[5] Two people are talking on the phone when they are suddenly cut off. They cannot communicate with each other and yet both want to continue the conversation. Moreover each knows the other wishes the same. How are they to re-establish contact? Each has the option of either calling the other or waiting. For them to succeed in re-establishing contact, clearly one must wait and the other must call; but there is no feature of their situation that would tell either of them who should call and who should wait.

In one-off situations, like the telephone game, where the game is only played once, nothing either of these people knows about the situation or each other prompts them towards choosing a strategy. If they knew more about each other, perhaps, they might know how the other would reason. But they do not. So there is no solution.

Lewis recognized that people do solve many coordination problems in everyday life and that, therefore, in many situations there must be some features that do "stand out" for all the participants in light of which they make their choices. He also realized that what made those features stand out is *external* to the terms of the coordination problem itself. To illustrate this, change the telephone game as follows. First Person knows that Second Person has a white telephone and that Second Person knows that he himself has a black telephone. First Person and Second Person are inveterate chess players and each knows this about the other. Since white always goes first in chess, First Person reasons he should wait for Second Person's call and reasons that Second Person will reason in the same way. Seamus Miller sums up Lewis's view of the externality of salience in this way.

> Agents have desires and aversions, modes of apprehending the world, histories, and exist in environments that impinge upon them. But in that case certain aspects of certain things are going to come to their attention, and others not, and some of these are going to strike them more forcefully than others. In short, some things are going to stand out; for any agents, including rational agents, some things are salient, others not.[6]

That a feature is salient is a result of *non-rational* tendencies to notice some features and to choose strategies because those features are present.[7] A tendency to notice that a feature is salient is "non-rational" when there is no reason, related to what is being coordinated, for preferring one choice to another. This does not mean that no one is doing any reasoning. Indeed:

> In finding a feature salient, each party is making a guess as to what feature others will respond to, and reasoning from that to the conclusion that the same feature will stand out for the others and that they too will reason as he is reasoning: and thence reasoning to a conclusion about how to act.

In these kinds of situations, referred to as "standard" coordination problems,[8] people are analyzed as "players" engaged in determining courses of action that will have the optimal "payoff." There is symmetry between the players, both in respect of what they are trying to do – namely, the same thing – and in respect of what they know about each other. So some aspects of standard coordination problems are different from the situation of spectators in relation to a performance. In this regard, I follow Robert Sugden who modifies this model for use in analyzing situations of discovery. As a result I will not use the term "players" or take the people involved to be seeking certain "payoffs." Instead, I suggest we think of spectators as "*learners*"[9] seeking to acquire the ability to describe the object developed in the performance.

In most other respects the situation of spectators of performances is very like that of players in standard coordination problems. In sum:

> Features of a performer are salient to a spectator for a fact or set of facts just when the learner-spectator, under a suitable common knowledge requirement, can notice those features as regularities in the behavior of the performer and when the learner-spectator concludes (1) that some pattern – and hence some set of facts – obtains, (2) that whenever those features appear in the same context then the same set of facts obtains, *and* (3) that every other learner-spectator will conclude both (1) and (2).

As in standard coordination problems, conditions (1) and (2) specify that a feature is salient if it is thought to guide responses, if it is seen as *projectible*. And, just as in standard coordination problems, condition (3) specifies that a feature is salient if it stands out as projectible *for a population*.

The situation spectators confront resembles closely in other respects the one confronted by players in standard coordination games. In some cases the player does not know anything at all about the other players, but in others there already exists a community in which each player knows how the game has been played by others in the population in the past. Similarly, most of the time spectators of theatrical performances just follow the presented features and project patterns that are familiar to them and then reason along. These features and patterns are familiar because, in nearly every culture that has theater at all, one or two kinds of theatrical performance are ubiquitous.

Consider the situation of a spectator watching and listening to a narrative theatrical performance of a *Hedda-to-Hedda* kind. Suppose she is quite familiar with this kind of performance. The observation that what is salient depends on context and history leads us to the thought that it is the fact that spectators and performers share contexts and histories that makes certain features and not others salient to spectators. Given common knowledge of the situation – that each is attending a narrative performance of the *Hedda-to-Hedda* kind – and given similarly and suitably backgrounded spectators, a performer's features will be salient to most spectators as the characteristics of an agent acting in an emerging set of circumstances. Recognition of these circumstances and of the actions of the agent, together with those of other agents, is what develops into recognition of the story that is eventually the object grasped by an audience.

6.3 A Thin Common Knowledge Requirement

The knowledge we have just supposed is common to theater spectators is relatively thin. And there are good reasons to think that the relatively thin common knowledge condition, even though it includes knowledge of past behavior, and even when spectators are in familiar circumstances and each knows that the others are as well, is not enough to explain convergence.

Consider two people, Sally and Joe, who are kidnapped and placed in separate rooms, unable to communicate with each other, and then given panels of four colored buttons. They are told that in a very short time they will each have to push one button and that they must push the same-colored button or they will both die. During the time they are waiting, their captor tells them he will offer some distraction; and at that point a radio comes on in each room, although neither is in a position to know what the other is listening to. After a bit of music an announcer starts talking about the President's birthday party. The announcer describes the red balloons, red tablecloths, red coats worn by the wait staff, and the President's wife's red dress, shoes, and stockings. The announcer makes it plain this is all being done because the President's favorite color is red.

This example and several variants have been developed by Margaret Gilbert in order to show that if either person chooses to push a button on the basis of its contextually salient feature, neither has any reason to believe the other will also choose the salient option and that, therefore, salience does not guarantee rational choice. The argument goes this way.

> Given that [choosing red] is salient, Sally can argue "[Choosing red] stands out for us both. Clearly I should do my part in [choosing red] if Joe does. But will he?" How can Sally figure out what Joe will do? Suppose she tries to look at things from Joe's point of view, that is, to figure out how Joe will reason. She will see by hypothesis that Joe also knows that [choosing red] stands out for both. She will also see that he is faced with the question whether to do his part in [choosing red]. He will see that he should do his part if Sally does hers, and he will ask himself whether he has reason to think she will do her part. But it is clear that he will find no such reason; in particular, an attempt to replicate Sally's reasoning will get him nowhere.[10]

The kind of situation described here by Gilbert is a one-off situation. And we might reply to this line of reasoning by pointing out that one-off problems do not provide the right model for discussing the typical situation of theatrical performances. Such one-off problems can be contrasted with coordination problems when there is a community with common knowledge of past behavior. Lewis's insight into this kind of case is that knowledge of past behavior provides each player with the precedent she or he needs to get this right most of the time. Precedence, Lewis saw, is a form of salience. This is why we are able to apply the proposal to cases of familiar performance kinds, just as we want to.

But we cannot apply it to performances that challenge spectators. At these performances, spectators are put in the position of not knowing how others will respond. So no spectator can know with certainty before the performance begins whether past behavior of performers and other spectators will be a reliable guide concerning to what to look for. More importantly, the practice of going to the theater must be taught; no one comes to the theater for the first time already knowing the 'rules' for finding the 'right' features salient for the characteristics of what is happening.

Therefore, any spectator's circumstance – even when presented with a familiar kind of performance – is far more like the circumstance of a spectator presented with an unfamiliar kind of performance than previously suggested. Unless spectators have additional information about other spectators in the situation, no spectator knows how any other spectator will reason about any feature. Even when spectators know the rules they still have reason to ask what makes a feature stick out in such a way that other spectators will have reason to think everyone else will notice it and forecast its pattern and implications as well. What grounds this?

6.4 A Plausibly Thickened Common Knowledge Requirement

Salience is the basis of choice when reason gives out. Consider two people who agree to meet each other at Piccadilly Circus in London on a given day; but for some reason they forget to agree when they will meet. Each of them realizes this fact while on the way to London on the day. Neither has a way of finding out when precisely the other will arrive at the meeting place. Empirical studies show that, without knowing what the other will do, they will choose noon.[11] Salience is dependent on context and history. So the question concerning what grounds any spectator's reason to think others will have reason to pick out the same things is the question what bits of context and history can be expected to make the same features salient.

To answer this question, we first note that what features a spectator thinks both are projectible and will stand out for others as projectible is dependent on what she brings to the performance. And we have to take that to mean that the features that stand out for her will be shaped by how she thinks what she is picking out is *reasonably related to her own perspective*. Accordingly, I propose we accept the following:

It is unlikely, if not impossible, that all members of an audience will find salient all and exactly the same features.

But this is not the disastrous conclusion it appears to be. The fact that each spectator does not find salient all and exactly the same features as all other spectators provides no reason to think that all other spectators or even many of them find mostly different features salient. So there is no reason to suppose that any spectator will experience a narrative performance and end up telling a *radically different* story from the story told by most other spectators. Fair enough, it may be argued, but this argument provides no positive reason for thinking that spectators with very different backgrounds will still find even roughly the same features salient simply because they know they are attending a theatrical performance.

The way forward is gained by examining the content of the common knowledge requirement more closely. The content we have adopted so far for this requirement includes only the knowledge each spectator has that each is at the theater, including knowledge of some past behavior of performers and other spectators. What more is plausibly part of what spectators know about each other or the situation of being at a theatrical performance?

One of the aims of spectators of theatrical performances is to understand the performance that they see. Each spectator also knows that whatever she says when discussing a performance with others will not be counted as demonstrating understanding if it does not agree in the main with the characteristics others are discussing. So there will be conservative social pressure both to look for and to respond to the features that others are likely to find salient and to track precisely those in developing the description of the content of the performance.[12]

Another fact is that spectators' physical reactions are 'catching.' When one laughs, for example, others tend to do as well. Laughter is often said to be "contagious." Anne Ubersfeld makes this and related observations the basis of a detailed analysis of spectator pleasures.[13] And, of course, laughter is but one of many involuntary or nearly involuntary responses that are contagious.

A further and crucial fact is this: spectators go to theatrical performances expecting performers to present them with an ordered sequence of materials to grasp, and they are rarely disappointed in that regard. When they are disappointed, spectators are apt to feel more keenly the conservative social pressure to figure things out as others do.

Knowledge that one is at a theatrical performance may be thickened in the following way:

> In knowing that she is at a theatrical performance, each spectator has knowledge of the interests of her fellow spectators and of their felt reactions, and also of the fact that each expects that something will be put forward for *all of them* to gain.

The first thing to notice is that this knowledge is not beyond the reach of what spectators can expect to know of each other. It is social knowledge that all spectators normally share. In particular, this kind of knowledge can be obtained without any spectator having access to others' disparate backgrounds concerning what they bring idiosyncratically to the performance.

Second, this knowledge is all that spectators need by way of common knowledge of each other's perspective. This is because knowing that one is attending a theatrical performance includes knowing that performers are going to present something to understand and in a way that makes it (not always easily) accessible to the spectator. Because spectators know this about performers they anticipate attending to the performers in order to get what the performers have arranged for them to observe. They watch for what the performers do to enable them to get that object. And performers do present things for spectators to attend to in order that spectators might observe the object the performers develop over the course of the performance.

Spectators do not know in advance *what* they will find. But, crucially, they know that everyone else will be looking *for the same things*. Thus, while spectators are not guaranteed to find exactly and all the same things salient, the thickened concept of common knowledge guarantees the possibility, indeed the likelihood, that they will find roughly the same set of features salient.

6.5 The Feature-Salience Model, "Reader-Response Theory," and "Intentionalism"

The feature-salience analysis of how spectators come to grasp characteristics of a performed object may be mistaken for a version of what is called "reader-response theory." That theory was devised to handle two problems, the "disappearance of the author" and the diversity of audiences for the reading and understanding of literary texts.[14] The first problem entails that we cannot appeal to the author's intended meaning of texts in order to settle interpretive disputes if only because we lack access to information about those intentions. So, lacking an authorial standard, we have only reader responses. The second problem entails that these responses may vary from reader to reader.

From these entailments, reader-response theorists conclude that each reader constructs the meaning of any given text for herself.[15] When this idea is applied to the situation confronting theater audiences, Patrice Pavis holds, there is an ambiguity in the "theatrical relationship" between "concretely, the position of the spectator facing the stage and, arbitrarily, his effort to constitute meaning by his act of reception."[16] Pavis's analysis depends on playing with this ambiguity to make out how a spectator's responses enable an interpretation of the "theatrical text" which is a decision about "the meaning of what he sees on stage."[17]

But on the feature-salience model, for a feature to be salient for some characteristic, each spectator must be thinking that all or most other similarly situated spectators are projecting the feature as part of the same pattern, for the same characteristic. So one way the feature-salience analysis diverges from reader-response theory is the social nature of the process of tracking a performance. A spectator may "propose a meaning,"[18] in some sense, but she is not satisfied unless she is tracking a pattern that she has reason to believe others are tracking.

The fact is that spectators mostly do get the same stories from narrative theatrical performances. On a reader-response theory, this is a lucky accident, or perhaps the result of social coercion. It is extrinsic to the process of understanding. On the feature-salience analysis, far from being accidental or coercive, the fact that most spectators agree about the characteristics they encounter is the key datum we seek to explain. And it explains that datum by noting how a feature becomes projectible for a pattern, for a spectator, in such a way that any spectator may plausibly conclude that any other spectator will also think the same feature reveals the same pattern.

This is not to dispute the motivation for reader-response theory. It is well motivated, in particular, in its rejection of authorial intentions. But we can go even further. For the feature-salience explanation is committed to the view that what the *performers* intend is also not what settles the issue of what is presented. So it is also not an intentionalist account of the mechanism of theatrical understanding.

Spectators frequently separate intentions from what is actually presented by performers. And so do performers. If performers notice what spectators are missing, and if they change their performances to accord better with their intentions, they must be able to grasp the distance between their intentions and what they actually present to an audience. This fact is what motivates the inclusion of the third condition in the feature-salience model, namely,

(3) feature f is salient for C's having an eager thirst.

An intentionalist might object that that condition has illicitly or inadvertently inserted appeal to the recognition of intentions of performers. That this is not so can be shown by imagining an alternative to that condition that makes such reference explicitly:

(3′) feature *f* is presented with the expectation and intention that it is salient for C's having an eager thirst.

Now suppose that in some performance a given spectator finds feature *f* salient for the fact that a character has an eager thirst and concludes that the character has a thirst. But also suppose that (3′) is not true: the performer did not exhibit *f* expecting or intending it to be salient to spectators for the fact that her character has an eager thirst, but instead thought that *f* would be salient to spectators for the fact that her character has a nervous tic that appears whenever she drinks water. In this case, our *spectator* will have concluded that C has an eager thirst and she will think that other spectators will conclude the same thing. And most of the time she will be right. When she is right, our *performer* will have conveyed to most of her spectators something she did not intend and did not expect to convey.

The third condition allows that a performer's expectations and intentions figure into basic understanding of theatrical performances in some way and that it is important that they do. But it does not allow that performers' intentions figure in for the reason that spectators must *recognize* those intentions in order to understand the performance. For in the end it is not performers' intentions that matter for spectators' basic comprehension. What matters is the *correctness* of their expectations concerning what is, in fact, salient for what. This is why there are acting classes and why theater programs have classes in theater history and the history of styles.

6.6 Generalizing the Salience Mechanism to Encompass Non-Narrative Performances

We may now also generalize the model to cover other kinds of features of both narrative and non-narrative performances.

"Spectator S understands, when presented with feature *f* of performance element K, that *p*" is true just in case, for some spectator S and some performance element K,

(1)   S responds to *f* of K as salient, under conditions of common knowledge that spectators are attending a theatrical performance, for a fact or facts that would lead one to conclude that *p* or that will be recognized as inconsistent with alternatives other than *p*,

(2)   S concludes that p,

(3)   feature f of K is salient for the fact that p.

I introduce reference to "performance elements" so that the formula includes features of the performance that spectators may find salient for intermediate and developing objects that are generated by features not just of performers, but also of props, the setting, lighting effects, and the like. I introduce the expression "fact that p," where p is a place-holder for any statement of fact belonging to a correct description of intermediate or developed objects in a performance, to allow for understanding of the objects of non-narrative performances. No other changes need be made to the feature-salience model.

6.7   Some Important Benefits of the Feature-Salience Model: Double-Focus, Slippage, "Performer Power," "Character Power," and the Materiality of the Means of Performance

You go to the theater to watch a performance called "Hedda Gabler." It is a narrative theatrical performance of a kind with which you are quite familiar. As you watch the first scenes unfold, you find yourself waiting for the appearance of the title character. When she does appear, however, you are immediately troubled. You have been led by the interchanges among the other characters already on view to specific expectations concerning many of Hedda's characteristics. You are not entirely disappointed: for example, her physical demeanor *is* imperious. But, as soon as she opens her mouth to speak, you are shocked. You cannot take your eyes off the gap caused by two missing front teeth. The lisp caused by the gap grates upon your ears. After some time you conclude that what shocked you are features only of the performer and not characteristics of Hedda.[19] After a while you may even forget about it. Or you may still find yourself noticing these features of the performer from time to time, but only as occasional distractions from the unfolding narrative of the play.

Features of performers are just anything about a performer to which a person's attention could be drawn. This may include what she is wearing, the mole on her neck, the flat twang in her voice, the lift of an eyebrow, the droop of a shoulder, her crooked-back posture, her blue eyeliner. Any regularly recurring feature could be considered separately and, hence, focused on for itself. Let us refer to the senses many spectators have, illustrated here by an extreme example, in the following ways:

The sense spectators can get, of having their attention drawn *both* to characteristics of the object being developed in the performance *and* to features of the performers, is the sense of "double focus." The correlative sense many spectators have, of finding their attention going back and forth between these, is the sense of "slippage."[20] The phenomena of double focus and of slippage are consistent with and, indeed, predictable by the feature-salience model for explaining convergence on characteristics of the characteristics of performance.

These are predictable effects because the salience model relies explicitly on the fact that spectators attend to performers' voices and bodies. In adopting the model, we have sought to explain which features are connected to characteristics of the object performed and which are not, given that there are many more features of a performer that spectators might attend to than performers plan to have noticed when developing and executing a performance. The bodies and voices of performers are notoriously distracting.[21] In attending to a performer a spectator may find herself uncommonly focused on his unusual hands. Accordingly, she may lose track of the performance. But she may, instead, observe how the events in the play are reflected in the movements and the stillnesses of those hands. Or she may not be aware of the direction of her attention, yet still track the developing object. Another spectator may be attending only and exactly to whatever regularly occurring features the performers had planned to be noticed and tracked by an audience.

The fact that double focus and slippage are predictable on the feature-salience model allows us to use it to clarify two significant phenomena, namely, "performer power" and "character power."

The phrase "performer power" refers to phenomena that have attracted attention in the philosophical and theater studies literatures.

One such phenomenon is an effect that Aaron Meskin and Jonathan Weinberg, following Stanley Cavell,[22] call "star power." Star power, as they understand it, is the effect that occurs when a "film star's identity as star carries significant weight, perhaps even more than the weight of the character he or she is portraying in any given film." Meskin and Weinberg refer to this effect as "psychological doubleness" and assert that it "is no mere side-effect or cognitive quirk . . . [because] filmmakers count on it and exploit it."[23]

Another phenomenon is an effect that Marvin Carlson calls "the 'ghosting' of previous roles in [the] reception of later ones."[24] This effect is part of "the normal theater experience . . . with an actor in previous roles," and is analyzed by Carlson as delivering "an aura of expectations based on past roles."[25]

Performer power is a wider phenomenon than star power or the social fact and aura of celebrity. It is wider because it applies both to filmic and to theatrical performances. It is also wider than either the "star system" or Carlson's "ghosting" because it is an effect exploited by many performers who are not stars and not familiar to spectators from past performances either. But it is, as Meskin and Weinberg assert, no mere side-effect of filmic and theatrical performance.

Performer power is to be anticipated on the feature-salience model. A performer in a play relies on the fact that spectators will pay attention to her features in order to gain information about the character she is playing. Her features may be compelling because she is a star, or because she is familiar from past theatrical encounters, or only because she is striking in appearance. If her features are compelling, for whatever reason, then in some performance practices she would be wise to exploit spectator's interest *in her features* in order to prime the feature-salience pump.

In contrast, "character power" refers to the familiar fact that performances are so striking that even those who know better attribute characteristics of a character to the performer. And again, the phenomenon is to be expected on the feature-salience model. For, in any performance, some of the characteristics of a character *are* identical to features of the performer. There is more to say about this phenomenon, especially concerning what it is to "know better." And I will return to that issue in the next chapter. But the predictability of this phenomenon on the feature-salience explanation of the mechanics of basic theatrical understanding surely counts in favor of the explanation.

The fact that double focus and slippage are predictable on the feature-salience model can shed light on two theoretical matters having to do with the materiality of the features presented to audiences, especially issues about the materiality of the performer's body.

First, the materiality of the actor's body has become a dominant theme in modernist drama and in theories of theatrical modernism. In a widely quoted remark Herbert Blau claims that "of all the performing arts, the theater stinks most of mortality."[26] Hollis Huston denies there is much else possible in theater but the persistent "gap . . . between the [material] performance and the thought performed."[27] And Stanton Garner defines the modernist aesthetic for theater this way: "to make the stage not simply stand in for reality but to become it."[28]

The feature-salience model for basic comprehension describes and explains the fact that lies behind discussions of this aspect of the modernist movement in theater. If spectators get the characteristics they grasp by attending to the features of performers, there is no reason that fact cannot become a theme of a movement in the history of theater. And if the movement is one that focuses upon the means by which the art form achieves its effects, as modernism is sometimes said to be, then it will be no surprise to find the fact of the performer's body figuring large in the themes and practices of the movement.

The second and related issue is that, ever since modernist theater practice and theory began to focus upon it, the materiality of performers and of other means of performance has come to be seen as a crucial point of division between semiotic and phenomenological theories of theater.

According to some, the materiality of the actor's body marks the limit of what can be analyzed in terms of semiotics, in terms of signs and meanings. For, in some performances, bodies seem not to mean something (else) but to *be* something (i.e., themselves).[29] Treating material things, such as props, as "signs" not only makes it difficult to say what *is* and what is *not* a material object; it also renders the pleasure to be found in them *qua* material objects inexplicable.[30]

According to others, the materiality of the performer's body, while challenging to semiotic analysis, is not a fact that a more sophisticated semiotic theory cannot handle; and we should move in this direction because nothing can be (just) itself once it is on the stage, which is a site of producing meanings.[31] A standard argument here is that, since anything can go as a prop for anything else in a theatrical performance, then anything must act as a "sign" when it appears in a performance.[32]

The feature-salience model provides clarification here in two ways. First, while it is probably impossible for all the features of a given object to be found salient by some population of spectators for all of its own actual characteristics, this does not entail that no features of an object can be found salient for some characteristics of the object itself on some occasion. For stylistic reasons, a company could call attention to the fact that they have been using plastic toys for pistols in their performance. They will do this by enabling spectators to focus on certain of the features of their props – those features that are projectible for *some of* the very same characteristics that the object happens to have. Second, when we ask what features of a performer, of a bit of the set or stage, or of a property are projectible for some pattern or characteristics of some characteristic in the performed object – of an agent, of a room, of a pistol – there is no *essential* on-principle restriction on what those characteristics could be. Whatever restrictions there may be are set by styles of performance.

In the end, therefore, this is not an issue about objects on stage being signs and meanings and so becoming unable to be themselves. Nor is it about the limits to what can be a sign on the grounds that a thing *is* just itself on stage in some performances. This is instead an issue about theatrical styles and the uses to which materials can be put. If there are limits to those uses, that will be a discovery in the historical practices of theater, not in its philosophy.

Of course what is gripping about this debate has to do with the fact that spectators get what they do by attending to performers, sets, and props. And that can be uncanny in some performance styles. But surely not in all. This is not, for example, a matter of real things breaking through the illusion common to all performances, as Bert States holds.[33] But the reason theatrical performance does not significantly involve illusions about performers' bodies has nothing to do with bodies being "signs," as Anne Ubersfeld holds.[34] The feature-salience explanation of basic understanding requires common knowledge among spectators that they are at a theatrical performance. And it is impossible to possess that knowledge in common with others and simultaneously to enter into an illusion that one is not.[35]

> The fact that slippage is predictable on the feature-salience model underwrites the explanation for why Goodmanian retrieval of literary texts is impossible.

The feature-salience model is able to explain the fact that spectators sometimes sense they have lost the thread of the developing object even when they have not. Spectators sometimes have basic comprehension of a performance but still experience the performance as containing gaps. This is the kind of phenomenon Goodman used to assert the primacy of the literary text over the other features of performance. Goodman asserted that, in the case of drama,

> the work is a compliance-class of performances. The text of the play, however, is a composite of score and script. The dialog is in a virtually notational system, with utterances as its compliants. This part of the text is a score, and performances compliant with it constitute the work. The stage directions, descriptions of scenery, etc., are scripts in a language that meets none of the semantic requirements for notationality; and a performance does not uniquely determine such a script or class of coextensive scripts.

> Given a performance, the dialog can be univocally transcribed: different correct ways of writing it down will have exactly the same performances as compliants. But this is not true of the rest of the text.[36]

But this misses the point. First, given the phenomenon of slippage, it is not to be expected that the dialog of a play can be univocally transcribed from a performance. The most we can hope for, and the most that we need for convergence on the same characteristics, is that spectators will come out describing *substantially* the same characteristics. Audiences do converge on pretty much the same characteristics, and the feature-salience model explains how they do that. But, secondly, it is also the case, and allowed for on the feature-salience model, that although spectators are not usually led to different descriptions of the characteristics of the characteristics in a performance, they may have quite different qualitative experiences of performers and other objects and, hence, of a performance. The feature-salience model shows that these qualitative inflections in the experiences cannot be avoided, are an important aspect of the experiences, and are not reducible by univocal transcription.

6.8 The Feature-Salience Model and Explaining How Basic Theatrical Understanding Occurs

The most important result derivable from the feature-salience model is that it shows how any single spectator of a narrative performance is able to describe *the* characteristics of the objects presented in the performance, not just *some* characteristics. Thus, we have achieved the goal of this chapter, namely, to show how the account of basic theatrical understanding satisfies the "cognitive uniformity" principle.

> Any spectator describes characteristics of the objects presented in a performance by means of finding some features salient and tying them together in some particular way if and only if most other spectators offer the same description for the same reasons.

This fact has a further important consequence: it demonstrates that there is a way to secure a convergence on characteristics of what is presented that needs no appeal to whatever texts act as resources for theatrical performances. And, since there is a way of securing convergence on characteristics, it may seem we now have a way to identify theatrical performances as individual works.

But this will seem unsatisfying. And it should: for our account is incomplete. Even though convergence on the same *characteristics* occurs in the way explained by the feature-salience analysis, we have not yet shown that the *objects* of a performance – things like characters, events, tables and pistols, and stories themselves – can be identified without reference to some textual substrate that helps us fix reference. To think otherwise is to accept "the list view."

> The "list view" is the view that possession of correct descriptions, correct lists of characteristics, is sufficient for identification of the thing possessing the characteristics. But the list view has things the wrong way round: we may not even realize we are in possession of a correct description until we recognize, or fail to recognize, the thing in question.

Consider what happens when spectators encounter Hedda for the first time in a familiar kind of narrative performance in some *Hedda-to-Hedda* style. In Act 1, Tesman and his Aunt Juliane discuss a number of things, including in their conversations some descriptive information regarding Hedda, her background, and her substantial possessions and demands. Audiences learn a good bit about Hedda, not only from the utterances of Tesman and his aunt, but also from their demeanor when discussing Hedda. And then, when Tesman says he thinks she is coming, a figure enters the room and Aunt Juliane says, "Good morning Hedda dear." At that point audiences see *her*.

How do they do this? Part of the answer has to do with the fact that spectators have been prepared to find certain features of some performer salient for characteristics of Hedda. But clearly this is insufficient grounds for the first identification of Hedda.

For, suppose a company has chosen to craft a short theater piece using only and most of the language of Ibsen's script, right up to the same point in the script, but to perform it as a spoken "choral" work including some contrapuntal part-work for five voices, and employing abstract movements based in the rhythms of the language uttered. The language of this piece is no less informative about Hedda's characteristics than is the language of the narrative performance just considered. Indeed the second performance might even aim at bringing out precisely these same characteristics and to reach a kind of climax at the last words of the piece, "Good morning Hedda dear."

But the features of performers that the spectators of the second piece find salient for characteristics of Hedda do not enable them to identify anyone who is Hedda. And that is because no individual (or even group of them) *appears* who could be identified as *her*. We must have a particular someone in mind in order to ascribe those characteristics to someone, and having someone or something in mind requires already having identified her or it. So having in mind a correct list of characteristics is not the same thing as having identified Hedda.

The final step we need to make is to show how the characteristics on which spectators converge are pegged onto the objects that, by being linked up in the right ways, turn into the stories and descriptions of developed objects that are touchstones of basic theatrical understanding.

Only at that point will we have shown that in all respects theatrical performances can be identified without reference to the texts they employ.

Notes

1   David Ball, *Backwards and Forwards: A Technical Manual for Reading Plays* (Carbondale: Southern Illinois University Press, 1983), pp. 60–1.
2   Ibid., p. 61. I will show later why the explanation he gives for this, namely that "play characters are not *real*," is seriously misleading.
3   Paul Ziff makes a related point about both theater and dance, especially regarding what can be taken in at any single auditing. Imagine, for instance, two people auditing the same performance but from different locations. In certain theater arrangements the position from which two people see the performance can make for many differences in what these spectators will have presented to them. Paul Ziff, *Antiaesthetics: An Appreciation of* The Cow with the Subtile Nose (Dordrecht, Holland: D. Reidel, 1984), p. 87.
4   The last clause is present to cover the non-discursive signs of performance as discussed in a previous chapter.
5   David Lewis, *Conventions* (Oxford: Blackwell, 2002; first published Cambridge, MA: Harvard University Press, 1969), p. 5. I am not concerned with the defense by Lewis and others of a general account of conventions in which reference to intentions can be eliminated and linguistic behavior naturalized. The appeal of this work in the present context is motivated by its consistency with the goal of seeking to understand first audience understanding and then performer meaning when and if that is necessary, and by the absence of reference to intentions in figuring out what conventions are in play in a given context of activity.

6   Seamus Miller, "Coordination, Salience and Rationality," *Southern Journal of Philosophy* 24/3 (1991), p. 362.

7   Lewis, *Conventions*, pp. 5–8.

8   Ibid., pp. 8–24 and 97–100, and Robert Sugden, "The Role of Inductive Reasoning in the Evolution of Conventions," *Law and Philosophy* 17 (1998), pp. 380–1.

9   Sugden, "Role of Inductive Reasoning", pp. 388–5.

10 Margaret Gilbert, "Rationality and Salience," *Philosophical Studies* 57 (1989), 61–77.

11 Judith Mehta, Chris Starmer, and Robert Sudgen, "The Nature of Salience: an Experimental Investigation of Pure Coordination Games," *American Economic Review* 84 (1994), 658–73.

12 For more technical discussions of these issues, see Miller, "Coordination," pp. 359–70, Sugden, "Role of Inductive Reasoning," and Peter Vanderschraaf, "Convention as Correlated Equilibrium," *Erkenntnis* 42 (1995), 65–87. Miller has used similar arguments to defend the general rationality guarantee deriving from choice based on salient features alone. I am less concerned with the rationality issue than with the question whether the fact that theater is a social institution gives us reason to suppose spectators will find pretty much the same features salient for roughly the same reasons and producing roughly the same outcomes.

13 Anne Ubersfeld, "The Pleasure of the Spectator," trans. Pierre Bouillaguet and Charles Jose, *Modern Drama* 25/1 (1982), p. 128.

14 Following Roland Barthes, many literature and theater theorists became convinced that we could never get a grip on authorial intentions. The reasons included the fact that we lack the relevant historical information and that, when we do possess it, that information can be subject to interpretation. But, for many, this was more a fact about the difference between texts and whatever Barthes meant by "textuality," itself a subject of some disagreement. Roland Barthes, "The Death of the Author," in *Image – Music – Text*, ed. and trans. Stephen Heath (New York: Hill and Wang, 1977), pp. 142–8.

15 Patrice Pavis, "The Aesthetics of Theatrical Reception: Variations on a Few Relationships," in *Languages of the Stage*, trans. Susan Melrose (New York: Performing Arts Journal Publications, 1993, first published 1982), pp. 67–94. Pavis notes there are two forms of reader-response theory, one that focuses on the theory of the reader's reception of any text and one that focuses on the history of the reception of a particular text. We are concerned only with the former.

16 Ibid., p. 70.

17 Ibid., p. 73. As we noticed in chapter 2, David Saltz shows that the two-text view fails to achieve what it sets out to do, namely, to accord the performance the same kind of importance that is usually attributed to the text. David Saltz, "When is the Play the Thing – Analytic Aesthetics and Dramatic Theory," *Theatre Research International* 20/3 (1995), 266–76. The present objection

may be seen as providing further reason to worry about the two-text theory.

18   Pavis, "Aesthetics," p. 80.

19   It is imaginable, though perhaps not without considerable stretch, that this company had prepared a production in which Hedda must have such a gap and must lisp. They may even have required the performer doing this role to agree to tooth removal before rehearsals in order to secure the part. But you are given no reason to think this has happened here. At no time and in no manner, for example, do the other characters make anything of Hedda's appearance and her manner of speaking.

20   I do not mean to suggest that double focus is the experience of having one's attention drawn to these things simultaneously. That may happen, but it is not crucial to anything we are about to investigate. It is enough that spectators commonly find themselves sometimes focusing on the performed object and sometimes focusing on the performers themselves.

21   See Jonas Barish, *The Anti-Theatrical Prejudice* (Berkeley: University of California Reprint Edition, 1985), for a detailed study of how performers' bodies in particular are at the root of common misgivings – moral and non-moral – about theatrical performers and performances.

22   Stanley Cavell, *The World Viewed* (New York: Viking Press, 1971).

23   Aaron Meskin and Jonathan Weinberg, "Imagine That!", in *Contemporary Debates in Aesthetics and the Philosophy of Art*, ed. Matthew Kieran (Oxford: Blackwell, 2005.)

24   Marvin Carlson, "Invisible Presences – Performance Intertextuality," *Theatre Research International* 19/2 (1994), 111–17, at 113.

25   Ibid., 112, 113.

26   Herbert Blau, *Take Up the Bodies: Theater and the Vanishing Point* (Urbana: University of Illinois Press, 1982), p. 83.

27   Hollis Huston, *The Actor's Instrument: Body, Theory, Stage* (Ann Arbor: University of Michigan Press, 1992), p. 45.

28   Stanton B. Garner, Jr., "Object, Objectivity, and the Phenomenal Body," in *Bodied Spaces: Phenomenology and Performance in Contemporary Drama* (Ithaca, NY: Cornell University Press, 1994), pp. 87–119.

29   Bert O. States, "Introduction," and "The World on Stage," in *Great Reckonings in Little Rooms: on the Phenomenology of Theater* (Los Angeles: University of California Press, 1985), pp. 1–15 and 19–47, especially 6–9 and 23–29. Another who shares States's worries about the refusal of semiotics to acknowledge the phenomenological impact of material things in performances, such as props, is Andrew Sofer, *The Stage Life of Props* (Ann Arbor: University of Michigan Press, 2003).

30   Sofer, *Props*, pp. 6–16 and 18–19.

31   Eli Rozik, "The Corporeality of the Actor's Body: The Boundaries of Theatre and the Limitations of Semiotic Methodology," *Theatre Research International* 24/2 (1999), 198–211. See also Umberto Eco, "Semiotics of Theatri-

cal Performance," *The Drama Review: TDR* 21/1 (1977), 107–17, and Kier Elam, *The Semiotics of Theatre and Drama* (London and New York: Routledge, 1980), pp. 4–27.

32 Elam, *Semiotics*, pp. 11–14.

33 States, "World on Stage," especially pp. 30–7, and "The Scenic Illusion: Shakespeare and Naturalism," in *Great Reckonings in Little Rooms*, pp. 48–79, especially 70–9.

34 Anne Ubersfeld, "Text-performance," in *Reading Theatre*, trans. Frank Collins, ed. Paul Perron and Patrick Debbèche (Toronto: University of Toronto Press, 1999), pp. 3–31, especially 24–6. (This is a translation of *Lire le théâtre*, vol. 1, Paris: Editions Belin, 1996.)

35 My analysis here is anticipated by my analysis of the same point in James R. Hamilton, " 'Illusion' and the Distrust of Theater," *Journal of Aesthetics and Art Criticism* 41/1 (1982), 39–50. However, there I had argued that there could be no illusion, because no one with the knowledge that she is in a theater can be taken in. Here I argue for the weaker claim that, for the same reason, illusion does not play a significant role in theater's deliverances. I thank Dom Lopes for pointing out that the stronger argument was invalid.

36 Nelson Goodman, *Languages of Art* (Indianapolis: Bobbs-Merrill, 1968), 210–11.

7
WHAT AUDIENCES SEE

Spectators demonstrate that they have basic comprehension of a theatrical performance by describing the object that was developed in the performance, for example, a story. When they describe or tell a story, they can be characterized as having been thinking about the objects of the story – its characters, events, and other objects such as skulls, hats, tables, books, pistols, and the like – and of the story itself, the object developed in the performance.[1] To have thoughts about characters and events in plays spectators must be able to identify characters when they appear and events when they happen and then to re-identify characters when they appear again.[2] And spectators appear to do just that.[3]

Spectators identify characters when they appear and events when they happen and re-identify characters when they appear again. Moreover, spectators appear to re-identify characters and other objects across performances and productions, even in radically different performance styles.

If Hedda Gabler appears in one performance of a typical production of a *Hedda-to-Hedda* kind, spectators expect to see her again in other performances in the same production. If spectators have seen one performance of that kind, they have no difficulty re-identifying Hedda if she subsequently appears in performances in very different productions from the one in which they first saw her. The first may have been a production with naturalistic setting, costumes, and props; the next with almost no props, no set, no period costumes; and a third might have naturalistic production values, but be set in a swimming pool outside a Malibu beachfront house with swimwear for costumes, and pool toys for props.[4] It does not matter in which order a spectator encounters such a performance. The ability to identify and re-identify characters – and all other objects as well – survives changes in performances within productions, changes in productions, changes in settings, and changes in performers as well.

Once introduced to a character, or to any other object of the content of a narrative performance, most spectators have no trouble re-identifying that object even in radically different kinds of narrative performances. If spectators first see Hedda in performances of the *Gabler at a Distance* kind, most will have little trouble re-identifying Hedda in performances of the *Spontaneous Beauty* or the *Hedda-to-Hedda* kinds. And, again, the order of encounters does not seem to matter. The ability to identify and re-identify objects of narrative theatrical performances survives even radical changes in the kind of narrative performance employing those objects.

Imagine a *Hedda-to-Hedda* kind of performance telling a story in which what had been supporting characters, such as Lovborg, Aunt Juliane, and Tesman, are now the performance's major characters, and their situation is the focus of the story. The company might be exploring the idea that we have limited knowledge of where we come from and too little time to figure life out before we die.[5] Or they might be exploring themes suggested by Elinor Fuchs's discussion of the Nietzschean conflict between Tesman and Lovborg.[6] The point is that, were Hedda to appear in this play, as Hamlet does in *Rosencrantz and Guildenstern are Dead*, spectators familiar with any of the productions we have been describing would still recognize her as Hedda. And once again, the order of the encounter does not seem to matter. The ability to identify and re-identify objects of narrative theatrical performances survives even some changes in the roles of the objects where those changes are due to changes in the story.

Characters are not the only objects in a story that get identified across performances by spectators. Andrew Sofer remarks that

> The stage life of props extends beyond their journey within a given play. As they move from play to play and from period to period, objects accrue intertextual resonance as they absorb and embody the theatrical past.[7]

Sofer is speaking here of props both as objects, parts of the contents of performance, and as performance elements. But, as we have seen in our discussion of the materiality of performance elements, there is no barrier to Sofer's conflation of these. And, as his case studies show, props have a variety of functions, some of which they can only play if they are objects recognized across performances.[8]

The question is, What underwrites our capacity to identify and re-identify the objects of the content of performances? I propose the following answer.

> The kind of mechanism that underwrites our capacity to demonstratively identify and recognitionally re-identify characters and events in narrative performances is the same kind of mechanism as the one that underwrites our capacities to demonstratively identify and recognitionally re-identify anything else in the world we can think about.

This demonstrative and recognition-based story of identification and re-identification is a natural extension of the feature-salience analysis that explains convergence on characteristics. Taken together, the resulting combined analysis allows us finally to show that spectators do identify performances – both in respect of the means of performances (the performers, the sets, the props) and in respect of all the objects included in their content – without reference to anything beyond what happens in performances. Moreover, as we shall see, the combined analysis provides a unified story of performance identification for performances of narrative fictions, narrative non-fictions, and non-narrative pieces.

7.1 Identifying Characters, Events, and Other Objects in Narrative Performances

We have seen that the ability to identify and re-identify characters – and all other objects as well – survives changes in performances within productions, changes in productions, changes in settings, and changes in performers. The ability to identify and re-identify objects in plays survives even radical changes in the kind of narrative performance employing those objects. The ability to identify and re-identify objects in plays survives even some changes in the role of the objects where those changes are due to changes in the narrative. We now want an explanation for these facts.

I propose that we begin by examining how it is spectators identify and re-identify these objects in familiar cases.[9] To facilitate that discussion, I will focus on identification of characters and ask how it is that spectators identify Hedda in any performance of the *Hedda-to-Hedda* kind.

We know that the list view of identification fails. If, in attending to some performers, an audience has found salient a list of predicates that characterize Hedda, that is not sufficient for having identified her. What else is needed?

> Demonstrative identification necessarily involves location of the object in egocentric space located within the framework of some kind of non-egocentric space.

This is what happens. In the opening act of a performance of a *Hedda-to-Hedda* kind, spectators are provided with a good deal of information of various kinds about Hedda. After some time, spectators see a figure arrive before them from or at a particular space. Or perhaps they hear utterances before they see anything, but these utterances come from some particular location in the space. Most spectators react physically to these movements or sounds. By these means, spectators are prepared to locate something or someone on which to hang the characteristics they have in mind; and, then, most spectators do identify someone as *that one* there. There is a spatial element in identification. It is by thinking about that one *there* that audiences are able to think about *that one* and ascribe characteristics they already have in mind to a particular individual. What happens in this case is consistent with what is called "demonstrative identification," first explored by Bertrand Russell and later developed by Gareth Evans.

Demonstrative identification necessarily involves location of the object in egocentric space. That is, to pick out something in the environment in the relevant way is to react to its location, as given by the senses, relative to oneself. This does not require *believing* something like "Oh, something is over there"; one's reaction to a thing's position is often nothing more than turning one's head or leaning one's body in the direction of some sound or movement, without any thought at all. It may not even be necessary that one be conscious in order to be disposed in this way.[10] The disposition to physical movement in reaction to the sensed place of things is what is central to the capacity to locate them in egocentric space.[11]

But it is not enough to be able to locate something in egocentric space, for this gets us at most a sense of "here," of "there," and perhaps "here and *then* there." What more is required[12] in most circumstances is that we impose our knowledge of some non-egocentric space in which things happen on our egocentric space or, to put it the other way round, to locate our egocentric space within the framework of non-egocentric space.

In everyday life, the relevant non-egocentric space is the public space of which we form cognitive maps, that is, the objective spatial relations among things. What non-egocentric space is in theatrical performance requires more detailed discussion (see section 7.3 below). But in either case the importance of demonstrative identification is that it grounds the capacity to have descriptive thoughts about an object in such a way that the descriptors are to be thought of *that* thing.[13]

This analysis of a spectator's ability to identify characters can be misunderstood in two directions. First, it can be taken to be a metaphysical claim about characters, namely, that they are spatio-temporal objects. But, although the fact that spectators identify characters in this way may raise metaphysical issues about the ontological status of characters and, indeed, any other objects in the content of a narrative performance, it does not settle such issues. Instead, this is only a description of the epistemological facts, the phenomenology, concerning how spectators identify objects in a performance. Presumably, any correct metaphysics of characters would have to be consistent with these facts, but that again is another issue.[14]

Secondly, the description of the mechanism by which spectators identify characters can be understood too narrowly. Surely spectators are frequently led to seek to identify the bearers of properties by already having some characteristics in mind, and then having an individual physically identified so that the list of properties gets its purchase on a character. But the point to notice here is that spectators do locate characters in egocentric space without prior lists of any characteristics in mind. This happens at the beginning of very nearly every narrative theatrical performance. Spectators may have no prior knowledge of the characters and events in the story – they may not even know it will be a *narrative* performance – and they still locate the things that are characters in the first moments of a performance. This fact highlights the point, already mentioned, that identification is largely a matter of responding behaviorally to the locations of sounds and movements of those characters.

> Three requirements are critical to our ability to attach descriptive thoughts to what is demonstratively identified. The first is that there must be some object that is identified; the second is that a subject must be able to track the same object through some substantial period of time;[15] and the third is that this ability to track over time must allow for changes in the positions, for movements, of both subject and object.[16]

It cannot be stressed enough that, read realistically,[17] the first requirement may be taken to exclude our ability to demonstratively identify characters and events in narrative performances and, so, to attach descriptive thoughts to them. But a realist reading of the first requirement is presumptive: we have no basis for introducing metaphysical concerns at this point. As regards the phenomenology of our perception of characters and events and the relation of that phenomenology to the epistemological analysis we connect with it, it appears so far that we just do demonstratively identify characters and events in performances. And it appears we use the same mechanisms to learn who characters are and what they are doing that we use regarding any other objects in the world. So, I read the first requirement as a description of our experience rather than as a metaphysical commitment. Taken as a reflection of our experience with these matters, therefore, the first requirement is satisfied. It is Hedda audiences are learning about, including the fact that *her* name is "Hedda."[18] The second and third requirements are likewise satisfied: once spectators have identified Hedda demonstratively, they track her in the first act during the time she is there and in the space where they first noticed her, now noting additional characteristics the performers make salient for them.

7.2 Re-identification of Characters and Other Objects in Narrative Performances

In the first act of the performance just described, Hedda is engaged in conversations with Tesman, Aunt Juliane, and Mrs. Elvsted. Spectators learn a good deal more about her in these conversations, and again much of what they learn comes from Hedda's reactions to others and their reactions to her.

At the appearance of Judge Brack, Hedda leaves to show Mrs. Elvsted out, then returns to finish a conversation with Tesman and Judge Brack. Upon her return, no spectator would be surprised to hear Judge Brack address her as "Mrs. Tesman." For it is the same character who left only moments before who has returned. But how do audiences know *this* figure is still Hedda?

It is natural to think the answer has mostly to do with the fact that audiences have been led to find certain features of the performer playing Hedda salient for characteristics of Hedda so that by now spectators have a fair list of characteristics of Hedda in mind. So, if this one fits that list and, above all, looks the same, then she is the same. But, if having a list fails to amount to identification, it also fails to amount to *re*-identification. And looking the same is not being the same; for this figure could look different yet be the same. So, how do audiences re-identify Hedda?

Spectators assume a relevant "area of search" which is defined by their estimate of how long a character has been gone, how far she could have gone, and from whence she left. It is the results of such estimates that underwrite a spectator's capacity to re-identify a person or thing within a performance.

The answer lies in the fact that spectators take that one *there* to be the same character that *only moments before* had left and who now has returned. That is, her location in space is linked to *the time* it takes for her to leave and come back. A figure appears and, to all appearances, is Hedda; but what actually underwrites an spectator's re-identification of Hedda is that her *appearance is distinctive enough, in the spatio-temporal setting of the performance*, to allow the spectators to locate her in egocentric space as the object of their continued thought. They are still thinking about *her*, *this one*, because they know that the spatio-temporal setting of the performance has not changed. And they also know that because they know *they* have not moved. They have thereby established a relevant "area of search."

Appeal to spectators' knowledge of their own spatio-temporal situations supports identification and re-identification within single performances. Spectators' knowledge of where *they* have been undergirds estimates of how long a character has been gone. And this works within a single performance of traditional duration because the time any character is out of sight and not tracked is relatively short.

But it is not obvious why such an appeal should work to support re-identification across performances, productions, performance kinds, changes in stories and so on. When there has been a substantial gap in time or place since the original sighting, it is implausible to think any spectator has been tracking any character's location. There is no plausible area of search that depends on the kinds of estimates that work within single performances. Spectators may not even know, in the relevant sense, where *they* have been.

Memory of a character will not serve. For the memory of the character a spectator has previously identified does not give that spectator reason to think that the individual before her now, which may have similar or even exactly the same characteristics, is the same thing she identified before. If the list view fails to deliver re-identification *within* single performances, it certainly also fails to do so *across* performances.

When a spectator has lost track of a character or when there has been a substantial gap in time or place since the original sighting, we seem to be in this situation: we can see how to show a spectator has identified *that one there*, but how do we show she has the *same character* in mind after some interval during which she has not kept track of the object? That one may be another character that looks just like the former character, or, worse, the character she once had in mind may have changed beyond recognition during the interval in which the spectator had not tracked her or him.[19]

7.3 The Special Nature of Theatrical (Uses of) Space: Performances and Performance Space

There are three ways to orient yourself that add up to subsuming egocentric space to non-egocentric space.

First, in most everyday circumstances the relevant non-egocentric space is simply the public space defined by our cognitive maps of the objective spatial relations among things. This can be thought of in two ways. Each corresponds to a way that people have a grasp of those objective spatial relations. Each can be illustrated by a way in which you might give directions. The first is by reference to compass points or street addresses: "from here you go north five blocks and turn west onto Laramie Street, and the address is 1702 Laramie Street." The second is by specifying a route: "from here you go alongside that long aluminum fence until it ends and then you turn left just before the big Lutheran Church; the bar is just ahead on your right; look for the big red dog on the roof of a building and it is just past that." We rely on knowing where we are in identifying objects (in this case, the bar) by reference to the space we are in subsumed under our cognitive map of public space in one of these two ways.

Second, in some circumstances the time and distance lapse may be so large you cannot say with precision where you have been in the interval. In these kinds of circumstances, you rely more heavily on familiarity with lists of characteristics. Even so, you still do so in relation to spatial location, as when you are trying to determine if the route you are following is the correct route to your friend's house in a city you have not visited in some years. In such circumstances you confirm that a given route is a route you have been down before because it prompts you to remember features, or you reject a given route as not familiar because it fails to prompt you to remember features, or the features it has are too dissimilar to secure recognition.

A third kind of circumstance involves a distinction among *kinds of spaces* or locations. And you appeal to the kind of locations you are in when recognition occurs independently of your knowledge of where you have been in an interval, no matter how long. For example, you are capable of recognizing your own radio in your own home even if there are thousands that look just like it somewhere and even if you have not been home for some time. In contrast, there are some location kinds that disable recognitional capacities. If your radio appeared in the police display of stolen goods, to use one of Evans's examples, it is unlikely you will be able to tell your own radio from any others in the universe. In this kind of location, having lost track of where the radio has been, and having no coherent story to tell about where you have been that would support a claim about the relevant area of search, you are unable to employ the techniques you have ready to hand in the other cases.[20] An important, even if completely obvious, aspect of this kind of circumstance is this: knowledge of the kinds of spaces that enable recognition is *a posteriori* knowledge, it is not something one comes to know without some experience.

I now suggest we define "performance space" as a particular kind of space. A definition of "performance space" should meet three desiderata. An adequate definition should encompass but also allow us to distinguish among performances, spectator sports, company picnics, and religious rituals. An adequate definition should not preclude a further distinction between artistic and non-artistic performances.[21] An adequate definition should not exclude from performances in general features we already know to be true of more specific kinds of performance types.[22]

In the present context the first of these desiderata is decisive; for a definition of performance space to meet this desideratum, it must entail that performance spaces are particular uses of literal space. Accordingly, and following out a line of thought suggested by Augusto Boal, Peter Brook, and Hollis Huston, I propose we define "performance space" as follows.[23]

> Broadly speaking, a "performance space" is an active observation space (1) that is created in literal space by the actions of some people who, by those actions, not only become either performers or spectators but also turn other people into either spectators or performers and (2) in which whatever spectators observe is observed in that literal space during the time those actions govern the behavior of the parties involved.

The definition does not pick out anything distinctive about theatrical space; but it does allow room to think of theatrical space as a species of performance space, more generally.

The fact that something is a performance space if and only if it involves the creation of an active observation space entails that performance spaces, including theatrical spaces, are kinds of places exactly analogous to other non-egocentric space kinds – i.e., uses of literal space – such as homes, police displays, and playing fields, under which a spectator's egocentric space can be subsumed. This fact ensures that performance spaces play the right kind of roles – as a way of specifying a relevant area of search – for underwriting the recognition of characters in the challenging cross-performance cases. Such spaces will be non-egocentric in the relevant way because they will be determined relative not to where spectators know they have been, but to their knowledge of the kind of place they were in when the original sightings took place. It is, we will now see, that because spectators originally identified Hedda in a theater space that they are able to recognize *her* again when watching a new theatrical performance of whatever kind in a relevantly similar (use of) space.

The fact that something is a theater space only if it is a species of performance space, involving the creation of active observation space, does not entail that there is anything of particular value in live performance that cannot be found in other forms of performance. There may be some value added by liveness; but that is not certain,[24] and it plays no factor in the issues we are discussing here.

7.4 Cross-Performance Re-identification

Earlier we saw that identification and re-identification of characters in theatrical performances survive more than one performance in the same production, more than one production, more than one performer, more than one interpretation, more than one style, more than one story. And our analysis must show how that is done.

We can begin with the rough idea that re-identification is a matter of an object striking a subject as being the same one encountered before. The challenges are these: when spectators identify Hedda in these cases, what grounds their capacity to distinguish her from all others? and is it possible to genuinely identify Hedda when she has "changed beyond recognition"? For the question is still this: what makes the thoughts spectators are having *thoughts about her*?

If a spectator has learned that the space in which she originally identified some object is theatrical space, then she has a grip on the use of space that is involved in re-identifications. And even if there are cases that are problematic in this regard, in most cases she has no expectation of recognizing that object again except in *that kind* of space, that is, in ordinary space used in *that kind* of way.

Suppose, late one evening on a street in Prague, you see a gymnastics routine performed by what appears at some distance to be a young man. You are struck by the singularity and precision of his movements and you share the awe he inspires in the other people standing and watching. Upon your return home, some weeks later, you are persuaded to attend a gymnastics meet in which one of your daughter's friends is competing. As you watch this young woman perform, you are suddenly struck with the thought that *this* is the same routine. For, as you watch the performance develop, some moves look the same to you and soon, perhaps, you begin to anticipate correctly what the next moves will be. You may not have been able to say in advance what moves defined the routine, but upon seeing them unfold you are prompted to remember them.

It is tempting to analyze this as a case of applying a list and recognizing the correct route because of the items on the list it prompts you to recall. For this example involves being struck by this routine of moves as something you have encountered before. This approach helps bring out what is tempting about the "list view" of identification, the suggestion that audiences re-identify characters by comparing lists of characteristics definitive of the characters to the characteristics being made salient in the performance they are presently watching. When watching a new play, for example, a spectator might think that *this one* could be the character encountered before. And this thought will be triggered if the spectator notices some similar characteristics.

That thought seems confirmed if there *is* something to identify as the one to whom to attach those descriptions and if the similarities pan out. Just as one confirms that a given route is the correct route because it prompts you to remember features, just as one rejects a given route as incorrect because it fails to prompt you to remember features and the features it has are too dissimilar, so audiences may come to accept or reject a character as being the one they encountered before on the basis of the descriptive facts about the character they remember as a result of their encounter with *this one* before them. And this is what is right about the claim that we identify by means of descriptions.

But this approach also brings out even more sharply why the list view and the analysis I have just connected to it cannot be the whole story or the fundamental one. For if you are reminded of Hedda Gabler by someone you encounter *in the street*, you probably do not think you have recognized Hedda. And no amount of subsequent, new, and confirming characteristics evident in this person's behavior would convince you otherwise. What is missing in the analysis, but what we all understand, is that a street is *the wrong kind of space* in which to meet Hedda. Just as the locale of the police display of stolen goods disables your ability to recognize your own radio, a street is the kind of place that disables recognition of theatrical characters.

To be sure, before you learn how to assess which non-egocentric spaces underwrite which re-identifications, it is completely open to you to suppose, for example, that you can identify your radio in the police display of stolen goods. You have to learn that this is a non-egocentric space in which, no matter that you can subsume egocentric space to it, you are still unable to pick out that radio which is the one you have encountered before, namely, yours.

But if you have learned that the space in which you originally saw Hedda is a theater space, then you have a grip on the kind of space that is involved in re-identifications. And even if there are cases that are problematic in this regard, in most cases you have no expectation of recognizing Hedda again except in that *kind* of space, that is, in ordinary space used in *that kind* of way.[25]

In the gymnastics case, what is the relevant non-egocentric space that underwrites your recognition of the movements and the routine of which they are the objects when, pretty obviously, the original sighting took place on a street in Prague and the second took place in the high school gymnasium in Powhattan, New York? The answer is that the relevant kind of space where the original sighting of this gymnastics routine took place is not the space describable by a cognitive map of Prague but rather a *performance space*, space used for performance (in Prague).

We may still worry about cases in which Hedda may have changed beyond all recognition. The fact is, we may not be able to re-identify characters or objects across some performances for this very reason.[26] And it may be that there are some of us who are better at this than others, or some cases where none of us can and some in which only some of us can. But the problem before us does not require that we can show that certitude exists in theory where it does not exist in practice. So these cases can be ignored.

7.5 Identifying and Re-identifying Objects in Non-narrative Performances

The analysis of identification and re-identification has been set out in terms of capacities for locating characters and events in narrative performances in the literal space of the theater in which the performance takes place. We have been led to this way of explaining audience encounters with characters and events by following out the thought that, to be thinking about characters and events, we must be able to identify them demonstratively and re-identify them by reliance on recognition capacities. Both of these centrally involve locating things in egocentric space subsumed under a sense of some non-egocentric space of which the spectator is aware. And that space, I have argued, is the space of the theater itself used as a space of observation.

In any of the non-narrative performance kinds imagined throughout this book – *Something to Tell You, Burning Child*, and *Pistols and Other Doors* – we identify the images, actions, and individuals we see within the space of the theatrical performance itself. In these, images, people, and actions are identified and re-identified, and re-identified across performances.

The idea of a special kind of space, where that is understood as "semic" or "fictive" or not otherwise identical to the literal ordinary space used in a certain recognizable way, is simply not plausible as a candidate for delivering an area of search that a spectator relies upon in determining which object she is thinking about. For there is no literal route for us to trace in determining the relevant area of search if one of the spaces we have to know how to get to is not a literal space. Re-identifications, across performances, of those same images, actions, and individuals are based upon a non-metaphorical appreciation of the fact that the original sightings were in ordinary space in which observation relationships are set up. This is literal space.

So here I appeal to an economy of thought. Theater space is what works as the non-egocentric kind of space to which spectator-subjects subsume their egocentric locations when demonstratively identifying who or what it is they are thinking about in all cases: cases of fictional narrative performances, of non-fictional narrative performances, and of non-narrative theatrical performances. The explanation is general, serving all identification and recognition.

Whatever turns out to be the correct metaphysical view of fictional characters, events, and other objects of fictional narrative performances – perhaps they are the kinds of things that can have qualitative but not numerical identity – this is the epistemological fact any metaphysical view must accommodate:

Spectators make use of acquired knowledge of the theatrical uses of literal space to identify and re-identify characters, events, images, performers, and so on, within and across performances, sometimes across performances of radically different kinds.

7.6 Added Benefits of the Demonstrative and Recognition-Based Approach to Identification and Re-identification

An added benefit of the analysis of identification and re-identification of the objects of a theatrical performance I have just provided is that it enables us to make more precise the feeling people have of "being in the presence of" characters and other objects of theatrical performance.[27]

In the normal case, if I am in your presence, then I could see or hear you if I looked in your direction or turned my head towards the sounds you are making, there would be some place quite nearby to which you could go such that I could not see or hear you even if I looked or turned in your direction, and there is some place quite nearby that I could go such that I could not see or hear you even if I looked or turned in the relevant direction. This suggests the sense in which we are in the presence of characters when watching theatrical performances.

The physical notions that are involved in describing what it is to be in the presence of another are the same ones that are involved in descriptions of demonstrative and recognitional identification of characters and other objects of theatrical performances. Both involve precognitive reactions to sounds and sights that trigger an organism's directional responses. Both involve tracking an object in space over a stretch of time and the same kinds of loss of contact and re-establishing-of-tracking contacts.

If this is roughly right, then it explains why we are much less in the presence of characters and events when reading novels or works of dramatic literature. For one thing we think is special about our encounters with characters and events in plays is that, in some sense, we are in their presence in a way that we are not in most other art forms capable of delivering narratives. No matter how close we may feel to a character in a novel, we are never in any doubt that we are not in that characters' presence. Even if we react physically to the movement (or apparent movement[28]) in movies, we are never in any doubt we are not in the presence of that movement. In this regard theatrical performance shares an important feature with dance performance.

Our analysis of identification and re-identification of the objects of a theatrical performance requires that spectators learn that theatrical space is a use of literal space that underwrites areas of search within which spectators are able to recognize and identify characters and other objects they have previously identified. The prominence of learning about kinds of (uses of) space is connected to a further added benefit of the analysis.

> The analysis positions us to finish explaining what I earlier called "character power."

Earlier I defined "character power" as the capacity of a performance to be so striking that even those who know better attribute characteristics of a character to the performer. What "knowing better" means was left undefined. We can now define it. In this context "knowing better" is, precisely, possessing acquired knowledge of the relevant kind of space within which to identify and re-identify characters in theatrical performances.

Character power involves mistakes in re-identification that take place when spectators encounter performers outside the theater. Why don't we anticipate seeing Hedda in the shopping mall next week? Why don't we see Hedda in the shopping mall? The answer to the former cannot be the same as the answer to the latter of these questions because on occasion we are indeed tempted to think we see Hedda in the mall, after all. And here is the sense of that: until an individual spectator learns that the theater space is the kind of space in which she can reliably identify and distinguish among certain individuals and that the shopping mall is not a relevant area of search for those individuals, a spectator might well expect the figure she picks out in the mall to have the characteristics of a character she has seen in a recent performance. Once she has the relevant knowledge, she does not make those mistakes.

7.7 Theatrical Performance as a Fully Independent Practice

The challenge in Part II has been to show that there is a way of identifying theatrical performances without reference to anything more than what happens in the performance itself and, in particular, without reference to the fact or contents of a text that is used. This could be done fully successfully only if we were able to show how we can talk about more than one performance with the same or similar content. This required an explanation of spectators' ability to identify the objects in one performance as the same objects in another.

Although the feature-salience analysis showed how spectators converge on roughly the same *characteristics* of the objects in a performance, the ability to identify the *objects* themselves required a further analysis. The list view proved inadequate to the task. But now we have seen that the demonstrative and recognition-based approach to the identification and re-identification of the objects of a theatrical performance *is* adequate to the task. Moreover, it relies on the same everyday physical reactions and cognitive methods that are found in the feature-salience analysis of convergence on characteristics. And it provides the last explanation we have needed for how audiences manage to understand, and identify, theatrical performances.

Not only have we demonstrated that there is a way to secure a convergence on characteristics of what is presented that needs no appeal to whatever texts act as resources for theatrical performances, we have also shown that there is a way of securing common basic theatrical understanding of the contents of performances without appealing to anything beyond what happens in performances. This means we also have shown that spectators do identify theatrical performances: ultimately, they are identifiable by appeal to what spectators say and do when demonstrating basic theatrical understanding. For what they say and do can be explained in terms of converging on the same characteristics and identifying the objects of the performances they see before them. In short, audiences do not, nor need they, appeal to texts to secure identification of theatrical performances. And, so, theatrical performance is a practice independent of literature.

But is it art?

Notes

1   Much of the work on this chapter was first done while I was the recipient of a two-week visit to Texas Tech University, in fall 2004, while on a Big 12 Fellowship. I appreciate the discussions I had there with Aaron Meskin and Danny Nathan. I would also like to thank Doug Patterson, for pushing me to make the phenomenological character of this chapter clearer, and Alberto Voltolini and Francesco Orilia for letting me read work in progress on the ontology of fictional agents and for making useful comments on earlier versions of this chapter.

2   It is common among philosophers to subsume whatever we say about char-
     acters and events in theatrical performances of narrative fictions to a general
     theory of fictions. In the end, this may be the right direction to take for the
     purposes of metaphysics. But in terms of the epistemology of theatrical per-
     formances – of how we understand the objects of what is presented to specta-
     tors in a performance – this is clearly not an option. Many theatrical
     performances are not narratives at all, let alone fictional narratives. If we want
     a general account of how the contents of performances are perceived, then
     starting with that particular and special subset of performances needs con-
     siderably more justification than is usually on offer. The main reason, I
     believe, is that the issues are usually taken to be metaphysical rather than
     epistemological.

3   In thinking this through, I rely heavily on the work regarding demonstrative
     and recognition-based identification developed by Gareth Evans in *The
     Varieties of Reference*, ed. John McDowell (Oxford: Clarendon Press, 1982),
     especially pp. 143–91 and 267–98.

4   This case is not entirely imagined: a film version of *Hedda Gabler* with a
     similar setting was released in November, 2004, at the Seattle Film Festival.
     A stage version was developed in Seattle in 2000. I have only transposed the
     setting to southern California from its native Washington.

5   The example is inspired by Tom Stoppard's script for *Rosencrantz and Guil-
     denstern are Dead* (London: Faber, 1967).

6   Elinor Fuchs, "Counter-Stagings: Ibsen against the Grain," in *The Death of
     Character: Perspectives on Theater after Modernism* (Bloomington: Indiana
     University Press, 1996), pp. 52–66. Fuchs's essay provides a basis of what
     could be a compelling performance, with Tesman and Lovborg in Nietz-
     schean conflict with Tesman as Apollonian and Lovborg as Dionysian, each
     writing a competing history of civilization, pp. 64–6.

7   Andrew Sofer, *The Stage Life of Props* (Ann Arbor: University of Michigan
     Press, 2003), p. 2.

8   Ibid., pp. 20–9.

9   As noted above, in most of the chapter I rely on Gareth Evans's work con-
     cerning demonstrative and recognition-based identification. Evans develops
     this material in an exploration of Bertrand Russell's claim that, as Evans puts
     it, "a subject cannot make a judgment about something unless he knows
     which object his judgment is about," *Varieties of Reference*, p. 89. Evans
     explores the idea that to assign predicates to a thing and assess the truth of
     the application, we must have what he calls "an Idea of the object," and he
     seeks to ground having an Idea of an object in having capacities to identify
     the thing demonstratively and recognitionally, without having to believe
     anything about the object to do so. The result is that Evans not only makes
     Russell's idea more precise, he also removes its unnecessary reference to
     knowledge or even belief content. Evans then builds a theory of varieties of
     reference on this largely, but reworked, Russellian base. It is the base-level

work that is of use in the present context. We can think of what follows as providing additional support for Evans's views on these matters even if, as I will point out soon, Evans would not be entirely happy with this application of that work.

10   The phenomena we are discussing resemble "flocking behavior" of birds, fish, and ourselves in a number of ways. But, in the case of human beings, it is especially important that flocking turns up in "cognitive and experiential variables" as well as in physical movements. James Kennedy and Russell Eberhart, "Particle Swarm Optimization," in *Proc. IEEE Int'l. Conf. on Neural Networks*, IV (1995), pp. 1942–8; the quotation is from p. 1943.

11   "Egocentric space can exist," Evans argues, "only for an animal in which a complex network of connections exists between perceptual input and behavioral output." Evans, *Varieties of Reference*, p. 154.

12   I leave on one side any complications that might attend the added fact that we are concerned from this point on only with organisms that are conscious and capable of reasoning.

13   And demonstrative identification is possible because we are the kinds of organisms that respond behaviorally to sensory inputs of spatio-temporal objects and can subsume those dispositions to knowledge of the spatial environment.

14   A separate defense of a similar constraint – a pragmatic constraint on ontology – requiring that ontological stories about works of art should conform to the facts of critical and appreciative practice is found in David Davies, *Art as Performance*, New Directions in Aesthetics Series (London and New York: Blackwell, 2004), pp. 16–24.

15   The idea that identification of characters and other objects in theatrical performances requires tracking in "continuous space" is a view familiar from Susan Sontag's "Theatre and Film," in *Styles of Radical Will* (New York: Farrar, Strous, Giroux, 1966), pp. 99–122, especially at 108ff. But I show that this tracking can admit of seriously, if not terrifically, lengthy gaps in time.

16   Evans, *Varieties of Reference*, pp. 173–6.

17   Evans intends a realist reading. He explicitly excludes the contents of hallucinations as capable of being identified demonstratively, ibid., p. 173. Nevertheless, for the reasons I offer in the body, I think the introduction of metaphysical considerations here is premature.

18   We can now explain why nothing is identifiable as Hedda in the chorus-like performance described earlier, in which spectators gain only a list of characteristics of Hedda. Nothing physical appears in that performance to which spectators are drawn to attach those characteristics. There is no experience of *that one there* that prompts such attachment. Accordingly there is nothing *about which* they are having thoughts; so those spectators are, in thinking about a possible someone called "Hedda," not thinking about *her*.

19   Ibid., pp. 272–3. Evans notes that this does indeed entail that there are cases that are undecidable, but this does not undermine the capacity to recognize or the concept of the capacity of recognitional identification. We will return to cases that are undecidable later in the chapter.

20   Ibid., p. 280.

21   Paul Thom, *For an Audience* (Philadelphia: Temple University Press, 1993), pp. 4–6.

22   See James R. Hamilton, "Theater," in *The Routledge Companion to Aesthetics*, 2nd edition, ed. Berys Gaut and Dominic McIver Lopes (London: Routledge, 2001), pp. 585–96.

23   Here I am developing ideas that are suggested in Augusto Boal, *Theatre of the Oppressed* (New York: Theatre Communications Group, 1990), Peter Brook, *The Empty Space* (London: Simon & Schuster, 1995), and Hollis Huston, *The Actor's Instrument: Body, Theory, Stage* (Ann Arbor: University of Michigan Press, 1992), pp. 1–16, 68–89, and 111–26. There is another strategy, derivable from H. P. Grice's theory of communication. The reason I do not pursue that here is that, for reasons discussed in Hamilton, "Theater," the strategy fails to meet the second desideratum.

24   The claim that "liveness" confers a value to theatrical performance in contrast to movie and other "mediated" performances is rightly and decisively contested, I believe, in Philip Auslander, *Liveness: Performance in a Mediatized Culture* (London and New York: Routledge, 1999), pp. 38–43.

25   The case I have been making is conceptual. Some empirical evidence related to the process I have described, and its reliance on spectators' ability to recognize objects because the spaces they occupy constitute a familiar locale, can be found in Steven P. Tipper and Bruce Weaver, "The Medium of Attention: Location-Based, Object-Centred, or Scene-Based?" in *Visual Attention*, ed. R. D. Wright (Oxford: Oxford University Press, 1998), pp. 77–107.

26   Francesco Orilia has convinced me that the Evans material does not provide the resources for solving most of these kinds of cases. He is more generally skeptical than I am that there can be perceptions independent of a certain set of features. He argues that Evans's idea of recognitional identification must involve the presence of perceptual features. I don't think I need to dispute that claim to still insist that there must be some sort of physical reaction to a something in space onto which the recognition of features is pegged. And, in any case, I now agree that Evans does not solve twin cases and so does not provide resources for solving cases in which characters have changed beyond recognition. See Francesco Orilia, "Identity across Time and Stories," in *Modes of Existence: Papers in Ontology and Philosophical Logic*, ed. Andrea Bottani and Richard Davies (Frankfurt: Ontos Verlag, 2006), pp. 191–220.

27   The idea itself is ubiquitous and important. See Marco De Marinis, "The Performance Text," in *The Semiotics of Performance*, trans. Aine O'Healy (Bloomington: Indiana University Press, 1993), pp. 47–59; reprinted in *The*

Performance Studies Reader, ed. Henry Bial (London and New York: Routledge, 2004), pp. 232–51, especially pp. 235, 242–4, and Alice Raynor, "The Audience: Subjectivity, Community and the Ethics of Listening," *Journal of Dramatic Theory and Criticism* 7/2 (1993), p. 9.

28 It is not clear that what is seen in movies is movement in space or only apparent movement. See Noël Carroll, *Theorizing the Moving Image* (Cambridge: Cambridge University Press, 1996) and Gregory Currie, *Image and Mind: Film, Philosophy, and Cognitive Science* (Cambridge: Cambridge University Press, 1995) for a good introduction to the details of this discussion. In either case, there will be some similarity between theater and movies insofar as movies are construed as a depictive art – so that the stage picture, moment to moment, plays a similar role in grasping a theatrical performance to that which it plays in grasping a movie.

PART III
THE ART OF
THEATRICAL
PERFORMANCE

8

DEEPER THEATRICAL UNDERSTANDING

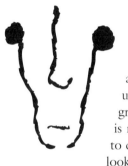

If theatrical performances are to be regarded as the products of a practice of art making, performances must be observable, appreciable and evaluable *as achievements*.[1] To correctly appreciate anything for the achievement it embodies, we must understand what that achievement is. This requires a grasp of the background against which any work is, or is not, an achievement and against which one is able to determine what kind of achievement one should be looking for. With respect to the latter, the kind of knowledge one needs to have involves knowing not only what to appreciate but also how to appreciate it – both what is to be looked for and how to go about looking.[2] An interest in achievement in works of art involves an interest in details, an interest in answering the questions why this detail is present and not that one and what this detail can tell us about the whole work.[3] Accordingly I propose the following working definition of *full appreciation* of a theatrical performance.

Full appreciation of a theatrical performance involves the ability to see the performance against a background that can inform the spectator what kind of achievement is or is not manifest in the performance, and, by reference to details in performances, to converse about how the performance practices contribute or detract from the performed object and about whether the performed object is achievable by certain kinds of performance practices rather than others.

We begin by discussing the fact that some people seem to get more out of what is presented to them in a theatrical performance than others do. Those who do get more seem to have a kind of background understanding that is of the relevant sort. These facts easily motivate a distinction between basic and some sort of "deeper" theatrical understanding. But again, it is one thing to motivate a distinction, another to defend it.

8.1   General Success Conditions for Deeper Theatrical Understanding

The success conditions I propose for "deeper theatrical understanding" are as follows:

> A spectator has deeper theatrical understanding if she is able to describe *either* (a) how the performers have achieved the presentation of the object *or* (b) how the object of the performance is structured.

Consider a parodic narrative performance delivering a *Hedda-to-Hedda* story based in Ibsen's script. Suppose nothing in the script is changed but that the performers play the beliefs, motives, actions, and principles of the characters so that the result is a parody. For example, the performance might induce the view that Hedda is unseemly for resenting a lack of freedom from which she takes no pains to free anyone else, does not acknowledge that this same lack of freedom binds her new aunts, and is completely oblivious to the social shackles on her serving staff. In the final scenes of the performance spectators might be induced to laughter at her suicide, to see it as silly and well deserved, an appropriate object of laughter and ridicule.

When a basically comprehending spectator tells the story presented to her in this case, she tells a story of some silly or perverse people who do silly or perverse things, appear to hold silly or perverse beliefs, and so on. She will not have missed the satire directed at the characters and their foibles. But surely she will still have missed something fairly crucial. For she will not notice that the piece she saw performed was in fact a parody. She will have grasped the satire that is the point of the parody, but she will not have understood it *as* parody.

A more experienced spectator may have sensed that there might have been more. And if the performers have signaled something more in the performance, a really experienced spectator is likely to respond to the calls the performers made on her capacities for assessing performance elements. But if a spectator, no matter how experienced, can demonstrate only basic comprehension, surely she has missed something present in the performance. In this case, the spectator will have missed something about the performance techniques employed.

Consider, in contrast, any more standard *Hedda-to-Hedda* performance based in Ibsen's script. Not all of these performances will look alike, of course. For example, different Naturalistic performances might focus on different inner demons, so to speak, or employ different Naturalistic techniques.[4] If a spectator reacts in appropriate ways or is able to tell the story and describe the character interactions with reasonable accuracy, given the emphases put in place by the performers, she has a basic theatrical understanding of the performance. But if this is all she can do, she has missed something. She will, *ex hypothesi*, have missed all of those large-scale features of which a grasp is unnecessary for basic comprehension. For example, she will miss the rhythmic pattern of the four-act structure, the overall rise and fall of intensifications in the story, and so on. She will have missed something about the structure of the content of this performance.

8.2 More Precise Success Conditions: Two Kinds of Deeper Understanding

By making suitable changes to the feature-salience model, we allow it to articulate what is going on when spectators meet the success conditions for deeper understanding. We also make precise the fact that there are two different kinds of specialized knowledge that could be required for a spectator to understand a performance more deeply than one who comprehends it only basically. The first change to the feature-salience model for basic theatrical understanding allows us to model *deeper performer understanding*.

> "Spectator S has deeper performer understanding, when presented feature *f* of performer J, that character C has an eager thirst" is true just in case, for some spectator S, some performer J, and some character C,
>
> (1) S responds to feature *f* as salient, under conditions of common knowledge that spectators are attending a theatrical performance, for a fact or facts that would lead one to conclude that C has an eager thirst or that will be recognized as inconsistent with alternatives to C's having an eager thirst
>
> (2) S concludes that C has an eager thirst

(3)   feature f is salient for C's having an eager thirst, and

(4)   S recognizes what it is that J likely intends to be made salient by exhibiting f, whether or not J is successful at realizing that intention.

This change is a simple extension of the feature-salience model consisting only in the addition of condition (4). For a spectator has *basic* comprehension of the fact that C has an eager thirst when conditions (1) through (3) are true but (4) is not. Under those conditions, S gets it that f is salient for C having an eager thirst and correctly concludes this by (1) through (3). But S does not have deeper understanding. Let us see what (4) contributes to explaining deeper performer understanding.

Suppose a performer draws spectators' attention to some features, intending that they be salient for the fact that C is trembling with a terrific fear of water or for the fact that C has a nervous tic that appears whenever she drinks water. However, what she actually succeeds in making salient is the fact that C has an eager thirst. Condition (4) allows us to capture the situation that obtains when a spectator recognizes that the performer is not doing what she thinks she is doing.

Possession of deeper performer understanding allows a spectator to recognize what performers are doing *and* to see the connection between that and the fact spelled out in condition (3). That is, if a spectator really does understand what a performer intends to do by the movement of the arm, she will not find that movement adventitious, she will know why that feature is in the performance even if she knows the performer is making some kind of performance mistake.

How would she know that? To achieve this, a spectator will have to be familiar with a good deal more than is required for basic understanding, even of fairly unusual theatrical performances. She will need to be familiar with at least one set of performance practices and, most likely, with some variety of performance practices. For she will have not only to find the same features salient as anyone else who has basically comprehended the performance, but also to recognize how those features are made salient by the performers. This is fairly specialized knowledge. By referencing that the spectator recognizes what performers intend, condition (4) captures this idea.

Finally, condition (4) allows us to explain what the spectator understands who grasps the fact that a performance is parodic in the way mentioned above. For, by condition (4), she understands why the performers have done what they are doing. To grasp that the performance is parodic – and to grasp what performers are doing even in non-parodic performances – requires the same kind of specialized knowledge that is needed in order to see when a performer is making a performance mistake. Again, it will be knowledge of performance practices that appear in other performances, usually performances she has attended. Accordingly I propose the following success conditions for *deeper performer understanding*.

> A spectator has deeper understanding of what the performers are doing and how they are doing it if she is familiar with performance traditions within or against which they are working, and able to describe what they are doing either to achieve the realization of those traditions or to challenge them.

No simple extension of the feature-salience model will deliver a model that can explain what goes on when a spectator grasps the inner structures of the object developed over the course of a performance. To have deeper understanding of this kind requires recognition of large-scale characteristics of a story, such as that it exhibits episodic plot structure. Grasping these kinds of characteristics is not necessary for basic theatrical understanding. But grasping them is precisely what distinguishes one kind of deeper understanding from basic comprehension.

A spectator who comprehends large-scale features thereby understands something about the performance that is beyond her own basic comprehension of the object developed in the performance. To express what is going on when this occurs we need the following (in which I use episodic plot structure as an illustrative example). Let us call the kind of comprehension modeled here *deeper object understanding*.

> "Spectator S has deeper object understanding, when presented with a story E, that E has an episodic structure" is true if and only if, for some spectator S, some performer J, and some story E,
>
> (1)   S has basic comprehension of the story E presented by J,
> (2)   S recognizes characteristics Z (under conditions of common knowledge among a population of suitably backgrounded spectators) as indicating facts that would lead one to conclude that E has an episodic structure,
> (3)   S encounters no characteristic Y of E that S would recognize, and that S has reason to think that any other suitably backgrounded spectator would recognize, as inconsistent with E having an episodic structure, and
> (4)   S concludes that E has an episodic structure.

The important structural changes in this adaptation of the feature-salience model are that, instead of considering what *features* of *performers or other performance elements* are salient to a population, we are considering what *characteristics* of *agents* (for example, characters), of their *actions*, and of *the resulting story itself* will be identifiable by the relevant population. The problems that prompt us to this way of explaining deeper object understanding are familiar: the plethora of characteristics of a story (or any developed object in a performance), not all of which would be salient to a population for large-scale characteristics; and the possibility of failed performer intentions.

We could have given a different statement of (2), namely,

(2′) S recognizes in the developing object E the conventional signposts of episodic structure.

But the original (2) reveals more explicitly how performer intentions drop out as irrelevant when it comes to spectators comprehending the internal structures of plays or whatever objects are developed over the course of performances. Performers sometimes fail to realize their intentions. It is not what performers intend that determines what spectators understand, however important what they intend may otherwise be. It is what performers actually do that counts. And (2), rather than (2′), which appeals to conventions and thereby to intentions,[5] gets us past the problem posed by failed performer intentions.

None of these conditions forces us to hold that a spectator cannot attain deeper understanding of the story while it is happening. But it is far more likely that suitably backgrounded spectators discover these kinds of characteristics in a performance upon reflection and, perhaps, after discussion with others following performances. It is common to hear spectators commenting after a performance that they do not yet know what it was they saw. This is best explained as putting off the demonstration of even basic theatrical understanding until the larger structures of what they saw have become clearer, upon reflection.

A spectator who has deeper understanding of the object she has seen develop over the course of a performance will have comprehended something about the fact expressed in condition (4) and its relation to the fact expressed in condition (1). That is, she will be assessing how it is that recognizing the structure of the story or sequence of images or what-have-you is connected to the fact that she has comprehended that story, sequence of images, and so on. And, once again, this entails that she has some experience with other performances. I therefore propose we adopt the following as a more precise statement of the success conditions for "deeper *object* understanding."

> A spectator has deeper understanding of the structures of the objects presented in a performance if she is able to demonstrate that she is familiar with the structures of other objects presented in other performances and to use that information to describe the structures internal to the performed object being developed in the performance at hand that make it the kind of object it is.

8.3 Some Puzzles about the Relation Between Understanding What is Performed and Understanding How it is Performed

We can imagine non-narrative performances, variations of *Something To Tell You* and *Burning Child*, for example, in which there is no underlying theme or principle that orders the images or image sequences. Spectators trying to sort out what they are seeing might well come to wonder if there actually is a single underlying sense of things in the object that had been presented.

Narrative performances lacking overall organizing principles are not hard to imagine either. Suppose there were a performance based on Ryunosuke Akutagawa's short story, "In a Grove."[6] A woman is raped and her husband murdered in a grove in a forest. Each of four witnesses tells what she or he saw. This comprises the story, namely, four distinct and disparate narratives. The result is that there is no single version of the story and spectators are left to decide what really happened or even if there is a 'true' version of the story at all. The result is a collage of competing, mutually inconsistent stories, ungoverned by any principle that would resolve the inconsistencies.

A spectator has a basic understanding of one of these performances if she is able either to tell the several stories and discuss the characters in the narrative performance with reasonable accuracy or to describe reasonably accurately the content of the juxtaposed images of a non-narrative performance. If that is all she is able to do, she has clearly missed something. That spectator may have a feeling that something is out of place. For there are competing elements in these cases that cannot be made to settle down, and that might be striking enough to be noticed.

If so, what the spectator notices has to do with the internal structure of the developing object performed. However, *ex hypothesi*, there is no coherent internal structure in such performances that she could discover. For these cases merely present juxtaposed and possibly inconsistent stories or image sequences without having a structure that resolves the tension between or among them.

> There can be performances of which no deeper *object* understanding is possible but that allow basic theatrical understanding (and may allow deeper *performer* understanding).

What kind of deeper understanding can be had of performances like *Pistols and Other Doors*, and others like it? For performances like these, it appears that there is little that could be comprehensible to a spectator at a basic level. At the basic level there is only nonsense, and so there is nothing coherently to comprehend. When there is comprehension, it involves grasping the ordering principles that are used to string the language and movement of the performance together. Since that ordering is part of the internal structure of the object that is developed in the performance, it now appears that there can be cases in which a spectator has deeper *object* understanding, but lacks *basic* theatrical understanding. And this sounds odd.

However, this analysis of what is available to spectators in such performances relies on an ambiguity in the idea of "comprehending" the details present in these performances. Comprehending those details may mean making sense of them, where that entails seeing how they are coherent. If the details themselves are incoherent, then of course there will be no comprehension of them in this sense. That, indeed, would be odd. On the other hand, if what demonstrates basic comprehension is a reasonably accurate *description* of what is seen and in what order, then the oddity vanishes. For one may accurately describe a sequence of images that is itself incoherent.

A further argument in favor of this position can be derived from the fact that such comprehension meets what David Novitz calls the "singularity constraint." According to Novitz, the singularity constraint "commits us to realism about cultural properties such that if a work really is vague at a certain time, then it cannot also have a precise and determinate meaning: if it is ambiguous at that time, it cannot also have a single meaning at that time."[7] It is therefore possible for a spectator coherently to describe the content she encounters in *Pistols and Other Doors*, even if that content is incoherent, as long as she does not also think her description makes the content coherent. Such a description counts as demonstrating basic theatrical understanding. So, we can conclude:

There are no cases in which deeper *object* understanding is possible but basic theatrical understanding impossible.

It would be convenient if deeper performer understanding and deeper object understanding were related to each other in some way that allowed the possession of one to lead inevitably to the possession of the other. But this is not so. Consider the position of a spectator who has basic comprehension of any performance that shares the distancing techniques characteristic of *Gabler at a Distance*.

A basically comprehending spectator will tell the tale and discuss the characters as they have appeared in this performance. Unless she knows something about more traditional *Hedda-to-Hedda* performances rooted in Ibsen's script, she will not realize how the internal structure of the object in a performance like *Gabler at a Distance* is getting developed. And, unless she has experience with performances employing these techniques, she will not realize how these performers are achieving the effects in this performance. This is just part of what it is to be only a basically comprehending spectator.

The performance practices employed in *Gabler at a Distance* have an effect on what internal structures the play has: they may change what would have been a climactic scene into something quite different. And the internal structures of *Gabler at a Distance* require the employment of certain kinds of performance practices, rather than others.

But, although those things are true, the background information informing deeper object understanding is quite different from that which informs deeper performer understanding. One has to do with familiarity with traditions of content of performances; the other has to do with traditions of practices, with how performers achieve those objects. So it is entirely possible that a spectator could notice, in a performance like *Gabler at a Distance*, the utter absence of a climactic scene, but not realize that this sense was induced by the performance practices, even had she noticed them. Conversely, a spectator could notice the performance practices but not realize what those techniques had produced with respect to differences between the developed object in this performance and those in other performances.

A highly experienced and reflective spectator may grasp some linkages between what she deeply comprehends. She may be led to deeper performer understanding by deeper object understanding, or vice versa. But there is nothing inevitable about that.

Although deeper *object* understanding and deeper *performer* understanding can find support for each other, so that grasp of one leads to grasp of the other and vice versa, a dialogic development of combined deeper understanding is not inevitable.

8.4 Deeper Theatrical Understanding and Full Appreciation of a Theatrical Performance

Is possession of deeper theatrical understanding sufficient for a full appreciation of a theatrical performance? The short answer is "no."

What the two modifications of the feature-salience model show us, and the more precise statements of success conditions therefore assert, is that both kinds of deeper understanding of a performance require comparison of characteristics in that performance to those in other performances, real or imagined. They both require familiarity with other performances. Without that sort of background a spectator is unable to see more deeply what is happening in any given performance.

On our working conception of full appreciation of a theatrical performance, full appreciation involves seeing that performance against a background that can inform a spectator what kind of achievement is manifest in the performance. And the kinds of special background knowledge needed for deeper theatrical understanding are surely the relevant kinds of information. It follows that:

> Possession of deeper theatrical understanding is *necessary* for a full appreciation of a theatrical performance.

But the working conception of full appreciation also holds that it will involve seeing how the performance practices contribute or detract from the performed object and how the performed object is achievable by certain kinds of performance practices rather than others. As we have just seen, however, possession of deeper *object* understanding does not lead inevitably to deeper *performer* understanding, and vice versa. So, it is possible for a spectator to have both forms of deeper understanding and still be missing something, in particular, any story about how the two things she understands in a given performance are connected or fail to connect. Lacking that, she is not positioned to tell a full story about what kind of achievement is manifest or missing in the performance. It follows that:

> Possession of deeper theatrical understanding is *not sufficient* for a full appreciation of a theatrical performance.

To see what more is required to put spectators in a position to tell a comprehensive story about the kind of achievement manifest or missing in a performance, I propose we describe in greater detail the kind of knowledge of performance practices that a spectator possessing deeper *performer* understanding has.

Notes

1   This idea is suggested by, among others, Denis Dutton. See his "Artistic Crimes: The Problem of Forgery in the Arts," *British Journal of Aesthetics* 19 (1979), 302–14.
2   For further discussion of these points, see Allen Carlson, "Appreciation and the Natural Environment," *Journal of Aesthetics and Art Criticism* 37/3 (1979), 267–8, and Paul Ziff, "Reasons in Art Criticism," in *Philosophy and Education: Modern Readings*, ed. I. Scheffler (Boston: Allyn and Bacon, 1958), pp. 219–36, especially §1, 220–33.
3   Roger Scruton, "Photography and Representation," in *The Aesthetic Understanding* (London and New York: Methuen, 1983), pp. 102–26, see especially §8, 116–19.
4   Also worth noting is that it is a matter of scholarly concern whether Ibsen wrote with Naturalistic performance techniques in mind. A nicely illustrative discussion of Ibsen's views on theater practices can be found in Inga-Stina Ewbank's Introduction to Geoffrey Hill's adaptation of Ibsen's *Brand*, 2nd edition (Minnesota: University of Minnesota Press, 1981), especially pp. xv–xx. So another set of questions might arise about the performance.
5   I argue this point in chapters 9 and 11.
6   Ryunosuke Akutagawa, *Rashomon and Other Stories*, trans. M. Kuwata, with an introduction by Howard Hibbett (New York and London: Liveright; reissue edition, 1999).
7   David Novitz, "Interpretation and Justification," in *The Philosophy of Interpretation*, ed. Joseph Margolis and Tom Rockmore (Oxford: Blackwell, 2000), p. 16. Novitz thinks of this as a constraint on *interpretation* and we are talking here about understanding. But since Novitz thinks of interpretation as filling in gaps in understanding (p. 5), and of interpretation as "extending understanding," I think it no distortion of his views to appeal to the constraint here.

9
WHAT PERFORMERS DO

In this chapter, I describe what is understood by spectators who have deeper understanding of performers. The goal is to discover whether deeply understanding spectators are positioned to have full appreciation of theatrical performances. My proposal for how to describe that material derives from the idea, set forth in chapter 4, that audiences attend to performers and that performers exploit that fact to arrange what audiences attend to so as to occasion audience responses to images, sequences of images, events, characters, situations, and actions in stories.

This idea entails that, for any specific performance, there is an answer to each of the following questions:

- What is the defining situation for this audience and these performers?
- What is the range of things this audience is to watch for in attending to these performers, given the defining situation?
- What are to be the relevant responses of this audience to what is watched for when it appears?
- What expressions and behavioral signs do these performers plan to display, given the defining situation? and
- How do these performers plan to manage their reactions to being attended to?

These questions offer guidelines for developing an adequate description of what is going on in any case of theatrical enactment whatever.

9.1 What Performers Do and What Audiences Can Know

In asking what it is that performers do to bring about basic (or deeper) understanding of theatrical performances, it will be useful to avoid some ways of prematurely theorizing about the question.

First, we should avoid adverting too quickly to generalized theories about acting. In seeking to ground our analysis of what performers do in descriptions of actual practices of theater, we run the risk of prematurely accepting as bedrock sets of practices that are in some fashion implicated in normative assumptions about what theater could or should be doing.[1] Shannon Jackson, like a number of others writing on this subject, treats the quest for "presence" in many performance practices of twentieth-century theater as implicated in a questionable "metaphysics."[2] The objection, at base, is that a practice aiming at making performers "present" gives a false picture of human life that underwrites and legitimizes oppressive practices in a variety of ways. And Jackson cites a number of performances that strove for reduction to real presence and, in the doing, "reified a number of gendered, racist, class conventions in order to stage absolute reduction."[3]

So we should avoid adopting as given, standard, or 'normal' any single group of the practices we discussed in the first chapter, all of which were invented or adopted in the name of theater as art but actually put forward in the pursuit of a specific vision "about the nature and purpose of theatre and what the responsibility of the actor was within the process of making it."[4]

However, attention to acting theories does give us something positive. For the techniques acting theories have espoused have in fact enabled performers to achieve success, understood as performances that have met with audience acceptance.[5] If we were to describe what performers do in such a way that it could not be achieved by most methods of acting, then clearly our description would not be correct. So, a description of what performers do should meet the following constraint.

A description of what performers do is adequate only if the description can be satisfied employing methods successfully used by theatrical performers.

Second, we should avoid adverting too readily to the terms of analysis put forward in discussions of performance and "performativity" that have come to prominence in theater and performance theory since the mid-

1980s. These discussions avoid the pitfall of unfounded generalization from particular, and possibly questionable, sets of practices. But they avoid such generalization at the price of reflecting on the concept of "performance" in abstraction from *any* actual practices. By this reasoning, a performance practice could only be questionable if it were entangled in questionable ideologies. But, if we think that, we will overlook the fact that sometimes a practice is questionable because some performers adhere to the practice out of cowardice, ignorance, or simple sloth.

There is something seductive about considering performance in the abstract. As Herbert Blau suggests, there seems to be a tension between the impulse to be real – to be non-theatrical in the theater – and the fact that, just because it is done on stage in front of an audience, everything the performer does in a theater is theatrical.[6] Theorists interested in this tension and the question of its relation to "modernism" in theater have found the notion of "performativity" useful. This term – initially borrowed from J. L. Austin to describe utterances by means of which something is done in addition to something being said[7] – has been used by literary and theater theorists since the 1980s to negotiate a series of disputes about modernism. For a variety of reasons, themselves still in dispute, the terms "performance" and "performativity" have sometimes been aligned with literalness and sometimes with theatricality. When aligned with literalness, the terms are taken to entail a commitment to the questionable claim that performers' intentions can be fully transparent to spectators.[8] When aligned with theatricality, the terms are taken to signal an unhealthy and slavish implication in being watched.[9]

Not only are these terms variously and inconsistently understood, sometimes they – and their original uses by Austin – are hopelessly misunderstood. Andrew Parker and Eve Kosofsky Sedgwick, for example, exhibit one glaring misunderstanding. They cite Austin's comment, that the possibility that performative utterances might not come off shows that they are liable to "an ill to which *all* acts are heir"[10] (Austin's emphasis), and then take that comment to mean that such liabilities are "intrinsic to and thus constitutive of the structure *of performance*" (my emphases).[11] Here Parker and Sedgwick make a claim about what is definitive of performance where Austin had made a broad and true empirical claim about the vicissitudes of any action, including performative utterances.

The main issue with this kind of theorizing, however, has to do with the fact that most of it never gets expressed in performance practices, let alone in a way that gets through to a spectator. Some of it does get through; and when it does, it is of serious interest to theater theory because it can become of serious interest to spectators, especially to deeply comprehending spectators. Suppose, for example, under the influence of theoretical worries about doing *versus* performance, a company undertakes to "reconceive of the breathing we take for granted as a bodily process to be explored or a spiritual discipline to be acquired,"[12] or thinks of what it is doing as "dying in front of your eyes"[13] or adopts a movement practice grounded in "Tai Chi Ch'uan rather than Yoga or Aikido or any other form of martial arts."[14] Not all of these may have an influence on that company's performances. And some seem more likely to show up in concrete performance practices available to an audience than others do. But we cannot rule out that some aspects of that company's performances will reflect one of these decisions; and if that did happen, the process by which the company came to those aspects of their performances would be critically relevant to a deeply comprehending spectator.

Unfortunately, however, most of the theorizing about performance and performativity has no such consequences.[15]

A more promising way to take up the legacy of Austin's concerns with performativity is represented by David Saltz.[16] In thinking about interpreting texts, Saltz makes the helpful suggestion that we think of texts as "scores for action." And he argues that, if we have an adequate idea of action, we can see how a performance and critical practice that treats texts in this way can be productive.[17] "Action," Saltz reminds us, is a "multidimensional concept" that, when it comes to theatrical action, has two crucial aspects: how we identify actions and how we are to describe their force. As both Austin and Saltz argue, each of these requires seeing what was done under the aspect of or set within a particular context.[18] Utilizing Austin's finely textured analysis of the concept of action, Saltz presents and analyzes a telling example of a textual poetics that is satisfactory for the literary analysis of a text but utterly useless in providing insight into the actions a performer can do.[19] And, in contrast, he is able to offer a useful story of how to employ the Austinian framework to "contextualize . . . texts in the scene of their performance."[20]

Saltz has employed these notions to good effect in a different direction as well, in particular in an antidote to John Searle's claim[21] (and Austin's too, by the way) that actors can do nothing other than "imitate" actions, that they cannot perform "real" actions, at least when performing their roles.[22] It is instructive to see how Saltz employs the details of the Austinian-Searlean analysis of action, and performative action in particular, to demonstrate that Searle's claim about performers is false. Were we thinking of performances as performances *of* texts, we would want to pursue this line of thinking more fully. But we are not.

In sum, most theories of "performance" and "performativity" are not constrained by what audiences can know, and those that are have so far focused only on the narrative, text-based tradition, and so are not sufficiently general.

The generality of the feature-salience model, exemplified in the way it sheds light on issues about materiality of and in performance, reveals that the issues discussed in most of the performance literature are particular to one theatrical tradition and do not concern the practices of theatrical performance *per se*. Moreover, although the feature-salience model for basic theatrical understanding concerns how *spectators* grasp performances, it does so by reference to any spectators attending to features *that performers present to them*. This suggests that we describe what it is that performers do in a way that is responsive to our descriptions of what spectators do. Accordingly, I propose a second constraint on the description of what performers do.

A description of what performers do is adequate only if it shows how ordered presentations of features are put in place by performers so as to be salient for characteristics of the object they develop over the course of a performance.

9.2 The Features of Performers and Choices That Performers Make

To develop an adequate description of what performers do, consider three motivating cases, each of which is a way of staging the burning of Lovborg's manuscript. This is the climactic event in most performances employing a reasonably traditional use of Ibsen's script for *Hedda Gabler*, and it is often referred to as the "child-killing scene." Here is a description of the scene from a standard acting edition of the script:

[Lovborg goes out by the hall door. Hedda listens for a moment at the door. Then she goes up to the writing-table, takes out the packet of manuscript, peeps under the cover, draws a few sheets half out, and looks at them. Next she goes over and seats herself in the arm-chair beside the stove, with the packet in her lap. Presently she opens the stove door, and then the packet.]

HEDDA. [Throws one of the quires into the fire and whispers to herself.] Now I am burning your child, Thea! – Burning it, curly-locks! [Throwing one or two more quires into the stove.] Your child and Eilert Lovborg's. [Throws the rest in.] I am burning – I am burning your child.

Let the first motivating case be a way of staging this scene in any performance of the *Hedda-to-Hedda* kind, and let us stipulate only that if the audience displays any overt reaction to the action, the performers have schooled themselves not to respond. Let the second motivating case be a way of staging consistent with *Gabler at a Distance*, stipulating that if the audience displays any overt reaction to the action, the performers will look directly into the audience, shrug as if to indicate they had no choice, and then continue the action of the scene. Finally, let the third motivating case be a way of staging the scene in any performance of the *Spontaneous Beauty* kind, stipulating that, if the audience displays any overt reaction to the action, the performers have trained themselves to stop for precisely three seconds and stare fixedly into the middle distance, and then go on.

These cases illustrate an important but simple and obvious set of things that performers do in the normal circumstances of preparing and performing what they prepare: they make choices about what *to utter* and what *to do*. Performers also choose *how* to utter what is uttered and *how* to do whatever it is they do. And, performers determine what to do and how to do it *for every moment* of the performance. The deliverances of these decisions are sequences of features determined by, and usually of, individual performers (even if they are rarely made in isolation).

But there is another aspect of basic-level decisions that requires concerted effort. Any company needs to decide where they wish to direct attention at each moment and how they will do that. Some of these decisions involve thinking about such things as how performers are situated in relation to each other and to the audience in the performance space. Determining how attention gets directed involves deciding the manner and timing of each performer's utterances in relation to the content, manner, and timing of the utterances of other performers. Similarly, to regulate the attention of audiences, companies think about how what each performer is doing relates to what the other performers are doing. The deliverances of these decisions frequently will be features of performers in relation to each other.

We can sum up these observations by suggesting a basic description of what performers do.[23] I will refer to this as "the simple suggestion."

The *features of performers* to which spectators attend are the result of a describable set of choices that a company of performers makes. The choices concern three general matters: (1) who utters what (including words, gestures, and so on) and how each utterance sounds or appears; (2) what each performer is doing at each moment in the performance and how she is doing it; and (3) where attention is to be directed at each moment and how that is to be achieved.

The simple suggestion meets the two standards of adequacy we have adopted. It describes the results of choices that go into preparing and presenting theatrical performances as collections of features that are intended to be salient for the characteristics or elements of the object they develop over the course of a performance. It describes what performers do with sufficient generality that it could be achieved by a variety of methods. Moreover, it responds to the intuitive idea that for any performance there is an answer to the questions, "What expressions and behavioral signs do these performers plan to display (given the specific defining situation)?" and "How do these performers plan to manage their reactions to being attended to?"

But the simple suggestion does not yet describe what performers do in a way that shows us how performers *shape the context* within which spectators grasp the developing objects of performance by attending to those collections of features. This is because each of the motivating cases for the simple suggestion omitted something important about the circumstances of the ways the incident is staged. What was missing in each was reference to a "specific defining situation" that is linked to and explains what is expected of audiences and what is chosen for presentation by performers. And this suggests a third constraint, applicable to a complete description of what performers do.

> A complete description of what performers do is adequate only if it is responsive to the fact that performers *shape the context* within which spectators grasp the developing objects of performance.

The simple suggestion is incomplete in another, albeit related, direction. The choices described in the motivating cases are not made as the expressions of sheer personal or collective whim. Therefore we need a fourth constraint on a complete description of what performers do.

> A complete description of what performers do is adequate only if the choices performers make are cast as the result of *deliberative practices* that, therefore, relate the choices to some ends they are thought to serve.

Getting a fuller description of what performers do that satisfies these constraints will respond to the intuitive idea that, for any performance, it should be possible to answer the questions, "What is the specific defining situation for this audience and these performers?," "What is the range of things this audience is to watch for in attending to these performers, given the specific defining situation?," and "What are to be the relevant responses of this audience to what is watched for when it appears?"

9.3 Theatrical Conventions as Sequences of Features having Specific "Weight"

Consider what would happen in any one of the motivating cases were a performer to fail to exit at the moment planned. If the company had planned the exit as comedic, and if the moment of confusion caused by the performer's missed exit cue were to get a laugh, then the unanticipated change in the performance would succeed in the company getting what it wanted. But it would not change the overall direction or movement of the performance nor any other effects the company anticipates from the choices they have made. The other performers must and would carry on, fully anticipating no further sudden changes in utterances or actions from their colleagues.

What this brings out, that is missing from the abstracted way the three cases were described, is that in any real performance it is *sequences of features* resulting from a *series of choices* that help give shape to the context in which spectators track the developing object of a performance. To take account of this fact, I suggest we build this on the simple suggestion: (4) when answering the performers' questions, companies seek to arrive at weakly coherent collections of means for displaying features in ordered sequences that constitute one way, among other possible and differently weighted ways, they could create the characteristics of the developed object in the performance. And I further suggest we define *theatrical conventions* as just such collections of features:

> Theatrical conventions are weakly coherent sequences of features selected for display that are differently weighted from conceivable alternatives and contingently salient for characteristics of the object developed in a performance.

Features collected in the ways we have described are coherently related to each other. But we need not think there is strong coherence within any grouping of features in these cases. There is nothing here that commits us to thinking, for example, that some of the detailed features presented to an audience in a performance of the *Hedda-to-Hedda* kind could never appear together with the choice, characteristic of a performance of the *Spontaneous Beauty* kind, of what to do in response to overt audience reaction. We can imagine a different staging of the destruction of Lovborg's manuscript that would present just that particular new combination of features.

The kind of coherence that exists here is a more after-the-fact affair. This should surprise no one familiar with rehearsal practices. A good deal of experimentation takes place in the rehearsal process: various moves and vocalizations are tried out, many are discarded, and those chosen are the ones that the company thinks will have the desired effects. It is by thinking of *effects* of the collection of features chosen for display that sequences of features are settled upon.

Another aspect of sequences of conventions is that there is something accomplished with them that can be accomplished by more than one of them. The motivating cases are, in one important sense, three ways of doing the same thing, namely, staging the destruction of Lovborg's manuscript. The fact there is another way of doing the same thing is connected to the fact that conventions are *weakly coherent*. The weakness of coherence within a sequence of features in each of these cases is a consequence of the fact that the results are determined externally, by reference to what are thought to be their actual effects, rather than by anything inherent in the features themselves. There is nothing inherent in any answer to any of the performers' questions that determines that it must have just one kind of effect on an audience. That is why there can be more than one way to stage the burning of Lovborg's manuscript; and it is why the relation between any given sequence of features that audiences find salient for the characteristics of a given developing object of a performance and that developing object itself is a *contingent relation*.

A third aspect of the conventions illustrated in the three motivating cases is that, even if each is a different way of staging the destruction of Lovborg's manuscript, there is something important about the differences among them. Were there not, no one would bother trying out different ways to stage the burning of Lovborg's manuscript. Each of them makes possible or at least more likely a different range of reactions by an audience. Each emphasizes something different about that event and, so, each is not *merely* another way of doing the same thing. Because of the differences in the reactions they induce, these alternative sequences of features are *differently "weighted."* That is, the effects they each have, understood as the range of reactions each makes possible, give point to performers' deliberations when considering alternatives.

9.4 What is Involved in Reference to Theatrical Styles

The definition of theatrical conventions has taken us some distance towards meeting the third and fourth constraints on an adequate complete description of what performers do. But the simple suggestion supplemented with the definition of conventions still underdetermines the shaping of performances. To complete the account, I propose we build one more element onto the simple suggestion: (5) when making choices companies seek to arrive at similar conventions throughout an entire performance, governed and connected by some conception or aims for the performance as a whole. Such conceptions or aims can be thought of as plans for other entire performances. And I suggest we define *theatrical styles* as just such collections of conventions.

> Theatrical styles are sets of similar conventions that are thought to serve a conception or set of aims that could govern one or more entire performances.

Performances of the *Gabler at a Distance* kind employ a variety of practices aimed to achieve distance between spectators and the events and emotions portrayed in the performance. An interesting fact about these practices is that they could do equally well to produce a reflective or a purely comedic version of the burning of Lovborg's manuscript. Brecht employed techniques consistent with *Gabler at a Distance* to achieve distanced political reflection. But the techniques Brecht used were also among those employed by *Monty Python's Flying Circus* to achieve a very different kind of distance. What makes the difference, in part, involves the precise ways in which this staging of the destruction of Lovborg's manuscript is *connected to the staged events coming before and after.*

Companies of performers deliberate about how the staging of each moment connects up with the staging of other moments, both those nearby and those remoter in time. They think about how the performance's beginning moments are related to its closing moments. They think about tempo, pacing, and rhythm. In the preparation of plays, scenes are often broken up into a series of "beats," that are the smallest units of "something happening." Beats have known structures to which audiences respond with understanding and which performers can take as units of work in preparing a scene. All of these provide ways of expressing the terms of the choices we have set forth in the simple suggestion. But they also provide ways to think about how groups of choices connect with each other. To choose among ways groups of choices connect with each other requires appeal to an aim, a goal, or some perhaps complex set of aims or goals.

One aspect of styles that these considerations bring out is that the governing aims in terms of which each sequence of features is selected are usually aims that *govern an entire performance*. When that is so, a performance is more or less unified in aims and conventions. Such a performance could inspire other performers to use similar conventions and aims in such a unified way for performances utilizing different scripts.

What I mean by "aims" can be brought out by the following example. At the risk of some oversimplification, it is plausible to say that Naturalism, as a group of styles of theatrical representation, was developed in the late nineteenth century to focus attention on the inner lives of the characters in plays, because that was thought to be the arena of human life about which the most significant lessons could be learned in theater.[24] In characterizing "Naturalism" in this way, I mean to call attention to what Raymond Williams calls "technical naturalism" and "naturalism as a dramatic form." "Technical naturalism" involves the representation of a 'natural'-looking physical environment, created by such devices as the picture-frame version of the proscenium, abolition of the apron, the stage as a room, and so on. "Naturalism as a dramatic form" uses this represented environment treated "as a symptom or cause . . . part of the action itself."[25] In "high naturalism," as Williams calls it, "the environment has soaked into [the characters'] lives" in such a way that "the actions of high naturalism are often struggles against this environment, of attempted extrication from it, and more often than not these fail." This is because the high naturalist's world is one "which has entwined itself in the deepest layers of the personality."[26] I think Williams is right that "the great majority of plays now produced, in all media, are technically naturalist, and . . . many [technically] 'non-naturalist' plays are evidently based on a naturalist philosophy . . . [about] character and environment."[27] I would only add to Williams's description of "technical naturalism" an emphasis on acting techniques as well as on the use of some specific conventions of theatrical narrative, both of which can and have been developed and refined for the purpose of achieving Naturalistic aims.

The importance of reference to aims can be stated as a corollary to our definition of theatrical style.

The conceptions or aims govern a style because they act as reasons companies have for convention selection and convention manipulation.

Understood this way, styles can be characterized as pairs of aims and sets of conventions, where the conventions function as the means believed appropriate to achieving the aims. As we have already seen, the link between aims and convention sets is weak. For example, the roughly diegetic style characteristic of Brechtian performance practices might be found serving very different aims in eighteenth-century acting practices in France. Williams offers another important example when he observes that "many 'non-naturalist' plays are evidently based on a naturalist philosophy."[28] This suggests another corollary to the definition of theatrical style:

> The convention sets characteristic of a style can come apart from the aims of the style (and from the style itself when understood as a historical phenomenon); and the same conventions can be governed by other aims and form other, phenomenally similar, styles.

The importance of this corollary lies in the fact that it allows us to characterize precisely one important way theatrical styles can be mixed. Theatrical styles can be mixed in many ways. But the subsumption of some conventions under even very different aims is of singular importance. This is because many popular techniques in contemporary theater that are said to "cross cultures" can be understood in this way – as they use the convention components of styles from alien cultures for domestic aims. And it is an empirical question of some importance whether this way of mixing convention sets from one culture to serve aims characteristic of another actually allows theatrical performances to bridge cultural divisions.[29]

9.5 More about Styles, as Produced and as Grasped

In a review of *Journey to the West*, adapted and directed by Mary Zimmerman, James Harbeck writes that the performance "does not play on the difference between Chinese and American theatrical styles but rather mixes and matches – the lines are spoken with American inflection, but much of the physical gesture (and the occasional acrobatics) owe more to movement training in the Chinese style."[30] Writing about the rise of performance studies departments and the problems of discussing performance practices that do not fall neatly into the study of literature or of drama, Roselyn Costantino writes that

> many Latin American performance practices are homegrown, deeply rooted in cultural traditions and theatrical styles not recognized by elite culture but

which nevertheless have existed for centuries as modes of expression for the peoples of the Americas. These include revue theatre, cabaret, street theatre, body art, religious rituals, popular celebrations . . .[31]

Similar comments appear in many articles regarding theater performance. The idea of a style in the academic literature about theatrical performance is very broad. It includes references to genre, nationally located traditions, performance kinds, and movements. Movements referred to in this litera-ture include "Naturalism," "Realism," "Expressionism" (from recent European culture), and "Arogoto or 'rough business'," "Jojuri," "the musical style known as Bungobushi," "Maruhonkabuki" (from a recently proposed catalog of styles of Japanese Kabuki theater).[32] Some styles are identified as styles of particular directors, performance groups, or even individual performers. Many distinctions among styles thought of as movements are made primarily by identification of characteristic conven-tions, although some are made by identification of differences in aims.

There is little systematic about the uses of these terms, and especially about the term "style" itself, in this literature. And there is nothing wrong with this. The lack of terminological discussion or precision does not interfere with communicative success among theater practitioners. But a philosophically adequate and complete definition of style requires greater precision. And to see if the definition offered here holds up, we need to see how it works to reconcile the demands placed upon the concept of style by art historians, interested in classifying works of art, and art critics, interested in explaining the work of particular artists.

Style as signature, and the classification project

The view of style as "signature" was initiated by Nelson Goodman.[33] Goodman argues that styles consist of specific features and that a feature of a work of art is stylistic "only when it associates a work with one rather than another artist, period, region, school, etc."[34] Goodman does not think every feature that enables us to identify provenance is stylistic. For not every such feature – for example, the age of the canvas on which it was painted – has to do with what the work does as a work of art. So his definition of style is this: "the style [of a work] consists of those features of the symbolic functioning of a work that are characteristic of author, period, place, or school." For this reason, Goodman concludes, style does *not* "depend upon an artist's conscious choice among alternatives."[35]

This view of style is called "style as signature" because, on Goodman's view, the primary function of style is that it functions as a kind of signature telling us the provenance of works. This definition of style clearly goes to the needs of art historians. And recognition of style, conceived in this way, falls clearly within the specialized knowledge base required for deeper performer understanding.

Individual style, and the explanation project

The leading view alternative to Goodman's originates with Richard Wollheim.[36] Wollheim argues that the analysis of style as signature results in the claim that the style of a work is exhaustively described by simply listing the stylistic features present in a work. Wollheim calls this "the description thesis."[37] And he notes that its chief consequence is the claim that anyone may be said to have a style. But clearly there is a difference between painting in a style and having a "style of one's own."

Wollheim argues that a function of style ascription is to explain the work of an artist. But if the description thesis were true, style ascription could not explain anything. For, attributing a style to a painter would not state a fact about the artist's work so much as a fact about the "existing condition of progressive art history." The attribution of styles consistent with the description thesis tells us nothing about the formation of that particular artist's style, only what style existing in a culture at a period some artist has learned. Instead, a style attribution should tell us something about the artist's work, rather than about his period, because "style is something formed, not learned."[38] In support of this view, Andrew Harrison quips "It is a dull skill to learn the trick of writing merely in the manner of [other] authors."[39] In contrast to the analysis of style as signature, Harrison suggests a concept of style as "direction of salience,"[40] where the conviction inspired by a work is a function of the artist's control of means in the service of her vision. And Jenefer Robinson[41] makes Harrison's idea of "control of means" clear by pointing out that a particular feature may be crucial to one painter's style but insignificant, although present, in another painter's work. This is a decisive consideration against the description thesis.

The concept of "individual style" comes to this set of claims. First, a style ascription that aims at explaining the work of an artist must do more than list the stylistic attributes of that artist's work. Second, to explain the work of an artist, we must think of the style as something formed, not merely learned. Third, a style ascription can explain the work of the artist if attention to the relevant attributes shows us the control the artist exercised over those attributes. And, fourth, this latter is why a particular attribute may be more important – either more controlling or more the evidence of control – in the work of one artist than in the work of another. This conception of style goes to the needs of art critics.

Theatrical styles

In stressing the importance of the connection of theater artists' aims to larger features of the artist's intellectual and political climate, our definition of theatrical style seems to move us in the direction of thinking of style as signature. But this is only apparent. Although the proposed definition of theatrical style holds that the convention sets that are the phenomenal features of a style are governed by specific aims that connect to issues of larger social scope, the mode of that governance is that these aims and conceptions *guide performers* in convention selection and convention manipulation. So the proposed definition runs counter to Goodman's conclusion that style does *not* "depend upon an artist's conscious choice among alternatives."[42]

Our definition also leads to a different emphasis in the explanation of what is characteristic of style attribution. Goodman contends that the importance of style attribution is primarily classificatory and he defines the style of a work as "those features of the symbolic functioning of a work that are characteristic of author, period, place, or school."[43] But the grasp of a style by a spectator of theatrical performance necessarily involves understanding the aims characteristic of a style and how they govern performers' choices of convention sets. Classificatory functions of theatrical style attribution are of secondary importance and follow from historical facts about the emergence of certain potential aims for theater on the cultural horizon. Since the aims of a style are what generate the need for the conventions that in retrospect come to be seen as characteristic of company, director, movement, and so on, the proposed definition of theatrical style commits us to analyzing the artist's role in developing or adopting a style. The conception of style as "individual," where that means it is something that can be "one's own," forces us to take artists' intentions seriously in thinking about their styles.[44]

> Reference to theatrical styles always includes reference to the reasons performers have for adopting particular sets of conventions and always makes reference to how those aims govern entire performances.

9.6 Grasp of Theatrical Style and Deeper Theatrical Understanding

In attaining *basic* theatrical understanding, ascription of intentions to performers is otiose. For what is decisive to basic comprehension is what *is* salient for characteristics of the elements of developing objects of a performance, not what performers intend to be salient. Nor does a spectator seeking *deeper* performer understanding of the performance need to guess the intentions of the performers. For what is decisive to deeper performer understanding is the spectator's knowledge of the actual conventions the performers have put into play. A suitably backgrounded spectator can know what conventions are in play even when the performers themselves do not or when the performers do not recognize the conventions they employ *as* conventions.

It may also seem that spectators need not make guesses as to performer intentions when they attribute stylistic commitments to them. For, we may think guessing is simply unnecessary for those familiar with the style of the performance. But another look at the notion of style we have been considering suggests this is not quite right. Apprehension of an individual style in a performance is not merely a matter of listing convention sets and linking them up with some statement of the apparent aims governing the choices and manipulations of the convention sets. A spectator establishes the link between aims and convention sets in a performance by seeing how the conventions are connected over time, through time, from beginning to end of an entire performance. So, to follow a performance in the mode of tracking its style is to follow how the performers' aims shape the context for and the particularity of each deployment of each and every theatrical technique. It is, as Wollheim suggests, to "retrieve the thought process" that yields just *that* performance.[45] These considerations drive us to the following conclusion.

> Since deeper theatrical understanding is not sufficient for full appreciation of a performance, and since full appreciation requires grasp of the individual style in a performance, and since grasp of individual style in a performance requires forming hypotheses about performer intentions, some form of interpretation, exceeding deeper performer understanding of the performance, is required.

The possession of deeper understanding of a theatrical performance requires the kind of specialized knowledge that would enable a spectator to assess achievement were she to go on to offer the relevant kinds of hypotheses. Moreover, by possessing deeper understanding of a performance, she has everything she needs to guide her thinking about what hypotheses are relevant. Further, her reflections on the performance guide her to look for the details that would enable her to confirm or disconfirm those hypotheses. A spectator who has deeper understanding of a performance is, therefore, poised to gain full appreciation of that performance. But to do so, she will have to engage in the interpretive process.

Notes

1   Shannon Jackson, "Practice and Performance: Modernist Paradoxes and Literalist Legacies," chapter 4 of *Professing Performance: Theatre in the Academy from Philology to Performativity* (Cambridge: Cambridge University Press, 2004), pp. 109–233, especially 112.
2   Ibid., pp. 115–20.
3   Ibid., p. 131. These are normative, not metaphysical, concerns. Were there no normative consequence, there would be no issue at all. It is only when metaphysics has consequences that anyone cares.
4   Alison Hodge, "Introduction," in *Twentieth Century Actor Training*, ed. Alison Hodge (London and New York: Routledge, 2000), p. 2.
5   Given the reservations we may rightly have about the normative consequences of certain techniques, even this minimal standard of success is questionable. But at this stage of the investigation, it is wise to keep the standards low.
6   Herbert Blau, "Universals of Performance: or Amortizing Play," in *By Means of Performance*, ed. Richard Schechner and Willa Appel (Cambridge: Cambridge University Press, 1990), pp. 250–72, especially 253.
7   J. L. Austin, *How to Do Things with Words* (Cambridge, MA: Harvard University Press, 1962), pp. 18–19.
8   Jackson, "Practice and performance," pp. 120–32.
9   Michael Fried, *Absorption and Theatricality: Painting and Beholder in the Age of Diderot* (Berkeley: University of California Press, 1980).
10   Austin, *How to Do Things with Words*, p. 18.
11   Andrew Parker and Eve Kosofsky Sedgwick, "Introduction: Performativity and Performance," in *Performativity and Performance*, ed. Andrew Parker and Eve Kosofsky Sedgewick (London and New York: Routledge, 1995), p. 3.
12   Blau, "Universals of performance," pp. 251–2.
13   Ibid., p. 267.
14   Ibid., p. 263.
15   Jackson, "Practice and performance," pp. 109–15, gives a telling example of the "conversational stall" that occurs between theater's most innovative practitioners and its typical theorists because of just this kind of theoretical orientation.
16   David Z. Saltz, "Texts in Action/Action in Texts: A Case Study in Critical Method," *Journal of Dramatic Theory and Criticism* 6/1 (1991), 29–44.
17   Ibid., pp. 33–4.

18   Ibid., p. 36.

19   Ibid., p. 38.

20   Ibid., pp. 39–44.

21   John Searle, "The Logical Status of Fictional Discourse," in *Expression and Meaning* (Cambridge: Cambridge University Press, 1979), pp. 58–75.

22   David Z. Saltz, "How to Do Things on Stage," *Journal of Aesthetics and Art Criticism* 49/1 (1991), 31–45.

23   The first two of these I heard from Herbert Blau, who suggested them as the core performer questions in a National Endowment for Humanities Summer Seminar he conducted on theater and performance at New York University in the summer of 1981. If these are wrong in any detail, it is my error. The third is suggested by Joseph Chaikin in *The Presence of the Actor* (New York: Atheneum, 1980), p. 59, where he writes, "Acting always has to do with attention, and with where the attention is."

24   See, for example, the account given of the development of Naturalism and Realism in O. G. Brockett, *History of the Theatre*, 4th edition (Boston and London: Allyn and Bacon, 1982), pp. 541–60.

25   Raymond Williams, "Social Environment and Theatrical Environment: The Case of English Naturalism," in *English Drama: Forms and Development*, ed. Marie Axton and Raymond Williams (Cambridge: Cambridge University Press, 1977), pp. 203–23.

26   Ibid., p. 217.

27   Ibid., p. 222.

28   Ibid.

29   See Rustom Bharucha, *The Politics of Cultural Practice: Thinking Through Theatre in an Age of Globalization* (Middletown, CT: Wesleyan University Press, 2000).

30   James Harbeck, "Performance Review: *Journey to the West*," *Theatre Journal* 49/3 (1997), 354–6.

31   Roselyn Costantino, "Latin American Performance Studies: Random Acts or Critical Moves?," *Theatre Journal* 56/3 (2004), 459–61.

32   Takechi Tetsuji, "Artistic Direction in Takechi Kabuki," trans. William Lee, *Asian Theatre Journal* 20/1 (2003), 12–24.

33   N. Goodman, "The Status of Style," in *Ways of Worldmaking* (Indianapolis: Hackett, 1978), pp. 23–40.

34   Ibid., p. 34.

35   Ibid., p. 23.

36   Richard Wollheim, "Pictorial Style: Two Views," in *The Concept of Style*, ed. Beryl Lang (Ithaca, NY: Cornell University Press, 1987), pp. 183–202.

37   Ibid., p. 194.

38   Ibid., pp. 194, 198.

39   A. Harrison, "Style," in *A Companion to Aesthetics*, ed. D. Cooper (Oxford: Blackwell, 1992), p. 406.

40   Ibid., p. 405. Here Harrison relies upon the notion of "thematization" as that is developed in Richard Wollheim, *Painting as an Art* (London: Thames & Hudson, 1987), pp. 19–36.

41   Jenefer Robinson, "Style and Significance in Art History," *Journal of Aesthetics and Art Criticism* 40/1 (Fall, 1981), 5–14.

42   Goodman, "Status of Style," p. 23.

43   Ibid., p. 35.

44   This is brought out clearly in Noël Carroll's comments on Arthur Danto's worries about narratives of style and Danto's objection to Wollheim's view, in Noël Carroll, "Danto, Style, and Intention," *Journal of Aesthetics and Art Criticism* 53/3 (Summer, 1995), 251–7. It also provides a way to respond to Harrison, even though he defends the conception of individual style. One way of staging the destruction of Lovborg's manuscript is, as we have seen, perfectly consistent with Brechtian aims and with the aims of *Monty Python's Flying Circus*. The example demonstrated the shaping role that aims have in determining exactly how various conventional devices are deployed. This aspect of the conception of theatrical styles opens up the possibility that even self-conscious adoption of a theatrical style originated by others does not preclude making work that is artistically convincing. Whatever may be the case in other art forms, theatrical work can be convincing because performers can own the aims and conventions they have adopted. They can own them because they can think through the aims governing their choices and work through how those aims shape the conventional devices deployed. So it need not be a "dull skill to learn the trick" of performing in the manner of another, at least if performing in the manner of another means adopting her theatrical style.

45   Richard Wollheim, "Criticism as Retrieval," in *Art and Its Objects*, 2nd edition (Cambridge: Cambridge University Press, 1980), pp. 185–204.

10
INTERPRETIVE GRASP
OF THEATRICAL
PERFORMANCES

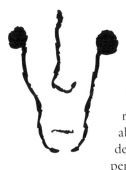

Our working conception of full appreciation of a theatrical performance involves two abilities. The first is the ability to see the performance against a background that can inform the spectator regarding the achievement that is or is not manifest in the performance. The second is the ability, by reference to details in performances, to converse about how the performance practices contribute to or detract from the performed object and whether the performed object is achievable by certain kinds of performance practices rather than others. A spectator in possession of deeper performer understanding is fully adequate to the first of these tasks. Determining how spectators succeed at the second task is what has brought us to examine the nature of gaining an interpretive grasp of a theatrical performance.

There are many reasons people find value in works of art. And many values can be served by interpretations of works of art. The discussion I undertake is narrower in scope, however, because the kinds of interpretations I wish to examine are those that lead to showing how theatrical performances can be appreciated for the achievements they represent, for "the ways in which [performers] solve problems, overcome obstacles, make do with available materials."[1]

Interpretation is frequently said to be a, or the, means by which we achieve understanding. This is a view common among those whose philosophical concerns about art interpretations are focused by reflection on more general kinds of interpretations. David Novitz puts the point this way:

[I]n one basic – perhaps the primary – sense of this word, "interpretation" mentions an activity that we wittingly perform in order to fill gaps in our understanding. In this sense, interpretation is called for only when we know that we have run out of established knowledge and belief in terms of which to dispel our confusion or ignorance. Put differently, interpretation (in the primary sense) always requires knowledge of one's own lack of comprehension . . . And the process of coming to understand . . . invariably involves the imaginative formulation of hypotheses that are expressly designed to dispel one's own incomprehension.[2]

Novitz's statement stresses two elements in this commonly held view: interpretation is aimed primarily at understanding; and interpretation is a process and interpretations are the results of those processes. Further, when we interpret correctly we come to understand something; and our interpretations just express what those understandings come to. In examining the interpretive grasp of a theatrical performance, I will argue that the second of these elements – the idea of interpretation as process of figuring things out – is crucial to explaining what goes on in interpreting a theatrical performance.

To assist in that examination, imagine two spectators whom we will call Petia and Thiago, who have just seen the same two performances – one 'straight,' the other parodic – and who have at least a basic understanding of both performances. When Petia sees the second performance, she is immediately aware of some differences and similarities. What she starts to think about first will depend on which performance she saw first and on whether any advance information she has been exposed to has led her to anticipate seeing a very different or a very similar performance. If she thought they were going to be very similar performances, she may begin to become aware of the differences when she notices differences in mood during the two performances: what she laughed at in one now seems much more serious; she notices, for example, genuine sexual tension in the scenes between Hedda and Judge Brack where before she saw only an old buffoon and a sharp-tongued dimwit whose interplay prompted derisive laughter. If she had been given to think these would be very different performances, her awareness may involve the unanticipated realization that she is hearing many of the same remarks and seeing many of the same actions that occurred in the other performance.

Petia has learned something about these performances from the experience of seeing them. She will start thinking about the differences between them. She is at least beginning to understand them more deeply. Let us therefore call her Practice-Perceiving Petia to register that she is prompted to think about theatrical practices and how they affect her perception of these performances.

Thiago is able to tell the story of what he has seen in these performances and to discuss the characters; during each performance, he reacted in a manner that was consistent with the stories as they were developed in the performance and that he was later able to tell. However, Thiago sees nothing to think about in the contrast, for example, between the encounters between Brack and Hedda in one performance and their encounters in the other. He makes nothing of the fact that many of the same remarks and many of the same actions occur in both performances. Since those remarks and actions occur in performances as different as these would be – as revealed by the quite different stories Thiago tells – we want to say that he has basic comprehension of the performances but has failed to learn something about them from the experience of seeing them. He certainly lacks deeper understanding.

Thiago may well see or hear some differences and similarities. But it is easy to imagine him discounting whatever differences he does see and hear simply because he does not grasp them as differences requiring something of him or prompting him to further thought about these performances. Perhaps he is otherwise frequently inclined to reflection about many things that affect his life and moods. But in these particular differences and similarities he simply finds no cause. So, at the risk of doing him serious injustice, let us call him Theatrically Thick Thiago to register that he is not prompted by his experiences of these performances to think about their respective theatrical practices.

10.1 Success Conditions for Interpreting What is Performed and Interpreting How it is Performed

There are at least two kinds of thoughts that are naturally grouped as "interpretations" of theatrical performances. The following characterization of success conditions for possessing an interpretive grasp of a theatrical performance captures both of them:

> A spectator has an interpretive grasp of a theatrical performance if she is able to offer *either*, first, a story about the connections the object of basic understanding has with other issues or themes being raised in contemporary culture (including her own reactions to the object) *or*, second, a set of reasons a company may have had for constructing and presenting the object of the performance in the way they did.

Robert Stecker holds that the questions that occasion interpretation are "(1) What is the object intended to mean (be, do)? (2) What could it mean (be, be doing)? (3) What does it mean (what it is; what it is doing)? (4) What is its significance to me (group g)?"[3] This looks pretty much right. Basic theatrical understanding and deeper theatrical understanding are aimed at answering question (3). The first sort of interpretive grasp I have suggested above is directly aimed at answering question (4). I will refer to that as "S-interpretation" to register the fact that a spectator making those kinds of connections is expressing her sense of the *significance* of the performance.

Although Theatrically Thick Thiago finds nothing to reflect on concerning the kinds of similarities and differences that Practice-Perceiving Petia sees between the straight and the parodic performances, he might still reflect sensitively on his own life and the lives of others as a result of experiencing these plays. One of the stories he tells may strike him as expressing a view of life that he regards as profoundly accurate while the other strikes him as revealing little or nothing that is plausible or even as profoundly mistaken. So Thiago, in respects other than those concerned with what is theatrically interesting, may be anything but thick; indeed he could be quite as sensitive and perceptive as Petia, perhaps even more so. But, in any case, when he tells anyone his view of these stories, he is offering an S-interpretation.

The second sort of interpretive grasp suggested above as appropriate for theatrical performance seems aimed at providing hypotheses that would explain why the *performers* are utilizing the practices in play in the performance. The questions to which this form of interpretation responds are a combination of Stecker's (1) and (3). I will refer to that kind of interpretive grasp as "P-interpretation."

Now a striking thing about Practice-Perceiving Petia is that she will have some questions for which she lacks the resources to provide answers. Her questions will be of two kinds. Since she is, *ex hypothesi*, a basically comprehending spectator, she will not know much about how the performers have managed to produce performances with so much in common and so much that is different. Many of her questions will be directed at finding out how this is done. Some of her questions, however, may be directed at discovering why the company or companies who presented these performances have done so in such different ways and to such different effects. Because she does not have answers to the first kind of question, she will be utterly devoid of resources to answer the second. Petia is beginning to comprehend deeply and what she is seeking are P-interpretations of these performances.

S-interpretations are stories about the perceived significance of a performance. P-interpretations are stories about the reasons a company undertook the manner and construction of their performance.

10.2 Eschewing Theories of "Work Meaning"

Many philosophers use the term "interpretation" to refer to *any* process that involves figuring things out and that leads to understanding. Perhaps some would insist that the salience model I have developed and deployed in previous chapters is, therefore, a model of interpretation. I think that is misleading; but I do not own the word and I would not object strenuously if someone insisted on it. What I would insist on is that the finer-grained approach is appropriate, and indeed required, whatever we wish to call things. I prefer to speak of processes by which comprehension is achieved at the basic and the deeper levels and to contrast that – as I think we do contrast it in everyday discourse about theatrical performances – with trying to say things that go beyond what we think just everyone can know, given sufficient experience and training.

I do not think that we should call claims "interpretive" on the grounds that we cannot know the truth about their content or that we cannot see a fact of the matter to appeal to in deciding truth. In the end, I think of interpretive grasp as a pretty natural extension of deeper performer understanding and deeper object understanding and, as such, as cognitive. But it is an extension, and I think we should start with that fact and explain it.

> Audience understanding and interpretation are complex affairs and we are wise to pay attention to the differences among the kinds of responses and thinking that go on when different aspects of a spectator's apprehension of a performance are being discussed.

This fine-grained approach may be given a sharper characterization by the following considerations. A fundamental source of worry about everything I have proposed concerning basic understanding, deeper understanding, and interpretive grasp derives from reflection on a standard view about the conditions for determining what a literary work *means*. The fine-grained approach I have taken can seem to be misleading if we think that all questions about understanding a work of theater boil down to a search for its meaning: for, if that is so, then what we should have been discussing all along is how spectators determine what a performance means.

The motivation for this objection can be found in the philosophical literature concerning what is frequently referred to as the search for determinants of "work meaning." And a particular view of work meaning has dominated discussion in the discipline since the mid-1990s. That view is that work meaning is to be understood as "utterance meaning." This view is called the "utterance model."[4]

Utterance meaning is distinguishable from utterer's meaning and word sequence meaning in the following ways. The same word sequence can be uttered on different occasions by a speaker and, in that case, she may have said different things. This will surely be so, for instance, if she is sincere in the first instance and ironic in the second. To mark this difference we adopt the term "utterer's meaning" to track the things she meant on the separate occasions. Now, since most of the time we mean what we say and say what we mean, we may be tempted to hold that what the utterance means is determined entirely by what a speaker means in uttering a given word sequence. To mark the fact that we sometimes do not say what we mean or mean what we say, however, we adopt the term "utterance meaning" to distinguish what we actually say from what we intend to say (which is, of course, "utterer's meaning"). In laying this out, I have been following the formulation of these concepts in William Tollhurst's influential essay in which he defends an identification of work meaning and utterance meaning.[5]

Jerrold Levinson argues the matter this way. Why can't work meaning be sentence meaning? Because it appears to be a condition of literary interpretation that sentences from a literary text be taken as intentional, sentence meaning is separable from work meaning.

Why can't work meaning be utterer's meaning? Because that would collapse the distinction between everyday communication, where we want to determine what an utterer meant, and literary communication, where we want the text to be an object independent of what the utterer meant. Were that distinction collapsed in the direction of treating literary communication as a species of everyday communication, we would no longer have need, on principle, of literary texts. For, as soon as we could determine what the utterer meant by the text, we could abandon the text.

Levinson also considers a third possibility, "ludic meaning" – "any meanings that can be attributed to a brute text . . . or text-as-utterance, by virtue of imaginative play, constrained only by the loosest requirements of plausibility, intelligibility, or interest." He dismisses this as "an inappropriate candidate for at least the fundamental meaning of literary texts, if only because [ludic meaning] presupposes [work meaning] in order to get off the ground."[6]

This leaves utterance meaning as the only plausible candidate for work meaning. But how are we to determine utterance meaning? Clearly it is related to sentence meaning and utterer's meaning, but how precisely does this relation go?

Here, briefly, are three views.

Levinson argues for a view he calls "Hypothetical Intentionalism" as the means by which to determine work meaning/utterance meaning and constrain possible interpretations of literary texts. On this view, "utterance meaning is logically distinct from utterer's meaning, while at the same time necessarily related to it conceptually: we arrive at utterance meaning in the most comprehensive and informed manner we can muster as the utterance's intended recipients. *Actual* utterer's intention, then, is not what is determinative of the meaning of a literary offering or other linguistic discourse, but rather such intention as optimally *hypothesized*, given all the resources available to us in the work's internal structure and the relevant surrounding context of creation, in all its *legitimately* invoked specificity."[7]

Not everyone thinks the best arguments favor Hypothetical Intentionalism as the appropriate view concerning what determines work meaning and constrains interpretation. Noël Carroll defends a view of what an utterance means (and hence what work meaning is) that aligns it more closely with utterer's meaning. His proposal, which he calls "modest actual intentionalism," is that "the intentions of authors that the modest actual intentionalist takes seriously are only those intentions of the author that the linguistic/literary unit can support (given the conventions of language and literature) . . . [so that] where the linguistic unit can support more than one possible meaning . . . the correct interpretation is the one that is compatible with the author's actual intention, which itself must be supportable by the language of the text."[8]

Robert Stecker stresses the conventionalist element implied in Levinson's approach to determining utterance meaning. He defines utterance meaning as follows: "A speaker, using a language L, means something by uttering x in L, only if she intends to do A by uttering x and intends the audience to recognize this, in part because of the conventional meanings of x or contextually supported extensions of those meanings."[9] When it comes to the determination of work meaning, however, although generally favoring a view that identifies work meaning with utterance meaning, the view he ultimately adopts, and which he calls the "Unified View" is "roughly, that work meaning is a function of both the actual intentions of the artist and the conventions in place when the work is created."[10]

Against that background, it may now seem that I have actually built into the analyses I have offered of basic understanding, deeper understanding, and interpretive grasp the unifying idea of "work meaning" I say I have avoided. This is because the way I have described what it is that performers do (so that audiences can grasp the content of what they do) has appealed centrally to choices and conventions. This seems to suggest that there is a substantial but unacknowledged role for theatrical conventions in the story I told about how audiences get the contents of theatrical performances. In fact, however, that is not the case.

In defending the appeal to conventions in his own view, Stecker rejects a criticism, due to Donald Davidson,[11] of the appeal to conventions in determining linguistic meaning. Davidson argues that "philosophers who make convention a necessary element of language have the matter backwards. The truth is rather that language is a condition for having conventions."[12] Stecker correctly observes that, since he is not offering a "bottom-up" theory of linguistic meaning, he is free to formulate a theory of art interpretation that appeals to the conventions of the artworld, in this case literary and art-historical conventions.[13]

We are free to do so; but, by itself, that does not warrant doing so. To be sure, audiences for theatrical performances possess the knowledge that they are confronting actions and objects in what Stecker calls "the intentional domain," actions and objects comprised of "intentional human behavior and its products – the things made as an intended consequence of the behavior." Indeed, the common knowledge requirement we adopted in chapter 6 entails that spectators possess a good deal more knowledge than the fact that they are confronting intentional human behavior. But this provides us no reason to suppose that they know the conventions in play in a particular performance, nor does it warrant the view that basically comprehending spectators grasp or determine the content of a performance only by first grasping the conventions in play and what those conventions can deliver.

Davidson argues specifically against the Lewis-style account of discovery of conventional norms that I employed in developing the salience model. And he is surely partly right when he claims that by appeals to the

> element of the conventional, or of the conditioning process that makes speakers rough facsimiles of their friends and parents, we explain no more than the convergence [and that thereby] we throw no light on the essential nature of the skills that are thus made to converge.[14]

Since, like Stecker, I have not aimed at a "bottom up" account of linguistic meaning, all that mattered to me in the Lewis-style analysis was precisely what Davidson agrees it *can* explain: convergence. Moreover, as I showed earlier, we needed an account of how audiences come to convergence that does not appeal to performer intentions. The Lewis-style account shows us how to achieve that.

Lewis contends that his account gives us a non-intentional story about conventions. But I have adopted a more robust sense of conventions – just as Stecker does. I have deployed the salience model to show how spectators come to grasp the same characteristics presented in a performance without having a prior grasp of either intentions or the more robustly conceived conventions.

Another reason to avoid a view that holds we grasp conventions in order to grasp content is that, even at the most basic level of understanding theatrical performances, the situation is simply much more complex than this story would allow. Some features of performers are salient for patterns that trigger recognitional capacities.[15] Some features are salient for patterns that spectators respond to in ways that support recognition but that audiences do not actually recognize: spectators react sub-doxastically to these features as salient for characteristics of the developing object of performance; and the relation between those reactions and what they do recognize is counterfactual.[16] There certainly could be conventions in play in these cases; indeed that is likely. But, although some spectators might grasp the content of a performance by means of recognizing those conventions, basically comprehending spectators need not grasp those conventions in order to comprehend the performance. To require it of them would be to require what Bernard Williams calls, in a very different context, "one thought too many."[17]

I conclude therefore that we should avoid a strategy that requires us first to determine the content of performances as utterances – whether that content is determined by intentions or conventions – and then to work back from there to explain how audiences respond comprehendingly to theatrical performances. We should maintain a commitment to a finer grained suite of accounts of spectators' comprehending responses, a suite of accounts that includes showing how responses at the sub-doxastic level contribute to understanding and also how and when performers' intentions and the conventions in play are grasped and can contribute to an spectator's comprehension and appreciation of the achievement in a given performance.

10.3 Interpretation and Significance

Some might think that simply finding something significant constitutes having an interpretation of that thing. An S-interpretation of a performance, in contrast, is an attempt to explain what aspects of the performance gave one the sense of significance it had for one. The fact that an S-interpretation is an *explanation* will be what distinguishes it, in a manner we will now address, from merely *finding* something significant in some way.

There seem to be only the loosest constraints, if any at all, on what an individual might find significant about anything. It may seem a little silly, but surely someone could 'see' the war between reason and irrationality embodied – somehow – in the fact that she encountered a coin in the dust of the middle of a country road at dusk. What people find significant is, as Stecker asserts, a matter entirely "contingent" on the history of the person or group to whom something appears significant (and, for that reason, it is likely to be "transient" as well).[18]

But if this is what is going on when a spectator expresses the significance she found in the performance, she has not yet offered an S-interpretation at all. Thus the question whether there are any constraints on the interpretation she can give has a very different look to it.

> An explanation of why a performance struck a spectator as significant is an S-interpretation of that performance only if the spectator, in offering the explanation, makes connecting references to specific characteristics of the performance.

The explanation could still be a little silly because what the spectator finds significant in the performance is rooted in a reaction that itself can only have an explanation at least as silly. But if a spectator offers an S-interpretation at all, she will connect her reactions to specific elements of the performance rooted in her having understood the performance. If her reactions are not tied to elements of what any other basically comprehending spectator would describe as the object of the performance, then (again) she is not offering an S-interpretation at all.

This is why some think S-interpretations are actually deeper, more profound, or richer than what I have called "deeper understanding." The latter is more a technical matter of the spectator having a background that enables her to see in the performance the means by which it is achieved or the larger-scale features that are present, reacted to, but not recognized by those who only basically comprehend the performance.

> S-interpretations are not mechanical and they go, as it were, to the soul of our felt responses to a performance. For that reason they have a claim on us that deeper performer understanding and deeper object understanding may only rarely do.

In fact, we can now explain why *basic* theatrical understanding may also strike us as more profound than "deeper understanding." When asked what a narrative performance was about, we may reply by telling the story. And, if we found the performance significant, it is likely we will tell the story that demonstrates our basic comprehension with inflections that reveal which elements we took to be significant *in* the story and, to some extent, why we did so. In short, the following is true.

> On some occasions, a spectator may express part of a particular S-interpretation by means of the same response that demonstrates she has basic comprehension.

It is always open for others, hearing a spectator tell the story in the way that reveals how she responded to it, to ask her to *explain* why she thinks of the story she has told in that way. This shows that demonstration of basic understanding and expression of S-interpretation, when offered together, can still come apart. What makes it sometimes seem that basic theatrical understanding is more profound than technically deeper understanding is that, when a spectator's demonstration of basic theatrical comprehension also expresses an S-interpretation, that demonstration can legitimately strike us as more profound than any amount of evidence of technically deeper understanding.

10.4 Interpreting Performers

A P-interpretation allows a spectator to explain something about a performance in a way that an understanding of its elements, however full and detailed, does not. Understanding yields descriptions. Interpretation, especially P-interpretation, yields explanations.

This can be brought out clearly by introducing a third spectator, Inka. Inka has made it her aim to get to know varieties of performance styles and the history of performance practices. She sees a lot of theater and theater in a lot of different styles. She is disposed to bring that information to bear on theatrical performances she witnesses. She has reflected on how such experience or independent knowledge could contribute to her understanding of any performance she witnesses and comes to the theater prepared to bring that reflection to bear on her experience.

Inka has at her disposal considerable resources for answering Petia's questions. Inka knows how performers prepare a production and, since she is familiar with different performance practices, she will tell the right story about how the performance devices employed have made both of these the kinds of performances they are. She will have a clear sense of both the similarities and the differences between these performances and will be able to tell Petia a good deal of what Petia wants to know. She will notice what Petia notices, albeit dimly, about the performances, and be able to explain how the performance practices shape their distinctive stories and moods. Of course, Inka may find one of them profoundly challenging and the other banal, just as Thiago does.

What makes Inka interesting is that she can do something that neither Thiago nor Petia can do: she can make plausible guesses as to the intentions performers may have had in utilizing the performance practices they have deployed *and* she is able to discuss how her own felt reactions to the wider significance of the performances relate to what she takes the performers' intentions to have been. She may, for example, think that her sense of the significance of one performance was not the product of the performers' intentions but was, instead, formed despite their efforts in another direction. Or she may think her sense of the significance of the performance was revealed to her as a result of the performers' intentions. So, let us call this spectator Intensively Interpreting Inka to register the fact that she has the background to do more by way of interpreting than either Thiago or Petia, however perceptive they may be.

Think of what it would take for Inka to explain the performance of *Spontaneous Beauty* to Petia. Petia had understood the story and begun to recognize the means by which the story had been told, but still felt puzzled. Critically, there is something to describe, namely the actual performance practices that took place. In the conversation, Inka will need to cite certain effects brought about at specific moments. If Petia now comes to remember those moments, Inka will describe what the performers did to achieve them. But Inka will not have explained the performance fully if she leaves the matter there. To explain this, Inka or Petia now have to offer a hypothesis as to what aims the performers had in deploying the range of devices they did, in the order in which they appeared, and so on. To figure out completely what had been done in the performance, and remove all puzzlement, they will need to work their way through the performance from beginning to end, seeing how the performance took shape and why it had the shape it had.

This should sound familiar. Here is why.

P-interpretations, concerning the reasons a company undertook a performance in a certain manner, are reflections of the grasp of styles.

Reference to theatrical styles always includes reference to the reasons performers have for adopting particular sets of conventions and always makes reference to how those aims are to govern entire performances. And the hypotheses spectators make in P-interpretations are about precisely those kinds of reasons. This is important because possession of deeper performer understanding offers a guide to what spectators are to look for and how to look at it. So, grasp of a style, by means of a P-interpretation, would seem to be all that is needed to obtain full appreciation of a performance.

Our working conception of full appreciation of a theatrical performance involved two things: first, the ability to see the performance against a background that can inform the spectator of what kind of achievement is or is not manifest in the performance; and second, the ability, by reference to details in performances, to converse about how the performance practices contribute to or detract from the performed object and whether the performed object is achievable by certain kinds of performance practices rather than others. A spectator in possession of deeper performer understanding is fully adequate to the first of these tasks.

P-interpretations are the means by which spectators succeed at the second task.

Notes

1   Denis Dutton, "Artistic Crimes: The Problem of Forgery in the Arts," *British Journal of Aesthetics* 19/4 (Autumn, 1979), p. 305.

2   David Novitz, "Interpretation and Justification," in *The Philosophy of Interpretation*, ed. Joseph Margolis and Tom Rockmore (Oxford: Blackwell, 2000), p. 5.

3   Stecker, *Interpretation and Construction: Art, Speech, and the Law* (London and New York: Blackwell, 2003), p. 4.

4   This latter term was coined, so far as I can tell, by Jack Meiland, "The Meanings of a Text," *British Journal of Aesthetics* 21/3 (Summer 1981), p. 197.

5   William Tollhurst, "On What a Text Means and How it Means," *British Journal of Aesthetics* 19/1 (Winter 1979), 4–5. Tollhurst does not use the term "work meaning," preferring to refer to this as "text meaning."

6   Jerrold Levinson, "Intention and Interpretation in Literature," in *The Pleasures of Aesthetics* (Ithaca, NY: Cornell University Press, 1996), p. 177.

7   Ibid., p. 178.

8   Noël Carroll, "Interpretation and Intention: The Debate between Hypothetical and Actual Intentionalism," in *The Philosophy of Interpretation*, ed. Joseph Margolis and Tom Rockmore (Oxford: Blackwell, 2000), p. 76.

9 Stecker, *Interpretation and Construction*, p. 13.

10 Ibid., p. 42.

11 The arguments Stecker discusses are those of Donald Davidson, "A Nice Derangement of Epitaphs," in *Actions and Events: Perspectives on the Philosophy of Donald Davidson*, ed. Ernest LePore and Brian McLaughlin (Oxford: Basil Blackwell, 1986), pp. 433–46.

12 Donald Davidson, "Communication and Convention," in *Inquiries into Truth and Interpretation*, 2nd edition (Oxford: Clarendon Press, 2001), p. 280.

13 Stecker, *Interpretation and Construction*, p. 13.

14 Davidson, "Communication and Convention," p. 278.

15 These were discussed in chapter 7, "What Audiences See."

16 We discussed these in chapters 5, "Basic Theatrical Understanding," and 6, "The Mechanics of Basic Theatrical Understanding."

17 Bernard Williams, "Persons, Character, and Morality," in *Moral Luck* (Cambridge: Cambridge University Press, 1981).

18 Stecker, *Interpretation and Construction*, pp. 4–5.

11
FULL APPRECIATION OF A THEATRICAL PERFORMANCE

Let us sum up the argument of part III. Full appreciation of a theatrical performance involves the ability to see the performance against a background that can inform the spectator of the achievement that is or is not manifest in the performance. If a spectator has comprehension of that background, she has "deeper performer understanding." But that is not sufficient for full appreciation of a performance unless she also exercises the ability that information gives her and forms hypotheses about the reasons the company undertook the performance in the manner in which they did. By forming these hypotheses, she traces how the performance practices contribute to or detract from the performed object. P-interpretations are the means by which spectators succeed at this latter task.

P-interpretations demonstrate a grasp of the style of the performance. Grasp of style involves hypotheses about performer aims and intentions for a performance and recognition of the convention sets that are gathered together to serve those aims and intentions. To recognize the convention sets, the spectator must know how weakly coherent sequences of features are selected for display: it is because they are differently weighted from conceivable alternatives and contingently salient for characteristics of a developed object of a performance.

Accordingly *full appreciation* of a theatrical performance can now be more precisely defined as follows:

> Full appreciation of a particular theatrical performance is a "reconstruction of the creative process"[1] which explains how *that* theatrical performance came about, in its entirety and in detail.

So, it would seem we have concluded our project. But there is an unresolved tension in the argument. This tension can be brought out sharply by considering the "Case of the Culturally Lethargic Company."

11.1 The Case of the Culturally Lethargic Company

The Culturally Lethargic Company (CLC) is a group of performers who assemble for a rehearsal and select some features for display acknowledging neither that they are engaged in making selections nor that there are any alternatives from which to select. CLC fails to deliberate about its selections. By something very close to chance their efforts could, on rare occasions, result in a performance resembling in nearly every respect one in which a particular aim is adopted, particular plans are made to achieve the aim, and the aim guides the execution of the plan from beginning to end.

On one such occasion, let us suppose, CLC plans and executes a performance called "Hamlet" that turns out to be moment for moment consonant with the laboriously considered Freudian performance, inspired by the Ernest Jones essay, undertaken and eventually filmed by Lawrence Olivier.[2] In CLC's production, the actor playing Hamlet really does have oedipal fantasies about his mother and father and delivers Hamlet's lines in the way he imagines to be just the natural way one might say them. The actress playing Gertrude really is in love with the (much younger) man who is playing Hamlet while also having what she herself considers a rather sordid affair with the man playing Claudius. Again, the way she delivers her lines seems completely natural to her. And so on . . . The set-builder has vague recollections of having seen a movie with a set that he thinks he can reproduce on a small budget – and it turns out to be the very womb-like studio set Olivier commissioned for the movie version of his production. And so on again . . . So there are decisions made, to be sure, and there is something roughly like deliberation. But there is no shared deliberation of the kind that creates conventions. Whatever deliberation does go on does not concern the kinds of aims and intentions that shape a performance in an individual style.

It is precisely the fact that CLC *assumes* sequences of features and sets of conventions rather than *thinking their way to* them that makes theirs a culturally lethargic company. It is not *just* by chance that they hit upon the features they select. But they are not hit upon as a result of anyone thinking about them in the way spectators would have in mind were they to ascribe aims and intentions to CLC.

Someone like Inka, who is suitably backgrounded to understand the conventions in play and to ascribe the relevant aims that guide the performance, will take what they present as the result of a resolution of some deliberative questions. A spectator like Inka will then ascribe aims and intentions to them. But she will do so falsely.

Even a spectator like Petia, who is backgrounded enough only to know what the conventions are and to be able to sense something that makes a call on her capacities for tracking how the aims of the performance make it what it is, will be led to make at least some guesses in this direction. But, again, the guesses of a spectator like Petia will be mistaken.

CLC has no intentions of the relevant kinds. There are elements in their performance that make a call on spectators' capacities to attend to the performance itself as part of their experience of the theatrical event. But if spectators do so attend, they are mistaken. There is behavior that indicates a resolution of some deliberative questions. However, there is, *ex hypothesi*, no deliberation. There is no consent to a common *stylistic* project. There is only acquiescence in what has always been done that has, purely by chance, resulted in a performance that looks exactly like one in which aims have been chosen, plans laid, and plans executed. How are we to assess the ascription of intentions even when no stylistic decisions were made?

Clearly, before spectators discover the truth about CLC – and, of course, they may never do – CLC's performance makes claims on spectators' capacities to assess the performance. In response, spectators like Inka and Petia would hazard more or less informed guesses about both the general aims and the particular plans of performers and would test those hypotheses against future developments. Inka would have resolved such hypotheses satisfactorily. She would not declare the project confused. She would have grounds *in the details of the performance* that supported her hypotheses and assessments. Indeed, it would be irrational for her to form such hypotheses if she had no reason to believe that the performance could be coherently shaped in that way. That she could find a way to track it as coherently governed by some aims shows that it could be so. From these considerations it seems spectators are justified in ascribing intentions to CLC.

Do we think the same thing if and after a spectator discovers the truth about CLC? Oddly, it seems we should. One thing that makes sticking with the ascriptions plausible is the fact that spectators are disappointed *with the company* when the revealing discovery is made; and they are not disappointed in themselves for having expected too much. If they were not onto something right about the details when they made the ascriptions in the first place, their disappointment in the company seems undermotivated. Why do we think it is the company that has let the spectators down and not the spectators that have expected too much? We think this because we can see ourselves recommending that others go attend *this* performance (even though we would surely warn them off CLC's upcoming production based in Ibsen's script for *Hedda Gabler*). In short, when Inka learns that CLC did not have the intentions she had ascribed to them, she would rightly conclude that CLC have failed to achieve intentionally what they have in fact presented. The performance may be a success, in some sense, even if that success no longer can be taken as an achievement of the company's.

But this means we have two, equally unpalatable, choices. First, perhaps we are wrong to follow our intuition that Inka's stylistic appraisal is justified in the case of CLC. Or, second, perhaps we are wrong to hold that stylistic grasp involves hypotheses regarding performer aims and intentions. For ascriptions of intentions are false when no corresponding intentions exist. So it appears one of these must be given up.

This is already a very serious matter since I have argued that style appraisal, by means of P-interpretations, is essential to full appreciation of a theatrical performance. But the problem is even more serious.

11.2 Broader Implications of the CLC Problem

If there is a problem for P-interpretations with features being selected without the selection being the result of a deliberative process, there will also be a problem for the definition of theatrical conventions as sequences of features *selected* for display.

The definition relied on the intuition that what makes conventions useful in artworks generally and theatrical performances in particular is that they are ways of enabling a particular focus on certain features that give rise to reactions supporting a particular way of apprehending some contents.[3] The selection of features involved is the result of processes of deliberation among conceivable alternatives. The notion of conceivable alternatives presumes that things could have been done otherwise. Do we now have to give all this up?

One way out is suggested by the fact that different kinds of practices can play a role in works of art and can be called "conventions,"[4] as Brian Baxter suggests. And not all of these involve deliberation. The first practices Baxter mentions are Lewis-conventions, with which we are already familiar.[5] Other notions of conventions that Baxter identifies as employed in artworks are (a) solutions to social problems that are not coordination problems – such as discovering how to present a kind of event or image to a particular audience without offending them, (b) conventions that "have symbolic significance for a certain population" but are not solutions to any problems at all, (c) conventions that are solutions to particular artistic problems, such as finding the right abstract "content" to go with a shaped canvas – and (d) conventions that are simply the habitual and customary practices of a group.[6]

Some notions in Baxter's taxonomy do not involve the idea of deliberation. We can readily imagine cases of devices whose use is conventional both in sense (b) and in sense (d), for it is not hard to think of cases of symbolic devices that are used out of mere habit rather than as the result of deliberation. And the same could be thought about devices that are conventional in sense (a). Unfortunately, this way out of the CLC problem is of no avail. For solutions to artistic problems, (c), pretty clearly do involve deliberation. Although such solutions may be produced accidentally, they are rarely if ever accidentally kept for presentation. And it would appear that conventions that are solutions to artistic problems are precisely the kind of conventions on which we need to focus.

Still, something has come of this. In accepting Inka's conclusions concerning CLC's "Hamlet," we have idealized the rehearsal process. Anyone familiar with how they actually go recognizes that frequently there are things a company could make choices about that, for one reason or another, they simply do not. For an obvious example, a company might assign a range of words a performer is to utter in a performance to the character suggested by the script. This is, of course, the standard practice in performances of the *Hedda-to-Hedda* kind: the performer portraying Hedda says the lines with the "Hedda" speech prefix. This is one of those choices aimed at solving particular some artistic problem. And the result of this kind of choice is rightly regarded as a convention. But performers may not notice this convention *as* a convention. Only when they do is the convention actually selected by them. Thus, we must acknowledge the following fact.

Theatrical conventions cannot be thought of as sequences of features that are always actually selected for display *as the result of deliberation.*

And so it appears that, when a spectator with deeper performer understanding describes even a convention (let alone a style), she is imputing deliberative activity to performers even when there may have been none at all. And this suggests another way out, namely that of accepting some version of "imputationalism."

11.3 The "Imputationalist" Solution

Do P-interpretations involve determining what performers intend or could intend a set of practices to achieve? Do descriptions of sequences of features as conventions require that the describer knows that performers chose those sequences because of their anticipated weight or only that he knows the reasons they could have had for choosing them? The distinction invoked in these questions is analogous to the distinction between what a text "does mean" and what a text "could mean."

Some philosophers hold that perfectly legitimate interpretations are *imputations* (or "constructions") of features of artworks. Imputations may be made with respect to meanings, aims, intentions, features, just about anything.

But other philosophers worry that, if an interpretation *imputes* rather than *ascribes* features or meanings to a work and aims or intentions to the author of a work, it changes what the work actually is. When we say, for example, that a text could mean M, M*, or M**, we may think that what we have in mind is that there is some one thing to which we could ascribe different meanings. But the imputationalist holds that in each case, for example when we say it could mean M, we are attributing properties to the text *that it would not have had* were we to say that it could mean M* or M**. Thus, if we say it could mean M *and* M* *and* M**, we are attributing three distinct sets of properties to the text. And now it would appear we have three works of literature, not just one. Corresponding to each attribution of features we have a different *constructed object*, constructed in part by the possession of just those properties. On the imputationalist view, it appears, this is the kind of thing literary works of art just happen to be.

Some might think we ought to reject imputationalism because it entails a position called "singularism." Singularism is the claim that each work of literature, *as interpreted*, is a distinct individual work. There is the text Maharat wrote, the text Maharat wrote as interpreted by Claudine, the text Maharat wrote as interpreted by Sebastian, and the text Maharat wrote as interpreted by Maharat. Since authors are notoriously unreliable about what their texts mean, we have no reason to regard the last of these as more determinative of what the work is than either of the others. The disturbing upshot, of course, is that we no longer have a work of literature with three interpretations, we have three works of literature. For some philosophers, the singularist consequence by itself shows that imputationalism is untenable.

But we should not be too hasty to conclude that singularism is a problem with respect to theatrical performances. After all, if we think theatrical performance is an art form in its own right and that performances are its artworks, we are already committed to singularism. For, theatrical performances last no longer than the run of the performances. And they do not endure when the run is over.

This version of singularism about theatrical performances is not the result of audiences' differing P-interpretations or of claims regarding conventions. But even so, it shows that the threat of singularism cannot be offered as a reason against holding an imputationalist view of the interpretive grasp of theatrical performances. Nor, for related reasons, should we attempt to avail ourselves of any arguments against imputationalism that depend on appeals to enduring features of works of art or on appeals to the claim that interpreters, not works, change over time.[7]

So, if we should reject an imputationalist account of spectators' interpretive grasp or of their understanding of conventions, we will have to appeal to other facts. Some of these, pointed out by Peter Lamarque, are that we typically think artists, not interpreters, create works of art, and that we normally think there is some sort of line between inherent and imputed properties.[8] It is not clear, however, why appeal to these facts should do the job.

11.4 Solving the CLC Problem Without Resorting to Imputationalism

We can preserve the idea that theatrical conventions are sequences of features for which there are decidable alternatives without accepting the most virulent implications of imputationalism.[9] And because we can do that, I maintain, we can preserve the justification for our intuitions about the P-interpretations a suitably backgrounded spectator will offer in cases like CLC. To see why this is so, let us examine more closely the conception of convention we have adopted. This conception was introduced because it reflected the thought that if a sequence of features is the result of choices, then each choice involved could always have been made differently, thus yielding a different sequence of features. What we will be able to preserve of this conception is the crucial idea that conventions are practices that could have been done differently. And we will be able to preserve this even though, as we have seen, not all conventions consist of features selected for display *as the result of deliberation*. The resources we need for seeing that all this is so are to be found in contemporary discussions of the nature of social conventions.

Prominent analyses of social conventions begin by acknowledging that explicit agreements do not initiate most social conventions. My second-year Italian language textbook lists the following "convenzioni sociali." Italians typically greet each other by shaking hands. Italians address those they know well with "familiar" linguistic constructions and those they do not know well and people older than themselves with "formal" linguistic constructions. Italians place more importance than North Americans do on titles, and the titles "dottore" and "dottoressa" are used not just in addressing physicians and PhDs but also in addressing anyone who has any university degree. These illustrate the kinds of things we think about when thinking about social conventions. Surely none of the three examples given by my Italian language textbook are examples of conventions formed by explicit agreement. So, many social conventions do not originate in the explicit agreements among those who are parties to them. Nevertheless it makes sense to call these conventions in part because something in their formation, adoption, and continuance *plays the role of explicit agreement*.

A standard way to investigate what plays that role is to examine unproblematic cases of convention by agreement in order to see what aspects of conventions are still crucially in play in cases where there is no explicit agreement. In the most traditional and perhaps its original usage the term "convention" refers to groups of people who have voluntarily come together for some purpose, who have convened. In another early usage, it refers to the acts of groups of people who have convened to establish those acts.[10] What stands out in the original circumstance of convention formation is that it pertains to the actual convening of people to solve some common problems, to the practices established by people who convened precisely for the purpose of establishing such practices, and to the fact that parties to those agreements are bound to keep to what has been established.

Several approaches to analyzing social conventions have arisen since the 1970s about what we should focus on in the original circumstance. One approach, beginning with the seminal work of David Lewis,[11] has focused on the idea of conventions as solutions to common problems. This approach asked how to think of those problems so that we can see how people, without making explicit agreements, arrive at solutions that in some way command the consent of most of the people who are party to the solutions.[12] The importance of Lewis's analysis in the present context has to do with his analysis of what we mean when we say a choice "could have been made differently," or that some actions "could have been done differently."

Part of what these locutions mean, regarding the preparation and execution of a theatrical performance, can be illustrated this way: when a group of performers arrive at their first rehearsal and are handed the script upon which they are to base a performance, given the complete generality of the issues confronting them, there is no logically predetermined way they are to use that script. There is not even a requirement that they use it at all. Each of these issues must be decided, or for each a decision must be assumed. There is something to be decided even if no one decides it.

Lewis proposes that we understand the idea that things could have been done otherwise as a conjunction of two claims: that for a given population some alternative action would have served the same purpose just as well; and that, if almost all others in the population had done that alternative action instead, then any one of them would have had a rational and decisive reason to do that alternative as well. This "equally satisfactory alternative" analysis would yield what we want by way of a mechanism for establishing and maintaining conventions were it not for the fact that it distorts some aspects of social conventions and, for similar reasons, will not capture important features of artistic conventions.

Against the first part of Lewis's analysis, Tyler Burge[13] has argued that this cannot be the right sense in which social conventions are arbitrary. Burge offers a hypothetical case of a group of people in a society who, while acknowledging that there are other languages and that using one of the other languages, as many of their fellows are now doing, has as many advantages as using their own, still believe that their language has a specific religious weight and so "insist they would retain 'the god's language' even if the others went astray."[14] And he observes that, although the belief itself might be unreasonable, the knowledge that others had switched would not provide these people with reasons, let alone decisive reasons, to switch to the alternative language.[15] The upshot is that even when a group of people conforming to a convention recognize there are alternatives – alternatives whose existence demonstrates they are conforming to a tradition – they may not view the alternatives as *equally satisfactory alternatives* to what they are doing.[16]

We have reason to avoid the second part of Lewis's analysis as well. Catherine Lord argues that artistic conventions are not inherently conservative in the way that social conventions are.[17] Given Lewis's model of social conventions, if there is no reason to prefer one alternative over another and if conventional actions are those that have been done before because a precedent makes a solution salient to a population, then there is almost never a reason to change. But artistic conventions change with considerable frequency. So, whether or not Lewis's analysis is adequate for social conventions, it is not adequate for analyzing the artistically relevant conventions in which we are interested.

A theatrical convention, like any social convention, represents something that could have been done another way. When it is the results of deliberation, what is at issue has to do with the fact that each alternative sequence has a different weight. The alternatives have foreseeable cognitive and non-cognitive effects on spectators, and so, when performers do deliberate, they base their choices of which sequence to present by considering such ranges of effects. Thus, performers *may* consider something more substantive than knowledge of their own preferences and of the preferences of others when they deliberate among alternatives. And this factor alters the equation with respect to performers' alternatives in something like the way that the belief that one's language is "the god's language" affects the alternatives facing Burge's tribe.

Still, there must be some standard for determining that something is a decidable alternative *in those cases where no deliberation takes place*. I propose the following.

> For each sequence of features performers use in a performance there is a decidable alternative, where "decidable" means "available to a company to decide."

This will be vacuous unless we can say more precisely what it is for an alternative to be available to a company to decide. It is too strong to insist that they must have thought of it themselves. For the case we are trying to resolve is precisely when they have not done so. It is also too strong to insist that others within their temporal, cultural, geographical, or ideological frame of reference have already considered it. A company could make even an explicit decision to do something or to do it in a certain manner without realizing that there is an alternative; and this may hold for any and every other company within the same frame of reference.

Yet I think we are moving in the right direction. We can get what we want by reference to the deliberations of an "ideal companion company." An ideal companion company is a possible company working within the same historical, cultural, geographical, or ideological framework as some actual company. It is ideal in the sense that its members have as much knowledge as is possible within that framework and as much self-aware-ness as the framework allows concerning the framework itself and the position of theater within it. It is also ideal in the sense that the company would consider anything they could consider.

> If an ideal companion company would consider an alternative way of doing something, then that alternative is decidable by any other company working within that same historical, cultural, geographical, or ideological framework.

Taken this way, the claim that conventional actions could have been done differently does not mean, *pace* Lewis, that any other plan of action would do the same job equally well. Nor does it require that there is always a "same job." Nor does the fact that a sequence of features could have been done differently entail that it would be irrational not to choose the alternative if almost all the other performers chose the alterna-tive, even when each one preferred that everyone choose the same alternative.

It might be irrational not to choose the alternative without argument; but even that is not obvious. Suppose one performer, Rebecca, prefers to perform her role in conformity to sequences of features consistent with *Gabler at a Distance*. All the others prefer to perform in conformity to the sequences of features consistent with *Hedda-to-Hedda*. It is not irra-tional for Rebecca to reason that the weight of the sequence of features consistent with *Gabler at a Distance* is the right weight *for her – and for the performance as a whole* – when others are performing in conformity to sequences consistent with *Hedda-to-Hedda*. In fact, in this case she prefers that everyone else choose the same alternative sequence of features for display, different from those she chooses.

It might be objected that I have not given Lewis's analysis of "could have been done differently" its due. I have stressed that performers rely on other factors beyond those having to do with being in a condition of common knowledge with respect to our own and others' preferences. But Lewis claims that the fact that a "person works out the consequences of his beliefs about the world – a world he believes to include other people who are working out the consequences of their beliefs, including their belief in other people" – provides added resources for our reasoning: "by our interaction in the world we acquire various high-order expectations that can serve us as premises."[18] Can a defender of Lewis's position appeal to high-order expectations of the kind referenced here to describe Rebecca's reasoning? I think not. Rebecca does consider what her expectations are regarding the conduct of the others. But it is not those expectations *as* expectations that make a difference to her. The difference she considers has to do with the weight, as determined by the range of *effects*, of the rest of the company acting in accord with their common expectations while she acts counter to those expectations.[19]

In some respects the appeal to what an ideal companion company deliberates about in order to settle what is decidable by any actual company resembles Richard Wollheim's claim that, because there may be many more things that form the background against which an artist forms her intentions than she is aware of, when we "reconstruct [her] creative process" we are not constrained to report her intentions from her point of view nor even "in terms to which the artist could give conscious or unconscious recognition."[20] And this is an advantage of the strategy I am arguing for. For it links the analysis of what it means to say a company "could have done otherwise" directly with a solution to the CLC problem, both as regards P-interpretations and as regards judgments that a company is using a particular convention.

> We do not need to avoid imputationalism altogether, for in grasping a performance style or understanding a convention, spectators avail themselves of knowledge about alternatives that may exceed what performers know.

The conceit of the ideal companion company is a convenient way to express this fact in a relatively formal way. The upshot is that, in referring to performers' intentions, or to the weight that sequences of features actually have as factors in performers' deliberations, spectators are focused on reconstructing a creative process the terms of which performers themselves may be unaware.

If this still seems like imputationalism, because it still seems spectators are imputing intentions to companies rather than reporting their actual intentions, it is at least without one of the crucial damaging aspects of that view. For the comparison to a companion company ensures it is the *actual* company whose achievements are being assessed – their particular choices and failures to choose – that are thought to be responsible for the actual details of any given performance. And, although I offer no distinction between inherent and imputed properties of performers as agents of a creative process, we do not end up with a view on which it is spectators rather than performers who create theatrical performances.

11.5 Full Appreciation of a Theatrical Performance and the Detection of Theatrical Failures

It is true, and important to the view I have been developing, that if a spectator is unaware of a convention *as a convention*, and if the presence of that convention is responsible for the aspects of the work that are present to be appreciated, then that spectator simply cannot appreciate that work, at least not for those aspects. This is because appreciation depends on having some level of understanding of what one is experiencing, where that comes to having a concept of what one is experiencing.[21]

Having such a concept requires spectators to offer hypotheses regarding what performers are up to in a performance, testing those hypotheses against the actual details of the performance, usually as it unfolds, and assessing the achievement the performance manifests given its aims and its context. Only spectators who have deeper performer understanding are able to offer the relevant kinds of hypotheses.

Spectators with deeper understanding are able to detect and explain failures of skill. A suitably backgrounded spectator is one who understands, or is coming to understand, the conventions and styles in play. She will know what to watch for. A performer will fail who does not exhibit the relevant features in voice, speech, mood, movement, or action. Such a failure to exhibit the relevant features may be a result of lack of skill. A spectator who possesses deeper performer understanding will not only notice this but will also be able to explain this to other spectators. Even a spectator capable only of basic comprehension will have some sense of this sort of thing, although she will be unable to explain what it is she is sensing.

A spectator may gain basic understanding of parts of a performance but not be able to describe the complete developed object of the performance. This can occur in at least three ways. It can occur if some of the features grouped together into conventions do not clearly and coherently induce the effects at which they are aimed. Or it may occur if the performers do not understand what effects the conventions they have adopted actually induce, and so have made choices quite at odds with their own conscious aims. It may also occur if the aims of the company are unclear and they have selected a mix of conventions that is confusing to an audience. If a spectator is tracking the adequacy of a P-interpretation she has offered and possesses deeper performer understanding, she will notice these failures and be able to explain them to others.

Basically comprehending spectators can find themselves alienated from a performance even while they follow it and understand the developed object of the performance. There are several ways in which this can happen. It can occur if the performers present a story to an audience only to find that the audience is committed, in some sense, to the values of a more familiar manner of presenting that particular story. Or it may occur if the audience is committed to a different manner of story presentation no matter what the story; and in this sort of circumstance it is even possible that that manner of presentation could be unfamiliar to the performers. Cross-cultural failures can occur in this way. Again, while the basically comprehending spectator feels alienated in these cases, a deeply informed spectator can, if she attempts to track what is going on over the course of the performance, explain what is creating this failure and this alienation.

The description I have just given of what positions a spectator to appreciate a theatrical performance in the fullest sense might be taken to entail that a person who lacks such positioning is unable to make any plausible critical judgments about a performance. But that harsh conclusion is not entailed by the view I have developed. The view I have offered does not hold that any given spectator has the capacities she possesses only as fully developed capacities across the board. She may be able to attain deeper performer understanding of some kinds of theatrical performance but be too inexperienced, or simply lack suitable background, to have deeper performer understanding of different kinds of performance. The capacity to understand one set of practices deeply does not ensure that one can understand another set of practices deeply. Moreover, nothing in the account I have given should be taken to suggest that spectators are frozen in place with respect to their capacities.

The kinds of failures a spectator with deep performer understanding can explain, if she has made the relevant P-interpretations, are many and varied. This may suggest that success at theatrical performance is a fragile thing. And that may be. But I have mentioned them only to demonstrate the assessments of failure *or success* that lie within the scope of the spectator who has full appreciation of a theatrical performance. And this allows us to present our final precise characterization of the full appreciation of a theatrical performance.

Full appreciation of a theatrical performance is a reconstruction of the creative process which explains how a particular theatrical performance came about, in its entirety and in detail, whether successfully or unsuccessfully.

This is the same sense in which anyone appreciates any work of any art.

Notes

1   The phrase is Richard Wollheim's, and the solution to the imputation problem that I offer in this chapter is based on some aspects of the view he develops in "Criticism as Retrieval," in *Art and Its Objects* (Cambridge: Cambridge University Press, 1980), pp. 185–204.

2   Ernest Jones, "The Problem of Hamlet and the Oedipus-complex," in William Shakespeare, *Hamlet* (London: Vision, 1947). The film version of Olivier's production is dated 1948.

3   Carolyn Wilde, "On Style: Wittgenstein's Writing and the Art of Painting," in *Wittgenstein and Aesthetics: Proceedings from the Skjolden Symposium*, ed. Kjell S. Johannessen, Skriftserien no. 14: (Bergen, Norway: University of Bergen, Department of Philosophy, 1997, 136–60).

4   Brian Baxter, "Conventions and Art," *British Journal of Aesthetics* 23/4 (Autumn, 1983), 319–32.

5   I used a modified version of some parts of Lewis's account of the grasp of conventional norms as a model for thinking about how spectators grasp the developing objects of theatrical performances. I have so far not used any part of that account in explaining theatrical conventions. Instead I have presented theatrical conventions as delivering features that spectators can grasp as salient for characteristics of the developing objects of performances, but as originating in the possibly explicit decisions of performance companies. We turn to the issues besetting that idea soon.

6   Baxter, "Conventions and Art," pp. 320–1.

7   These arguments against imputationalist accounts of interpretation are offered by Jerrold Levinson in *Music, Art, & Metaphysics: Essays in Philosophical Aesthetics* (Ithaca, NY: Cornell University Press, 1990), pp. 180–1.

8   Peter Lamarque, "Objects of Interpretation," in *The Philosophy of Interpretation*, ed. Joseph Margolis and Tom Rockmore (Oxford: Blackwell, 2000), pp. 110 and 115 respectively. Lamarque is not sanguine about the second of these lines of argument; nor will we be when we return to it.

9   The part of this section that deals with decidable alternatives and arbitrariness was made clearer following discussions with Laurie Anne Pieper, who also read the entire first draft of the manuscript. I thank her for both of those things.

10 There is a methodological issue, and four substantive ideas each of which brings with it a set of issues. The methodological issue that arises for attempts to provide a precise notion of convention concerns whether the responses we give to the substantive issues will be constrained by the doctrine of "methodological individualism." That doctrine holds that there are no

intentions but those of individual minds, and so all social phenomena that are to be explained in terms of intentions must be explicable by appeal to the intentions of the individuals involved, considered separately. Methodological pluralism, in contrast, can be defined simply as the thought that there might be or must be genuinely plural – and perhaps shared – intentions, beliefs, or obligations. The four substantive ideas are dealt with in the body of the text.

11 Lewis offers the following final statement of his theory of social conventions:

> "A regularity R in the behavior of members of a population P when they are agents in a recurrent situation S is a *convention* if and only if it is true that, and it is common knowledge in P that, in almost any instance of S among members of P,
>
> (1) almost everyone conforms to R:
> (2) almost everyone expects everyone else to conform to R:
> (3) almost everyone has approximately the same preferences regarding all possible combinations of actions;
> (4) almost everyone prefers that any one more conform to R, on condition that almost everyone conform to R;
> (5) almost everyone would prefer that any one more conform to R', on condition that almost everyone conform to R',
>
> where R' is some possible regularity in the behavior of members of P in S, such that almost no one in almost any instance of S among members of P could conform both to R' and to R." David Lewis, *Convention* (Oxford: Blackwell, 2002; first published Cambridge, MA: Harvard University Press, 1969), p. 78.

12 Another strategy, developing from important work on social facts by Margaret Gilbert, has focused on the fact that conventions originating in the original circumstance are binding on parties to them in fairly specific ways. Conventions, she observes, command the consent of the parties and also authorize stronger bonds than individual consent. They appear to give something like rights of expectation to each party against the others. We may take Gilbert's most settled position to be this: "a social convention is a jointly accepted fiat, a rule of the fiat form that is properly seen as 'ours' by the members of some population: a 'group principle.'" Margaret Gilbert, "Rationality, Coordination, and Convention," in *Living Together* (New York: Rowman & Littlefield, 1996), p. 56 (previously published in *Synthese* 84 (1990), 1–21). A "group principle" for us would be a principle with these two characteristics: first, that "each of us has reason to follow it" and, second, that "neither is entitled unilaterally to give it up without the acquiescence of the other." For a principle to *become* "our principle . . . we must have expressed to each other our willingness to so regard it." This does not entail that such

a principle is *established* by explicit agreement; but it does require that some form of acknowledgment be given before each of us is *entitled* to the expectations we have regarding each other's conduct. And it is this idea of being entitled to our expectations that has motivated Gilbert's analysis of social conventions from the outset. See also, for example, her "Walking Together: A Paradigmatic Social Phenomenon," in *The Philosophy of the Human Sciences*, ed. P. A. French, T. E. Uehling, and H. K. Wettstein, Midwest Studies in Philosophy 15 (1990), 1–14, reprinted as chapter 6 of *Living Together*. Most of the debate in this area has focused upon whether the commitment to methodological individualism is justified and whether there are genuine collective intentions. It may be that the facts concerning the generation and reception of theatrical performances show that there are genuine collective intentions. But that is not to the point in the present context. If the account developed here of conventions without deliberation holds (or fails), that will be independent of the issue of shared intentions.

13 Tyler Burge, "On Knowledge and Convention," *Philosophical Review* 84/2 (April 1975), 249–55.

14 Ibid., p. 251. Burge notes "they might refuse to entertain the possibility that the gods might switch languages, insisting that nothing could persuade them that this had happened."

15 It is important to note that Burge is not disputing whether conventions are arbitrary. What is at issue is how to characterize arbitrariness and whether Lewis's specific characterization is satisfactory. Of course if we did say his characterization is adequate and agreed that Burge's hypothetical case is plausible, then we would have to conclude that the choice among languages in this case is, *pace* Lewis, not arbitrary.

16 Henry Jackman provides Lewis something of a way out here, proposing that Lewis might avail himself of a distinction between a practice being a "convention *for*" a population, which would require that they acknowledge at least one equally satisfactory alternative, and a practice being simply a "convention in" a population, which would not have this requirement. Henry Jackman, "Convention and Language," *Synthese* 117/3 (January, 1998), 295–312.

17 Catherine Lord, "Convention and Dickie's Institutional Theory of Art," *British Journal of Aesthetics* 20/4 (1980), 322–8.

18 Ibid.

19 Of course the company could have a convention about how conflicts are resolved. And that could be a Lewis convention, I suppose. Depending on the details of that convention, Rebecca's insistence or her unwillingness to explain her insistence might turn out to be irrational. But absent such a mechanism or an explicit agreement, it will not. So Lewis's characterization of arbitrariness is still not appropriate for catching what we mean by saying theatrical performance conventions are actions that could have been done differently.

20 Wollheim, "Criticism as Retrieval," p. 201.

21 See part II of Roger Scruton, *Art and Imagination: A Study in the Philosophy of Mind* (London: Methuen, 1974) for an extended discussion of the relationship among achievement, awareness (in the sense of having a concept of what one has experienced), and appreciation.

EPILOGUE

By way of drawing to a close, let us examine directly the fact that many people still think of theatrical performances as performances *of* something else, usually works of literary art. There is a good reason they think this, even though it is mistaken. It has to do with the nature of what has been the dominant tradition of theater in Western culture at least since the late 1700s.

Let us begin this examination by reminding ourselves of some of the reasons adduced earlier in the book for why this belief is mistaken. Not everything we regard as a performance is intentional. Consider what you have in mind when you compliment your friend after watching her deftly wriggle out of a very public and socially awkward moment. "Good performance," you say, after the dust has settled. You feel no need to think there must be a something *of which* hers was a performance. For there is nothing that corresponds to that "of." The "ingredients model" of the text–performance relation in theater generalizes this idea to all theatrical performances.

More specifically, adherents of the ingredients model hold these claims to be true.

(1) Theatrical performances are not presentations *of* works of literature, nor are they "performance texts" arrived at by the transformation *of* a written text, nor are they the completion or execution *of* works that are initiated – in any substantive sense – in written texts of any kind.

(2) Performance identity is established by reference to aspects of, or facts about, the performance itself and sometimes to aspects of and facts about other performances too.

(3) A performance is, accordingly, never a performance *of* some other work nor is it ever a performance *of* a text or *of* anything initiated in a text; so no faithfulness standard – of any kind – is required for determining what work a performance is of.

(4) Theatrical performances are artworks in their own right.

(5) A text used as a source of verbal and other ingredients in a theatrical performance may have another life as a work of literary art. But it need not. Moreover, whether the text has a literary life of its own is a question logically unrelated to the use of any materials from that text in a theatrical performance. That is, there simply is no theatrical mode of presentation of works of dramatic literature: as works of dramatic literature they are *only* texts to be read.

To defend this model of the text–performance relation, I have argued that spectators identify theatrical performances by reference to what they understand when they have basic comprehension of a performance. If asked to identify the performance they saw on any occasion they can respond by describing the performance. That description will be the same description they would give were they to demonstrate they had basic comprehension of that performance. So, *that* is the performance.

But suppose you see your friend extracting herself in the same way on another occasion. In that case you might be inclined to compliment her, saying, "You did it again!" By the pronoun "it" you intend to refer to a social routine of some sort she seems to have for getting out of tough social situations. The social routine your friend has performed is analogous to the performed routines of gymnasts; and many of those have names. Olena Kvasha is described as beginning her routine for the asymmetric bars in this way:

> She mounts the apparatus by a stretched *Hecht* over the low bar to hang from the high bar. She immediately kips and casts a rearways uprise to handstand, followed by a clear hip circle into the *Healy* turn.[1]

And once a routine has a name, the intentional idiom, "of," reappears. Those of us with a suitable background can assess how well a gymnast has done a "stretched *Hecht*," for example, or a "rearways uprise." So we can speak of Kvasha's performance "of" a stretched *Hecht* and the *Healy* turn; and once that is established, we can imagine gymnasts all over the world practicing and presenting performances "of" *Kvasha's Routine on the Asymmetric Bars*.

And so it is with the "of" of theatrical performance. For, in a similar fashion, the ingredients model leaves room for performances of such routines as are found in other theatrical performances. Some of those routines, or longer sequences of routines called "scenarios," have such appeal that they are done again and again; and often they then have names. So there are performances, for example, of the "Lazzo of the tooth extractor" and of *Hedda Gabler*.

But we should be careful here. The ingredients model does not commit us to the view that theater's routines and scenarios must have originated in written texts. Nor does it commit us to the view that anything about the origination of some performances in written texts constrains a performance. In many traditions, these claims are not even entertained. But in one particular tradition, the "text-based tradition," both of these claims have been thought to be true.

I want now to focus only on the text-based tradition. What is definitive of that tradition? Do the facts of origination in a written text actually constrain performances? If not, what does constrain performances in the text-based tradition? And why does it still seem to some that the facts of origination do, and ought to do, the constraining?

I believe we already have laid down the resources to answer these questions; it is only a matter of bringing them to bear.

A. The Idea of a Tradition and Tradition-Defining Constraints

To gain some perspective on the text-based tradition, it will be useful first to develop a definition of a *theatrical tradition* that follows from claims defended earlier in the book. The *features of performers* to which spectators attend are the result of a describable set of choices that a company of performers makes by a deliberative process. The choices concern five general matters: (1) who utters what (including words, gestures, and so on) and how that utterance sounds or appears; (2) what each performer is doing at each moment in the performance and how she is doing it; (3) where attention is to be directed and how that is to be done; (4) when answering the foregoing questions, companies seek to arrive at weakly coherent collections of means for displaying features in ordered sequences that constitute one way, among other possible and differently weighted ways, they could create the characteristics of the developed object in the performance; and (5) when making choices companies seek to arrive at similar conventions throughout an entire performance, governed and connected by some conception or aims for the performance as a whole. For each sequence of features performers use in a performance there is a decidable alternative, where "decidable" means "available to a company to decide." An "ideal" companion company is a possible company working within the same historical, cultural, geographical, or ideological framework that has as much knowledge as is possible within that framework and as much self-awareness as the framework allows concerning the framework itself and the position of theater within the framework. If an ideal companion company would have considered an alternative way of doing something, then that alternative is decidable by any other company working within that same framework. So a deliberative process either is actually involved or can be rationally assumed to be at work in the selection of features for display.

Theatrical conventions and theatrical styles can be defined by reference to the features selected for display and to the deliberative process involved in such selection. *Theatrical conventions* are weakly coherent sequences of features selected for display that are differently weighted from conceivable alternatives and contingently salient for characteristics of a developed object of a performance. The weighting involved in the selection of features in the forming of a convention is crucial. The effects each sequence of features has, understood as the range of reactions each makes possible, give point to performers' deliberations when considering them as alternatives.

Theatrical styles are sets of similar conventions that are thought to serve a conception or set of aims that could govern an entire performance as well as other performances. Theatrical styles can command significant followings and have influence over a good number of performances, even performances that no longer serve exactly the same aims. The influence of Naturalism is a case in point. Its initial focus on "presenting characters as case studies in human behavior or social problems" was motivated by "the perceptions that all life, human as well as animal, is in a continual process of evolution, and that human behavior can be explained through scientific analysis."[2] But the focus on inner lives of characters, supported by the techniques adopted for that purpose, has survived in performances not at all motivated by these considerations and convictions.

There can be frameworks in which differences among decidable alternatives are fairly small. This often results in styles that resemble each other closely. And this observation affords a natural and plausible way to think about a *theatrical tradition*. Here is what I propose.

A theatrical tradition is a group of styles that employ conventions not distant from each other in means and effects, have similar but not precisely identical aims, and foreclose on the choice of alternative styles, conventions, and aims in such a way that many of those who work within the favored group of styles may not even notice the alternatives.

The key feature of this definition is the foreclosure clause. What is decidable by any given company – at the level of feature selection, of adoption of conventions, or of developing a style – is a matter of a company's objective framework. But, as an empirical matter, judgments that any company actually makes are governed not by their objective framework but by their perception of it. And they can be blind to their objective framework. Catherine Lord is right that artistic conventions are not as conservative as social conventions are.[3] But artistic *traditions* are frequently every bit as conservative. They are most especially so when a tradition has been so dominant that anyone who tries to think in other than its terms appears to be thinking about something else altogether. As David Summers puts it, in the service of a parallel distinction between "conditions" and "conventions," a tradition is "conventional in the sense that it always assumes specific historical form, but it is not *primarily* conventional: that is, there is no alternative in the making of [a work]" to the manner in which the work is made. And here he means no "historical" alternative, no *perceived* alternative.[4]

A company arrive at the first rehearsal and are given a script. There is no logically predetermined way for them to use the script. There is not even a requirement, of logic or of art, that they actually do use it. This is a situation in which a number of things can be decided. We can easily imagine many of those things not being decided: indeed, many companies do things in the way they have always done them and never think about it at all. Despite the exciting challenges in theater in the past hundred years or so, in most cultures and periods innovation in theatrical traditions has been pretty rare. What kinds of things account for the foreclosure on perceived alternatives among the many ways a performance can be developed?

Some of this may be due to culturally shaped ideas about what is possible in theatrical performance. An interest in character and motivation may be thought to be a fairly natural expression of a culture whose philosophical traditions have held as a "broad consensus" that "in addition to the flux of experience there are *subjects* of experience . . . that persist through time" and that "a necessary condition of personal identity across time is some kind of *coherence* or *connectedness* in a person's life."[5] But a tradition that rejects both of these seminal claims might instead pursue an intensification of "individuality without personality" by means of emphasizing "emotion rather than motivation."[6]

But cultural differences will not explain every foreclosure characteristic of a tradition. Sometimes the reason is simpler than that. We can easily extend Burge's remark that the stability of *social* conventions "is safeguarded not only by enlightened self-interest, but by inertia, superstition, and ignorance"[7] to cover *theatrical traditions*. If a tradition has been in place long enough in a population, it can so dominate the thinking of performers and audiences that they come to think that theater in the styles that comprise the tradition is just what it is to be theater. And this begets a species of ignorance that readily explains the persistence of theatrical traditions.

It provides a ready explanation of the persistence of the belief that the text-based tradition is equivalent to theater itself, even among theater people who, of all people, ought to know better.[8] Hence the temptation of many theater people in the 1980s and 90s who thought that, when abandoning only dramatic literature and its agonistic structure, they were abandoning theater for performance.[9]

B. Constraints Derived from Origins in Written Texts

The text-based tradition can be defined as follows:

> The text-based tradition is a condition of theatrical performance in which performances are generated by a use of texts that, typically, are written for the purpose, and the written text is used to determine, reasonably precisely, what is said, who says what and in what order, and sometimes who does what and when. The rest of the issues about which performers must deliberate are left open.

How the words are to sound, at what speed they are to be delivered and in what tone(s), what gestures are to be made, and where attention is to be focused at each moment – all these decisions and more are usually taken to be unspecified in the text-based tradition. The aims in the service of which such decisions are made are also taken to be unspecified. In short, there is room for stylistic variation in the tradition; and the concrete performance use of any text is subject to substantive variance in conventions and aims.

This openness to stylistic variation has two results. The tradition can seem to its practitioners to be more open than it is and, relatedly, the tradition is riven by debates over how much further the written text can be taken to constrain performances. Nothing in the history of performance practices in this (largely Western European) tradition actually settles this matter. So people argue with each other about it. One often repeated position is that there are indeed some elements in the written text itself that should be taken to guide performers when they decide these matters. But this is false.

> Performances in the text-based tradition are not further constrained by facts about the written origins of the performance.

The false position will be tempting if we have not abandoned the deeper view that theatrical performances are performances *of* something independent of the performance itself or of collections of performances. This idea is embodied in the mistaken thought that "the performance exists to give audiences access to the play . . . [and] the audience reads *through* the performance to the play."[10] But that this thought is mistaken is immediately evident, as David Saltz shows, from the fact that in seeing a performance of a play a spectator is seeing the play itself.[11]

Still the thought persists. In a review for the *New York Times*, Charles Isherwood complains about a performance of *Hedda Gabler* at the Brooklyn Academy of Music because the company does not "let the text speak for itself even for a minute." In contrast, he claims, "their first responsibility [should] be to give us what Ibsen wanted."[12] Now of course he does not mean the first of these claims literally: he is not imagining it would be preferable to any spectator, including himself, to come to the theater and be handed a script to read so that, without any interference from actors, lights, the stage, he and other spectators could "let the text to speak for itself."

There have been those who claimed a script was always a better read than a vehicle for performance. And some who think about works of dramatic literature still worry about the effects of the fact that most works in that literature were written to be performed.[13] But this is not Isherwood's complaint. So, what does he mean?

It is clear that the second claim expresses his objections. Isherwood's complaints are against a set of performance practices that do not bring out those aspects of the scenario he takes to have been Ibsen's central concerns, "the ever-pertinent question of the anguish and corruption bred in the heart when a questing soul is trapped in small circumstance." Like the ART's "scandalous"[14] production of *Endgame*, this performance is not marked by significant deviation from the words, the assignment of words, the order of the words, or the sequence of actions. He is not faced with the prospect of reactions to Ibsen's text that Herbert Blau focuses on when he writes:

> Where it [meaning] doesn't seem to matter at all – *Ibsen's* lines and *Ibsen's* meaning – it's not necessarily anymore because the playwright isn't a thinker, but because he *is*, and because the actor has become something of a thinker too, encouraged by Brecht and then Grotowski to *confront* a text and if it goes against her conviction to change the lines and the meaning s/he doesn't like.[15]

Instead Isherwood objects to the effects of the specific conventions employed to further the style of the performance. He objects to the performance's "ill-conceived humor," its "showy bits of business," the fact that this Hedda "kills herself in full view of the audience."[16]

The fact that Isherwood is mistaken about what Ibsen wanted is irrelevant.[17] For had he been right, we would still have cause to wonder why his claim *about Ibsen* should have been thought decisive.

> The facts about the written origins of performances still appear to do the constraining in the text-based tradition because performances in that tradition are said to be "interpretations of plays" and this induces a misunderstanding of what it is that is being performed.

As David Saltz has shown, the idea that performances are interpretations of plays underlies the common practice of critics who claim, as Isherwood does, that a performance should deliver the effects and bring us to appreciate the aims of "the text itself." He also shows why this is mistaken. Something can be a performance, and an interpretation of a text, and not be a performance of the text. To exclude this range of counter-examples requires specifying what a performance is in a manner that is not equivalent to treating the performance as an interpretation. And this consideration shows that not only is interpretation not sufficient to establish the relation between a text and a performance, it is not even necessary.[18] Even if we do not give up the intentionality of theatrical performances (as the type-token views discussed in chapter 2 do not), it is clear that performances are not *of texts*. Appeals to let the text speak for itself are deeply misguided about what is being performed; and the issue of what it is, if anything, about the written text that constrains any performance that it originates is still an open question.

C. What Really Constrains Performances in the Text-Based Tradition

I propose an analysis of the constraints on performance in the text-based tradition that locates the source of constraints in histories of performance practices. Rather than settling disputes about constraints, this analysis provides a guide to understanding, participating in, and assessing disputes about appropriate constraints in particular cases.

> Since the change or omission of features for display can alter what basically comprehending spectators describe when displaying understanding and identifying a performance, such changes alter what can be learned from the routine presented: accordingly, in the text-based tradition, detailed changes from one performance to another are justified by appeal to chains of performance histories back to the initial *performances* of each text-based scenario.

This analysis is suggested by the following example. A teacher of playwriting tells some struggling students to write out their favorite jokes and then transform the writing into dialog. He is asked to provide an example and does. Since the example is pretty funny, a local company that produces evenings of short new one-act plays asks to use it. He agrees. The joke's punch line is scabrous. The director changes it. But through this change, the point of the original joke gets lost, and in its place is a moment of complete absurdity. Surely, if the author had objections, we should hesitate to credit them were they merely addressed to the single fact that changes had been made. Where we get interested in deciding whether to credit a complaint is when the joke has been made funnier, or worse, or different in some interesting way.[19]

In short, what is to be credited is a complaint when changes in the details alter what the joke has to tell us. The proposal I have made is a generalization of this claim and a specification of how justifications of detailed changes are made. This view invokes what David Best calls "the particularity thesis," the idea that "there are particularly stringent demands on details in a work of art, and that this is a central aspect of the concept of art."[20] Some changes will do little to alter what can be learned from the work; some unchanged features for display will become more or less important in relation to changes in other aspects of the work.[21] But there is a logical relation between the particularity of a work, its details, and what can be learned from it.[22] And this shows us why companies working in the text-based tradition study performance histories before launching their own performances of any scenario.

Herbert Blau remarks that "Beckett direct[ed] his own plays like musical scores, with unyielding rigor." The connection between Beckett and directing musical works is entirely apt. Stephen Davies shows that in the Western classical music tradition there are standard ways composers have used for giving "work-determinative instructions" and any performance *of* such a work must conform to those instructions.[23] Moreover, there has been a trend since the middle of the twentieth century for classical composers to try to "thicken" the specification of the constitutive properties of their works. But clearly, despite Beckett's desires in this direction, that same kind of gesture can have no success in theater. As we have seen, everything in performance practice and spectator reception practice cuts against it. Even Beckett seems to have known this, for as Blau also remarks, this was quite "another story" from the one Beckett was telling in "his essay on Proust, not to mention the subversiveness of his texts."[24] So once again the practices of Samuel Beckett provide useful illustration. In this case, they neatly illustrate the importance and relevance of the particularity thesis. Two examples of Beckett's practice are especially illuminating.

The first has to do with his grounds for objecting to the American Repertory Theatre's "scandalous" production of *Endgame*, in 1984. Directed by JoAnne Akalaitis, a director and performer with one of America's most experimental arts collectives, Mabou Mines, it nevertheless was a performance that signaled a return from many bolder experiments of the 1960s and 70s to the use of texts written by playwrights. It employed almost all and only the words written by Samuel Beckett in the script for *Endgame*. And, as Gerald Rabkin puts it, "according to the traditional theatre model, the production was meant to interpret with fidelity the 'text and spirit of the play'."[25] But controversy arose, despite its use of a not significantly altered text, because Beckett thought Akalaitis's setting of the play in an abandoned subway station and the adding of incidental music (by Philip Glass) was, as he put it, "a complete parody of the play as conceived by me."[26]

Notice these features of the case. The Beckett–Akalaitis controversy arose within the text-based tradition. The controversy had nothing to do with alterations in the words, the assignment of words, or the order of words. Nor did it have to do with such directions as were in the text regarding who did what and when. Rather, the controversy concerned the manner of staging. Even some detractors of the performance held that its performance conventions captured crucial aspects of a performance with which Beckett should have been happy. For example, Jonathan Kalb claims that the "primitivism" in the techniques employed by Akalaitis had captured much of the "reflexivity of the play."[27]

The second example has to do with facts about Beckett as a translator of his own scripts and prose pieces. Dina Sherzer remarks that "it is a commonplace that Beckett distrusts language," and cites specific characters who express this view for him. One case is that of Mrs. Rooney in *All that Fall* who "explains that she uses the simplest words and yet she finds her way of speaking very bizarre."[28] It is important to bear this in mind when considering the differences in meaning between the French and English versions of his texts because, as Marjorie Perloff remarks, we cannot suppose that "they were quite simply identical."[29] Beckett's distrust of language, and the fact that there are numerous shifts in meaning between the French and English versions of most of his texts, push us to ask what must have concerned him other than meanings?

On a familiar account of meaning,[30] if Beckett's characters hold the same things true when uttering their English sentences and when uttering their French sentences, their sentences mean the same. But they can mean the same things, as understood on this theory of meaning, and still give very different weight to those meanings. This is done by paying attention to what Sherzer calls "the materiality of language, . . . [to] sounds, . . . [and] syntax."[31] This is an interest in "the form of language," in the use of "clichés, proverbs, or sayings," in the use of invented proverbs and "maximlike utterances," and repetitions which tend to make the sound of language more prominent.[32] And these are precisely the kinds of materials that get changed in Beckett's translations of his own texts.

In short, Beckett's translation practice is a practice of giving specific weight to given verbal vehicles of performance. It is a practice of shifts in effects. These are effects that result from word choices and not from sequences of features chosen for display, i.e., conventions. But this grounds his objection to the Akalaitis production: that production had made certain features prominent for the performance that gave it a specific weight with which he could not agree.

It makes only a legal difference that the person who voiced this concern was the writer of the text used in the performance. If the claim had been well founded, it would have detailed the kind of changes that altered what could be learned from the piece (which Beckett's complaint did) and showed that the alteration of what could be learned lacked suitable justification, given a history of performance practice and a suitable understanding of the context in which the performance was created (which Beckett's complaint did not do). If both those showings had been made, it would not have mattered that it was Beckett who put forward the complaint.

Beckett made no attempt to do the latter of these two tasks: indeed his own failure to object to Andrei Gregory's 1979 production which employed far more significant technical changes is correctly taken to be a relevant fact in assessing Beckett's objections to the ART production. So, we should conclude Beckett offered exactly half of the reasons he should have done, given the assumption of a text-based tradition. His failure even to address the second part of a reasonable criticism of ART's production reveals that he had not learned the lessons the ART production was even then making evident – the lessons now stated, explained, and defended in this book.

D. The Myth of "Of"

Once the text-based tradition and false views about what constrains performances within that tradition no longer have us in their thrall, we have a way of describing its characteristic theatrical performances within the general scope of the view defended in the book. These are performances that adopt constraints that are not binding in the tradition, but are taken as though they were. It is false to hold that there is something in or about texts written for performance that must guide performers when they decide how the words are to sound, at what speed and in what tone(s) they are to be delivered, what gestures are to be made, and where attention is to be focused at each moment. All these decisions and more are usually taken to be unspecified in the text-based tradition. The aims in the service of which such decisions are made are also taken to be unspecified. In short, there is room for stylistic variation in the tradition; and the concrete performance use of any text, even within the text-based tradition, is subject to substantive variance in conventions and aims. But a company can develop a performance as though there were greater constraints than there are.

A spectator of a performance conceived within the text-based tradition who sees the text-based tradition as one among others – and gets the point of this book – will understand something other spectators, lacking her acumen, will miss. She will be able to reconstruct the creative process of the performing company, explaining to herself (and others) how the particular theatrical performance came about, in its entirety and in detail, whether successfully or unsuccessfully. And part of what she will be able to explain is that the performing company have chosen to constrain their choices *as though* certain false views were true.

A major advantage of this approach is that, while we can continue to judge performers' success in terms of the text-based tradition, just as we could before, we can now also judge something else about the performers' success. Namely, we can assess their choice to be so constrained in the aesthetic and cultural environment in which a company find themselves. Where the text-based tradition had obscured the fact, the most basic decisions about how to employ a text are finally seen as choices concerning which spectators can make appropriate aesthetic and artistic judgments.

Notes

1 www.olympic-eurogym.demon.nl/ukraine/kva/kva_gym.htm.
2 Christopher Innes, "Contextual Overview," in *A Routledge Literary Sourcebook on Henrik Ibsen's* Hedda Gabler, ed. Christopher Innes (London and New York: Routledge, 2003), p. 12.
3 Catherine Lord, "Convention and Dickie's Institutional Theory of Art," *British Journal of Aesthetics* 20/4 (1980), 322–8.
4 David Summers, "Conditions and Conventions: On the Disanalogy of Art and Language," in *The Language of Art History*, ed. Salim Kemal and Ivan Gaskell (Cambridge: Cambridge University Press, 1991), pp. 181–212, quotation from p. 184.
5 Peter Lamarque, "Expression and the Mask: The Dissolution of Personality in Noh," *Journal of Aesthetics and Art Criticism* 47/2 (1989), 157–68, quotation from 165.
6 Ibid., pp. 165–6, 159. See also Philip B. Zarrilli, "What Does It Mean to 'Become the Character'?: Power, Presence, and Transcendence in Asian Inbody Disciplines of Performance," in *By Means of Performance*, ed. Richard Schechner and Willa Appel (Cambridge: Cambridge University Press, 1990), pp. 131–48, especially 131, 144, 145, and 146.
7 Tyler Burge, "On Knowledge and Convention," *Philosophical Review* 84/2 (April 1975), 253.
8 See an informative analysis of this situation in Marvin Carlson, "The Resistance to Theatricality," *SubStance 98/99*, 31/1–2 (2002), 238–50, especially 246–9.
9 The situation is more complicated, of course. The phenomena of performance comprise a larger field than theatrical performance, and one need not give up the study of theater to study performance. But see the terms in which Richard Schechner claims theater ought to be studied, in "A New Paradigm for Theatre in the Academy," *TDR* 36/4 (1992), 7–10. It is also instructive to see the terms on which he recants part of that position, in "Theatre in the 21st Century," *TDR* 41/2 (1997), 5–6.

10   David Z. Saltz, "What Theatrical Performance Is (Not): The Interpretation Fallacy," *Journal of Aesthetics and Art Criticism* 59/3 (2001), 299–306, quotation from 299.

11   David Z. Saltz, "When is the Play the Thing?: Analytic Aesthetics and Dramatic Theory," *Theatre Research International* 20/3 (Fall, 1995), 266–76, quotation from 266.

12   Charles Isherwood, "An Actress Upstaging Her Talent and Ibsen," *The New York Times*, Critic's Notebook, March 18, 2006.

13   Benjamin Bennett, *Theater as Problem* (Ithaca, NY, and London: Cornell University Press, 1990), pp. 2, 13, 15–16, 66ff., and 253–67.

14   And Isherwood does describe the Sydney Theater Company's production as "scandalous."

15   Herbert Blau, "The Impossible Takes a Little Time," *Performing Arts Journal (PAJ)* 7/3 (1984), 29–30.

16   Ibid.

17   Christopher Innes, "Critical History," in *A Routledge Literary Sourcebook on Henrik Ibsen's* Hedda Gabler, ed. Christopher Innes (London and New York: Routledge, 2003), pp. 41–8. Innes notes that Ibsen's intention is now widely recognized to have focused on contemporary social critique, especially of *fin-de-siècle* decadence, and that the view Isherwood and others have attributed to Ibsen falsifies his skill as a playwright because it entails that the other figures who surround Hedda are "insignificant ciphers" (pp. 44–5). Isherwood also omits mention of the many performance practices appearing here that had been used before in performing this scenario. The dark humor in the play has been obscured by views like Isherwood's (p. 47). And, finally, no less a director than Ingmar Bergman has staged the death of Hedda in full view (pp. 47–8).

18   Saltz, "What Theatrical Performance," pp. 300–1.

19   I thank Ron Willis of the University of Kansas theater program for the example, which he insists is real.

20   David Best, "Logic, Particularity and Art," *British Journal of Aesthetics* 23/4 (1983), 306–18, quotation from 307.

21   Ibid., p. 309.

22   Ibid., p. 310. Best is hesitant to explain what kind of logical relationship he has in mind because, as he says, there are plenty of counter-examples to many formulations of this idea. He is content to leave it as an intuition. And so am I.

23   Stephen Davies, "Ontologies of Musical Works," "Authenticity in Musical Performance," and "The Multiple Interpretability of Musical Works," in *Themes in the Philosophy of Music* (Oxford: Oxford University Press, 2003), pp. 30–46, 81–93, and 245–63.

24   Blau, "The Impossible," p. 30. The full passage in which these phrases appear is worth quoting: "Certain of the authors, dead or alive, whose consciousness turned us almost inevitably to the performative dismantling of texts, want to

do the preempting in precisely their own way. Brecht left behind his model books and Beckett directs his own plays like musical scores, with unyielding rigor. But as far back as his essay on Proust, not to mention the subversiveness of his texts, he was telling another story . . ."

25 Gerald Rabkin, "Is There a Text on This Stage? Theatre/Authorship/ Interpretation," *Performing Arts Journal (PAJ)* 9/2–3 (1985), p. 146.

26 Quoted ibid., p. 146. A slightly fuller excerpt is found in Jonathan Kalb, *Beckett in Performance* (Cambridge: Cambridge University Press, 1989), p. 79.

27 Kalb, *Beckett*, pp. 82–4.

28 Dina Sherzer, "Words about Words: Beckett and Language," in *Beckett Translating/Translating Beckett*, ed. Alan Warren Friedman, Charles Rossman, and Dina Sherzer (University Park, PA, and London: Pennsylvania State University Press, 1987), pp. 49–54, quotation from 49.

29 Marjorie Perloff, "Une Voix pas la mienne: French/English Beckett and the French/English reader," in *Beckett Translating/Translating Beckett*, ed. Alan Warren Friedman, Charles Rossman, and Dina Sherzer (University Park, PA, and London: Pennsylvania State University Press, 1987), pp. 36–48, quotation from p. 36.

30 Donald Davidson, *Inquiries into Truth and Meaning* (Oxford: Clarendon Press, 1984).

31 Sherzer, "Words about Words", p. 50.

32 Ibid., pp. 50, 51, 52.

GLOSSARY

Some of the terms that appear in the glossary are not technical terms in philosophy. But they are defined in the book, are frequently used or referred to, and are central to the argument.

Idealized Cases

The book relies on a set of idealized performance kinds. These cases are introduced in chapter 3 and are referred to throughout the book. They are cases designed to highlight features needing analysis on any adequate general account of theatrical performance.

The cases used in the book are idealized in three senses. First, they ignore the actual circumstance that might have prompted the kind of performance they illustrate. Second, they involve the use of scripts (which is not characteristic of all forms of theater). And third, they involve the reworking of material in previously written texts for performance (whereas that is a minority practice in the actual history of theater). The features they do illustrate are mentioned in the following brief descriptions. The idealized cases used in the book are as follows.

Hedda-to-Hedda: a class of narrative performances involving the use of scripts written for performance in which performers play characters by uttering words assigned to those characters (by speech prefixes) and moving in ways that will be grasped by spectators as the actions of the characters. The manner, rhythm, tone and speed of word delivery, as well as of movement, are usually governed by some interpretive ideas concerning the play as a whole.

Gabler at a Distance: a class of narrative performances involving the use of scripts written for performance in which performers play characters by uttering words usually assigned to those characters (by speech prefixes) and moving in ways that will be grasped by spectators as the actions of the characters *but also* by uttering words and engaging in movements that will undermine simple acceptance by audiences of some aspects of the story being presented. Interpretive ideas of the play govern which elements of the play are to be presented for straightforward acceptance and which are not.

Spontaneous Beauty: a class of narrative performances involving the use of scripts written for performance – and possibly other texts as well – in which performers may sometimes utter words assigned to characters but may sometimes utter other words or sounds for various acoustic effects, and in which some performers (not necessarily the performers identified as playing the relevant characters) move in ways that will be grasped as the actions of characters. Performances in this class use a variety of techniques to examine the content of the scripts written for performance while simultaneously presenting the story it lays out.

Burning Child: the first class of non-narrative performances discussed and referred to in the book, a performance consisting of sequences of words, chosen from one or more texts – in the imagined case only from the script Ibsen wrote for *Hedda Gabler* – that performers think can be said honestly, coupled with images created to accompany the words (or vice versa), and movements to get from image to image.

Something to Tell You: a second class of non-narrative performances consisting of sequences of whole sentences the performers deliver directly to the spectators, with a minimum of movement, and where the movement is aimed at reinforcing the sonic effect of the barrage of language directed at the spectators. Some of the themes of this kind of performance include references to aspects of the performing conditions at the time of the performance.

Pistols and Other Doors: a class of dance-like movement performances whose texts are sentences and language fragments, from whatever sources, arranged to create rhythmic effects, and in some cases underlying themes, that emerge and disappear unpredictably during the performance. The texts may be generated by automatic or mechanized randomizing processes, but the effect is of a kind of nonsense just on the edge of sense.

Models of the Text–Performance Relation

Models of the text–performance relation are discussed in detail in chapter 2. Since the book is a defense of the last of the four models discussed, references to it and its properties occur in a number of places in the book.

The four models discussed represent fundamentally different ways to conceive what is happening when a performance makes use of a written text in performance and what happens when a performance makes use of no text. Each model articulates five things: what aspect of the text is presented in the performance; what audiences refer to when identifying a performance; what criterion or standard, if any, secures such reference; whether the performance is understood as a work of art on that model; and whether, and if so how, the written text is itself understood as a work of art. The four models are, very roughly, as follows.

The literary model: the idea that theatrical performances are illustrations or interpretations of works of dramatic literature.

The two-text model: the idea that theatrical performances consist of "theatrical texts" to be read and are something like translations of their corresponding literary texts.

The type-token model: an idea developed by reflecting on the ontology of theatrical (and musical) performances, holding that a performance is an instance (or "token") of a kind (or "type") that may have other (and other kinds of) instances, for example, a text or score.

The ingredients model: the idea that texts are used in performances in much the same way people use ingredients when they cook.

Definitions of Terms Used to Describe What Spectators Do

Basic theatrical understanding (chapter 5): A spectator has basic understanding of a theatrical performance if she (1) can describe the object that was presented over the course of the performance, (2) reacts physically in the right ways to what is happening in the performance as those things happen, *or* (3) adopts the moods responsive to what is happening in the performance as those things happen.

Deeper performer understanding (chapter 8): A spectator has deeper understanding of what the performers are doing and how they are doing it if she is able to demonstrate that she is familiar with the performance traditions within or against which they are working and to describe what they are doing either to achieve the realization of those traditions or to challenge them.

Deeper object understanding (chapter 8): A spectator has deeper understanding of the structures of the objects presented in a performance if she is able to demonstrate that she is familiar with the structures of other objects presented in other performances and to use that information to describe the structures internal to the performed object being developed in the performance at hand that makes it the kind of object it is.

Interpretive grasp of a theatrical performance (chapter 10): A spectator has an interpretive grasp of a theatrical performance if she is able to offer *either* (1) a story about connections the object of basic understanding has with other issues or themes being raised in contemporary culture (including her own reactions to the object) *or* (2) a set of reasons a company may have had for constructing and presenting the object of the performance in the way they did. The two clauses suggest two different kinds of interpretive grasp. *S-interpretations* are stories about the perceived significance of a performance. *P-interpretations* are stories about the reasons a company undertook the manner and construction of their performance.

Full appreciation (working definition, chapter 8): Full appreciation of a theatrical performance involves the ability to see the performance against a background that can inform the spectator of what kind of achievement is or is not manifest in the performance and the ability, by reference to details in performances, to converse about how the performance practices contribute to or detract from the performed object and about whether the performed object is achievable by certain kinds of performance practices rather than others.

Full appreciation (final version, chapter 11): Full appreciation of a theatrical performance is a reconstruction of the creative process which explains how a particular theatrical performance came about, in its entirety and in detail, whether successfully or unsuccessfully.

Definitions of Terms Used to Describe What Performers Do

The simple suggestion (chapter 9): The *features of performers* to which spectators attend are the result of a describable set of choices that a company of performers makes. The choices concern three general matters: (1) who utters what (including words, gestures, and so on) and how each utterance sounds or appears; (2) what each performer is doing at each moment in the performance and how she is doing it; and (3) where attention is to be directed at each moment and how that is to be achieved.

Theatrical conventions (chapter 9): Theatrical conventions are weakly coherent sequences of features selected for display that are differently weighted from conceivable alternatives and contingently salient for characteristics of the object developed in a performance.

Theatrical styles (chapter 9): Theatrical styles are sets of similar conventions that are thought to serve a conception or set of aims that could govern one or more entire performances.

Theatrical traditions (Epilogue): A theatrical tradition is a group of styles that (1) employ conventions not distant from each other in means and effects, (2) have similar but not precisely identical aims, and (3) foreclose on the choice of alternative styles, conventions, and aims in such a way that many of those who work within the favored group of styles may not even notice the alternatives.

Some of the technical philosophical terms used in the book are defined on the spot, usually in endnotes. Because they may not be familiar, most of the important ones also appear in this glossary.

Counterfactual Conditionals

Conditionals are sentences of the form if . . . then . . . , where the ellipses following "if" and "then" represent claims. The "if"-clause is called the "antecedent" of the conditional, and the "then"-clause is called the conditional's "consequent."

Counterfactual conditionals are conditionals in the subjunctive mood that presuppose their antecedents are false. They assert that something would have been the case had something else been the case (with the explicit assumption that the latter was not, in fact, the case).

Counterfactuals are thought to be useful in explaining how physical laws – expressed in sentences like "All copper conducts electricity" – differ from other generalizations that might happen to be true – for example, "Every object on my dining-room table conducts electricity." The idea is that if anything were copper – which my pencil is not – it would conduct electricity, but not just anything would conduct electricity were it on my dining-room table.

Counterfactuals are also thought to be useful in explaining dispositional properties. Saying this lump of sugar is soluble in water just comes to this: it would dissolve, if it were in water (which it is not).

Counterfactual conditionals were appealed to directly in chapter 5, in explaining how to distinguish the physical reactions and mood shifts that are evidence of basic theatrical comprehensions from those that are not. They were also appealed to indirectly in chapter 3, in explaining how the thought that theatrical performance is a social phenomenon should be understood. The thought is that being a form that has no non-audience practice is a dispositional property of theatrical performances.

Demonstrative and Recognition-Based Identification

An approach to the identification of objects pioneered by Bertrand Russell and developed by Gareth Evans. The underlying idea is that in order to have a thought about something, one has to have an idea of that thing first. That claim appears to entail that the first idea of a thing has to be devoid of any content. Evans develops the idea, by appeal to some empirical work on organisms' basic physical reactions to items in spatial locations, into a rigorous and complete analysis of reference.

An epistemological variation of this approach was deployed in chapter 7 to show how spectators identify and re-identify immediate objects (for example, characters) and developed objects within performances, across performances, including across performances at some stylistic distance from each other. The approach is consistent with the feature-salience model of convergence of disparate spectators on the same characteristics of objects in a performance in several ways.

Feature-salience Model

This model is designed to show why even quite disparate spectators gravitate towards attending to the same features of performers and finding those features projectible – for themselves and for other spectators – for the same characteristics of the objects presented in the content of a theatrical performance. The model is based on accounts of feature salience developed in game-theoretical approaches in decision theory, first studied in the manner employed here by David Lewis, Margaret Gilbert, and others.

The model is first developed in chapter 6. Changes made to the model in chapter 8 are used to bring out the differences between basic and deeper understanding, on the one hand, and between two different kinds of deeper understanding, on the other.

Metaphysical Realism

Metaphysical Realism is the view that, for some domain of discourse, the objects it discusses are real objects, having existence independent of our experience of, knowledge of, or interaction with them. So they may have interactions with each other about which we may not know. As applied to the world of everyday objects, metaphysical realism is just a kind of commonsense view that is also found in the natural and social sciences. Naturally, one might have real reservations about holding that we ought to be metaphysical realists about characters in plays. And this provides a reason for being careful about the commitments of one's theory about how spectators identify the objects presented in theatrical performances.

Necessary and Sufficient Conditions

Reference is made to this distinction in several places in the book. A set of conditions is said to be necessary for some further item just when the set of conditions must be in place for the item itself to be in place. For example: one may play for France in the World Cup only if one is a citizen of France; a figure is a square only if it is a closed plane figure. That some condition, C, is necessary for some state of affairs, A, is usually expressed in the form of the conditional, "If A then C."

A condition is said to be sufficient for the application of a term if the presence of that condition is all that it takes to justify applying the term. As the examples just used suggest, individual conditions are rarely sufficient conditions. Sufficiency is most frequently achieved by sets of conditions that are required conjointly. That some condition, C, is sufficient for some state of affairs, A, is usually expressed in the form of the conditional, "If C then A."

The importance of the expression of necessary or sufficient conditions in the form of conditionals is that this provides a guide for testing whether a claim of necessity or sufficiency is true. If someone claims that A is necessary for C – that "if C then A" is true – she can be rebutted if we locate some item that is undeniably a C but does not satisfy A. A conditional is false just when its antecedent is true and its consequent is false. In chapter 8, it is argued that having deeper understanding of a theatrical performance is not sufficient for having full appreciation of the performance. And the argument proceeded by seeking to find a case, a counter-example, in which a spectator had deeper understanding but lacked full appreciation.

Ontology, Metaphysics, Epistemology

In this book, ontological questions are set aside or avoided, as studiously as possible, in favor of epistemological questions. The contrast between them is first mentioned in chapter 2, but it runs through most of the book.

As Willard Van Orman Quine quipped – in his famous essay, "On What There Is" – the ontological problem "can be put in three Anglo-Saxon monosyllables – 'What is there?'" And, he continued, "it can be answered in a word – 'Everything' . . . but there remains room for disagreements over cases; and so the issue has stayed alive down the centuries."[1] Ontology, understood in Quine's way, is that branch of metaphysics concerned with what kinds of things our best theories in science and art commit us to believing exist, if any.

Ontological questions about theatrical performance may have good answers, and those answers may be illuminating about the art of theatrical performance. But this book focuses on asking and answering epistemological questions. These are questions about what we can know and how we know those things. An unargued premise of the book is that whatever ontology may be worked out for theatrical performance, it must be consistent with what we can know about performances and how we do know those things.

The distinction is especially important to the argument in chapter 7 because the idea, defended there, that we identify characters and other objects presented in the contents of theatrical performances can readily be misconstrued as the claim that fictional (i.e., non-existent) objects exist. But, if the claim is understood as tracking the epistemology of theatrical performances, it need not have that absurd implication. The facts that we do identify characters and that doing so is a crucial part of how we know what is going on in a play should be important data for an ontological investigation to address. The trick would be to try to figure out what kinds of things those have to be for the epistemology to work out as it does. That issue is not addressed in this book.

Note

1 Willard Van Orman Quine, "On What There Is," in *From a Logical Point of View*, 2nd edition, revised (Cambridge, MA, and London: Harvard University Press, 1980), p. 1.

INDEX